Praise for *Cover Him with Darkness* and Janine Ashbless

"Thrilling.... Milja has to choose whether to betray the lover she risked everything to rescue, or go against the divine plan, while staying true to her own values—all while navigating a rocky romance with an appealing supernatural creature who feeds off her desire for him...sharp and enticing."

—*Publishers Weekly*

"Calling *Cover Him with Darkness* a romance is like calling a Lamborghini a cute little car. Janine Ashbless has broken every unwritten rule of writing romance and makes it work most spectacularly—it's dark and gritty and so beautifully written that the words are pure poetry."

—Kate Douglas, author of the Wolf Tales series

"Janine Ashbless has long been a master at conjuring the erotic in myths and legends. Now she's taking on religion and all I can say is wow. Just wow! What is evil? What is good? Could the faithful have completely missed the point? Sexy food for thought: *Cover Him with Darkness* is an intensely wild ride."

—D. L. King, editor of *Seductress* and *The Sweetest Kiss*

"This book was truly a fantastic read. Janine Ashbless amazed me over and over again with her presentation of the sort of tribal, religious mystique of Montenegro and especially with her detail of its jagged scenery. I felt I was on a tour and actually bearing witness to the stunning mountainous landscape—I walked along the narrowest of goat trails, could feel the drafty little church atop its cold mountain, taste the bean soup... and the dream sequences between it all?... Help me. No... Gimme."

—Rose Caraway, editor of *The Sexy Librarian's Big Book of Erotica*

COVER HIM WITH DARKNESS

COVER HIM WITH DARKNESS

A Romance

THE BOOK OF THE WATCHERS
PART ONE

JANINE ASHBLESS

TEMPTED
ROMANCE

Published in the United States by Tempted Romance,
an imprint of Cleis Press Inc., 2246 Sixth Street, Berkeley, California 94710.

Printed in the United States.
Cover design: Scott Idleman/Blink
Cover photograph: Robert Daly/Getty Images
Text design: Frank Wiedemann

First Edition.
10 9 8 7 6 5 4 3 2 1

Trade paper ISBN: 978-1-940550-01-5
E-book ISBN: 978-1-940550-06-0

NB: All Bible quotes are from the King James version. All quotes from the *Book of Enoch* are from the R. H. Charles translation (1917). *An Evil Cradling* was written by Brian Keenan (Vintage, 1992). Milja's father quotes from St. Nicholas Cabasilas (fourteenth century), and sings lines from a prayer by St. Dimitri of Rostov (seventeenth century).

For Phil, my rock of ages

And with huge thanks to Brenda at Cleis, who read my short story "Cover Him with Darkness" (*Red Velvet and Absinthe,* 2011), and wanted to know what happened next.

And it came to pass, when men began to multiply on the face of the earth, and daughters were born unto them, that the Sons of God saw the daughters of man, that they were fair. And they took them wives of all which they chose.

Genesis 6:1-2

Contents

PROLOGUE

*F*our of them accompanied the prisoner: a lion, a bull, an eagle and a man. At least, that was what they looked like—except that the lion and the bull were both winged, with six wings each, and they beat the air with the sound of a hurricane as they flew. And the man was winged too, and bore fire in his open palms, and his face was a blur of flickering light crowned with stars. The eagle, shining like hammered gold, was three times the size of the naked, wounded human body it carried in its claws.

They swooped down onto the mountainside, and in that moonless night the light the crowned one shed turned the jumble of bare rock to shifting bars of black shadow. When the snow-white bull put its head down and charged the cliff face, the earth shook and crumbled. Beneath that blow the mountain split in two, revealing a deep ravine.

The eagle had dropped its prey as they landed. Now the lion, crimson and pinioned with flame like a phoenix, went over to the unconscious man. He was already bleeding from dozens of places, and his hands and feet were tied together with slick red cords. The lion stooped its huge head and closed its jaws about the man's shoulder and chest, lifting him. As the teeth bit into his flesh, the prisoner moaned in pain.

The crowned and shining figure led the way into the mountain cleft and the lion followed, dragging their captive across the broken stones. The bull brought up the rear.

They took him deep into the mountain, to a place where a great rock lay fallen, and they laid him on his back across the stone like a sacrifice upon an altar. Then the burning seraph untied his hands and feet enough to spread his limbs out. The broken man looked tiny beneath their huge, effulgent forms. Their light bleached him of color.

With hooves of glittering diamond, the winged bull stamped the loose ends of the bloody rope into the stone, and the rock gave like dough beneath the blows and then closed up around the tethers, holding the man fast. He roused from unconsciousness as his last limb was pinned, and lifted his head, screaming defiance and spitting blood, then arching his back and trying to tear free from his bonds.

The crowned figure stepped back a little, as if to protect its shining robes that glittered with all the colors of precious stones, from the spatter of blood and sweat and spittle.

But the eagle hopped closer. It darted its hooked beak to the prisoner's stretched stomach and tore open the skin, rummaging about in the bloody entrails within and pulling shreds out through the open wound.

Their captive screamed in pain, and the earth shuddered.

They left him there, vanishing from within the bowels of the mountain and reappearing outside in a sunburst of glory. With a wave of his hand, the crowned one closed the mountain up once more.

The lion disappeared.

The eagle disappeared.

The bull disappeared.

The seraph lingered a moment, thoughtfully.

It started to rain. Softly at first, but then hard and steady, like it would never stop.

And I woke up, hands clenched so tight that my nails had dug into my palms, my body aching with tension from my spasming muscles. The pillow slip under my cheek was soggy with tears.

What was it I had been dreaming? The last shreds of vision flickered away into the dark. *Something awful*, I thought, feeling my heart pound. *Something about rain?*

Outside the window of my Boston student apartment, the rain fell like it wanted to drown the world.

chapter one

THE PRISONER

The first time I saw him fettered there in the dark, I wept.

I was seven years old. My father led me by the hand down the steps behind the church altar, through a passage hewn into the mountainside. I'd never been permitted through that door before, though I knew that the key was kept under a loose floor tile beneath the icon of St. Michael. In those days that picture made me nervous: the archangel's painted eyes always seemed to watch me, even though the rest of him was busy throwing down the Devil and trampling him underfoot.

All along the narrow tunnel beyond the door there were niches cut into the rock walls, and near our church these were filled with painted and gilded icons of the saints and of Our Lord, but farther back those gave way to statuettes of blank-eyed pagan gods, growing cruder in execution and less human in appearance as we walked on. I clung to Father's hand and cringed from the darkness closing in behind me, as his kerosene lamp picked out the rock-cut steps at our feet and our breathing sounded loud in our ears. The journey seemed to take forever, to my child's mind. I couldn't help imagining the carved and painted eyes in the tunnel behind me: glowing pinpoints of light that watched my retreating back—and I kept looking over my shoulder to see.

Finally we came out into a roofless chamber, where the walls leaned inward a hundred feet over our heads and the floor was nothing but a mass of loosely tumbled boulders. I looked up, blinking at the light that seemed blinding, though in fact this was a dim and shadowed place. I could see a wisp of cloud against the seam of blue sky overhead, and the black speck of a mountain eagle soaring across the gap.

There he lay, upon a great tilted slab of pale limestone, his wrists and ankles spread and bound by twisted leather ropes whose farther ends seemed to be set into the rock itself. It was hard to say whether the slab had always been underground or had fallen long ago from the mountain above; our little country is, after all, prone to earthquakes. Dirt washed down with the rain had stained him gray, but I could make out the muscled lines of his bare arms and legs and the bars of his ribs. There was an old altar cloth draped across his lower torso—and only much later did I realize that Father had done that, to spare his small daughter the man's nakedness.

"Here, Milja," said my father, pushing me forward. "It is time you knew. This is the charge of our family. This is what we guard day and night. It is our holy duty never to let him be found or escape."

I was only little: he looked huge to me, huge and filthy and all but naked. I stared at the ropes, as thick as my skinny wrists, knotted cruelly tight about his broader ones. They stretched his arms above his head so that one hand could not touch the other, and matching tethers held his ankles apart. I felt a terrible ache gather in my chest. I pressed backward, into Father's black robes.

"Who is he?" I whispered.

"He is a very bad man."

That was when the prisoner moved for the first time. He rolled his head and turned his face toward us. I saw the whites of his eyes gleam in his gray face. Even at seven, I could read the suffering and the despair burning there. I squirmed in Father's grip.

"I think he's hurt," I whimpered. "The ropes are hurting him."

"Milja," said Father, dropping to his knee and putting his arm around me. "Don't be fooled—this is not a human being. It just looks like one. Our family has guarded him here since the first people came to these mountains. Before the Communists. Before the Turks. Before the Romans, even. He has always been here. He is a prisoner of God."

"What did he do?"

"I don't know, little chick."

That was when I began to cry.

"What did he do?" became a question I repeated many times as I grew up, along with, "Who is he?" My father didn't lie, but neither could he answer my question truthfully. He was an educated man, though he had taken up the vocation of priest of an isolated village in one of the most barren, mountainous corners of our rugged country. He had studied engineering at university in Belgrade, but he admitted that the answers to my queries were unclear to him. "The gods have condemned him," he would say, with a sigh. That sounded so strange coming from an Orthodox priest that I didn't know what to think.

Every Sunday, after going down into the village to celebrate the Divine Liturgy with the congregation in the church there—nobody ever climbed up the two hundred steps to our dingy little chapel carved into the sheer rock—he would descend into the prisoner's cave. He would take the man water and bread, and wash his face. My father was not without compassion, even for a prisoner, and he felt the responsibility of his position.

"Is he...Prometheus?" I asked when I was ten, and had been reading the Greek myths in one of the dog-eared books Father had brought from the capital. "The gods chained up Prometheus forever. Is it him?"

"It may be."

"But...Prometheus was *good*, Papa. He taught us how to be civilized. He stole fire from the gods to bring it to men. He was on our side!"

"What did man do with fire, Milja?"

"Cook?"

"He smelted iron, little chick, and with iron he made swords. He made all the weapons of war, and men have slaughtered men in countless millions ever since. Are you sure Prometheus had our best interests at heart? Would we not have been happier if we'd stayed in the innocence of the Stone Age?"

I was too young to answer that. Father sighed and fetched a black-bound book, laying it on the table by the window where the light could fall upon it. He opened the pages to somewhere near the beginning.

"My grandfather told me that it is Azazel we hold in our keeping. Have you heard of him?"

"No," said I in a small voice.

"Neither man nor pagan titan, little chick, but a fallen angel. A leader of the Watchers: those Sons of God who lusted after mortal women. The Israelites dedicated their scapegoat sin-offering to Azazel every year when they drove it out into the wilderness. And just like the Greeks' Prometheus, he is credited with teaching men metalworking and war-craft—and women the arts of seduction and sorcery. Here in the *Book of Enoch*, see; the angel Raphael is commanded by God: *'bind Azazel hand and foot and cast him into the darkness. And lay upon him rough and jagged rocks, and cover him with darkness, and let him abide there forever.'*"

"Which is right, then?" I asked. "Is he a demon or is he Prometheus?"

"Maybe he is both, and it's the same story. Or maybe he is something else altogether. All I know is that he's been here since the beginning, and that it is our duty to keep him bound. It's what our family forefathers dedicated their lives to. And you must carry on when I am gone, Milja. You must marry and teach your husband and your sons, so that it is never forgotten. And you must *never* tell anyone else, all your life. It must not go beyond the family. Promise me!"

"Why not?"

"What if someone, someone who did not understand, felt sorry for him and set him free? What if he is one of the great demons, Milja? What would happen to this world?"

I was eleven when I started to visit him in secret. I took him food, because I couldn't bear any longer to lie awake in bed thinking of how hungry he must be. I knew he could get water—when it rained it would run down the rocks onto his face—but at eleven I was always ravenous myself, and starvation seemed the worst of tortures. And the image of him lying bound there haunted my dreams more and more, evoking feelings I had no words for—not then—until it seemed impossible for me to stay away.

Still, I went at midday, when the light was strongest and the cavern least frightening. I brought him bread crusts and cheese. I picked berries from the mountain bushes and fed them between his cracked lips.

I remember the first time I did it, the first time I went alone. I climbed up on that big rock slab and knelt over his dirt-streaked body, and he opened his eyes and looked up into mine. His irises were so dark that they couldn't be distinguished from the pupils, and in this half-light they looked like holes.

"What's your name?" I whispered.

I don't know if he heard me. He certainly didn't reply. He just looked at me, from the depths of his private torment.

"I brought you some milk." I tipped the teat of the little skin of goats' milk to his lips and let it trickle into the side of his mouth, carefully: I was scared of choking him. His throat worked and his lips twitched, bleeding. He drank it all and I sat back. That was when, with obvious and painful effort, the lines of his face pulled into a brief smile—a smile so fragile a butterfly might have trampled it underfoot.

That was when I was lost.

I was fourteen when I first heard him speak.

"Milja," he murmured, greeting me. His voice was hoarse from disuse, but its depths made the hair stir on my neck. I nearly fled.

"What's your name?" I asked once again, but he didn't answer, withdrawing instead, it seemed, into his anguish once more. He only twisted from one hip to the other to ease the strain on his back, and hissed with pain. The power of his corded body, terrible even under constraint, made me tremble.

He spoke only rarely in the years that followed, and what he said made little sense to me—often it wasn't even in any language I knew, and when I could make out the words they seemed to be nothing but fragments. "Leaves on the brown-bright water..." he might mutter to himself. I think he was remembering things he had seen before he was imprisoned. As I grew to realize how the uncountable years had stolen even his mind, I felt dizzy with horror.

I was eighteen when Father sent me away.

You have to understand: I grew up alone, set apart from the other village children. Oh, when I was a little child I ran and played with them, but as I grew older things changed. Our family had been here for centuries before the village of Stijenjarac was founded, fulfilling our ancient duty until war and political turmoil and expanding horizons had scattered and dwindled its numbers. We had always been treated as *separate* from the rest of the village; sometimes we would intermarry, but only our boys choosing their girls. I was the last of the line to grow up here. Schooling in the village was little more than rudimentary, and at fourteen I was the only girl still being taught; all the others my age were laboring with their mothers in the house and the fields. At sixteen I was still studying under my father's tutelage, and had become a freak in the eyes of the whole community. The girls turned as one and cut me off from their company, erecting a wall of sneering hostility. The boys just teased me unremittingly, their curiosity expressed in the crudest manner. Thrown stones were the least of my worries.

I think Father was secretly pleased I showed no interest in the village boys. He hoped I would go to university some day, like him.

Perhaps I should have made an effort to understand my peers more, and tried to make friends. Perhaps. But I was naive, and I thought all men should be like my gentle, scholarly father, so I was alone a great deal. I looked after the house when Father was out—his ability to fix generators and rotavators was something the villagers valued him for as much as his priestly status, I think. I cooked and did the laundry. I read. I climbed the hillsides on my own, being careful to avoid the shepherds up there. And I went to visit our prisoner, every day.

As I grew older I grew bolder too. I stole wine for him. I baked him honey cake. I would bring water to wash the grime off his body, slightly shocked by my own recklessness as I wiped down the heavy slabs of his muscles, or slid a hand under a lower leg so that I might massage his calf and relieve the ache of his trapped limbs to some tiny extent. Sometimes he would focus upon my face long enough to whisper my name.

His body fascinated me. I learned its illicit contours in the half dark, mostly by touch. He felt cold all over, like the rock he lay on, but there were smooth bits and there were places rough with hair. There were harder and softer stretches. There was a big, jagged scar over the right side of his abdomen, but it looked old.

There were things only a married woman should see.

I wanted to take his pain away.

I was book-smart, as they say in America—there was no such phrase in our village, though they understood the concept perfectly—and I was burning with curiosity, but not wise. One day I lay down beside him on the stone and nestled my head on his chest. I could hear the slow beat of his heart. The bars of his ribs were like carved prehistoric rock-glyphs, and I walked my fingertips across each ridge and furrow. The skin above his hip was so smooth it was like stroking feathers, but the old altar cloth felt damp and coarse in comparison. There was something repulsive about the feel of the grimy cloth that preserved his modesty. With my right hand I drew off that swatch, and then for the first time I touched him without the excuse that I was tending him. Without any excuse at all.

Hair, matted into curls. Below that, duskier skin. I shut my eyes. My hand, for once, was bolder than my gaze.

Soft.

Silky.

A small cool heft in my hand, yet heavy with a secret weight: the significance invested in the forbidden. My heart was racing, far faster than the heavy beat against my ear. My mind shied away from what I was doing. But my body seemed to be sure of what it wanted, and urged my hand to its task.

Tentatively I began to caress him.

He responded to that. Not just that sleeping creature stirring to wakefulness under my open palm, but his heartbeat waking with a kicking thud and then his whole frame following—his back stretching, his breath catching in his throat, his toes flexing and curling. I snatched my hand away, terrified and thrilled, and when he groaned deep in his chest I felt it through my bones.

"Ansha?"

I didn't recognize the name, if it was a name. His eyes were wide open, staring, but I couldn't be sure he saw anything. I pushed myself up into his line of sight.

"Milja," I whispered. "I'm Milja."

His cracked lips parted, and he made a sound of need. He was beautiful in a way I couldn't understand: so beautiful I felt it as pain. So I returned my hand to its former position and nearly jumped with shock when I found that everything had changed. Nothing soft anymore, and nothing cold, and just so much *more* of him, flesh brought into existence from the nothing, from the void. Like a miracle.

I wrapped my hand around that burgeoning miracle.

So heavy. So strong. My hand embraced that hardness, stroking. His breath started to come faster, with a little tremble at the end of each exhalation, interspersed with murmured, unintelligible words. Soon he was so eager that he was too thick for my grasp.

I paused. I wasn't entirely sure where this was going, or how long it would take to get there. My own body was a cauldron of conflicting needs and fears.

"Milja!" he groaned, desperate.

That was when I heard a noise, like an echo of his cry. My head snapped up.

There—again: "Milja? Where are you?" A footfall on rock.

My father, entering the cavern.

I slid off the prisoner's boulder, scraping raw lines on my bare shins. Clumsy with terror, I found the fallen altar-cloth in the gloom and threw it across his hips in an attempt to hide the evidence of my sin. Then I backed away, but a loose stone turned under my feet and fell clinking among the slabs.

"Who's there? Is that you, Milja?"

A light sprang out in the half darkness, as my father snapped on his flashlight. There was nowhere for me to hide. I blinked and cringed as the beam caught my eyes.

"Milja! What are you doing down here?"

I couldn't answer. My skin burned with shame, proclaiming my guilt. I felt like there was no air in my lungs.

Father hurried forward across the fallen stone, frowning. The light swept the agonized lines of our captive, from his clenched hands to the mounded folds draped over his groin and the dig of his heels against the rock, pushing his thighs and hips an inch higher in his vain quest for solace.

"Girl!" Father's brows were knotted in anger, as if he were the Patriarch Moses surveying the sinning Israelites when he came down from the mountain. I had never seen him with an expression like that. He'd always been so mild and gentle with me. "What have you been doing?" he thundered.

"Nothing!" I lied, shrinking into myself.

"You shouldn't be here alone!"

"I've not done anything!"

The prisoner groaned.

My father shook his head, like the tolling of an execution bell. His heavy voice and damning words made it clear that he believed the man and knew that I was the one bearing false witness. "Didn't I tell you, child, that Azazel is the teacher of seduction? Did you not *hear* what I said?"

I bit my lip and wondered if I was going to be sick.

"I will send you away, Milja. You cannot stay near him! Your cousin Vera is in Boston: I will send you to her."

America?

I was twenty-three before I saw him again.

I went to Boston, Massachusetts, as my father arranged. He sold several of the icons and statues from within the tunnel to pay for me; there's never any shortage of black-market buyers for that sort of thing. Wheels were greased—some of them, I know, less than legally. I went to college. I graduated as a structural engineer and got a promising job.

I was even engaged to be married, briefly. Father was delighted, although Vera and her husband Josif thought I could do better—by which they meant some Orthodox boy who'd been born in America but whose parents remembered the Black Mountain or at the very least spoke our language—and they only redoubled their efforts to set me up with some ethnic relative.

I never warmed to those young men my cousin steered to me. It wasn't that I wanted to be on my own…but they weren't what I dreamed of. Nor was I what they wanted: I wasn't ugly, I guess, but tallish and skinny, with breasts too small for American tastes, my wavy dark hair tied back and my nose buried in a book.

And anyway, I was no use at talking to men the way they wanted to be talked to. Growing up without a mother or sisters or girlfriends, I'd never learned how. There are ways of conversing, and laughing, and moving, and appearing; signals girls give off that say *I'm fun: I'm interested in guys: You want me.* I'd never learned how to do any of that. I was too earnest, and when men did hit on me I'd either respond to their flirtations with serious conversation, or curl my lip at their silliness. Aggressive teasing just made me recoil, offended and scared. I did once try dying my hair blonde, which I dimly realized was one of the Right Signals, but the sight of my big dark eyes staring out from among long yellow locks just freaked me out and I hennaed it dark again even before it grew out.

Ben Dearing was, to my cousin's consternation, as WASP as they come. I met him at college, where he was in a student metal band called *Loki Unbound*. That was the reason we started seeing each other. I was standing in front of the flyer pinned to the gigs board in the hall, staring, when he first came up to me.

"You going to come see us play, then?"

"What does it mean?" I demanded, pointing at the poster, not even looking up at him. The picture, clearly drawn by someone with crude talent but in need of a lot of training, showed a muscular man in a loin-cloth bound hand and foot in a cave—the jagged stalactites made the location clear. Over his rage-twisted face dangled a serpent, poison dripping from its fangs. "Who's that?"

"That's Loki. The Norse god."

I felt cold, like all the blood was running out of my body and pooling in my leaden limbs. "Norse?" I made myself look up at the guy, taking in his long fawn hair and happy smile. "Scandinavian, you mean?"

"That's right. Vikings. You heard of them, yeah? Loki was a trickster and a troublemaker: sometimes on the side of the gods, and sometimes on the side of their enemies the giants."

"*Giants?*" I repeated stupidly, like I believed every word.

"Uh, yeah. Eventually the gods got so mad they tied him up under the earth, using the sinews of his own murdered son, and placed a venomous snake over him. When the poison drips in his eyes he thrashes about, causing earthquakes."

"But he escapes?"

"He will, just before Ragnarok."

"And what's that?"

"The End of the World. Are you going to come and watch us? I'm the drummer. And...that's my picture. D'you like it? You can have a copy if you want one. I'm Ben."

"I'm Milja," I said, still not thinking straight.

"Cool!"

Loki. Prometheus. Azazel. Amirani in Georgia, as I found out later when I started searching on the Internet. All demiurges involved in the creation and nurture of mankind. All rebels fettered for eternity by a God or gods who would not tolerate insurrection.

I went to the gig. I didn't have to dance, which was a relief. I could just stand at the back with my plastic cup of cola and watch. I liked the guys' long unfashionable hair.

Despite his metal aspirations, Ben was really quite sweet. And I was a good girl from the old country, so we didn't actually sleep together until we were engaged. We fooled around, of course. I was an expert with my mouth and my hands long before I gave up my virginity. And he did a good job unknotting the insecurities and the ignorance tangled in my psyche. When we did finally go all the way, it was not such a big step as I'd feared.

But it didn't work out well in the end: on our third night of actually having sex together I begged leave to tie him up, spread-eagled on the bed. Then I straddled him, slipping him into my hungry embrace. Below me, in the warm, dim light of the candles we'd lit, his body lay stretched out like a sacrifice: narrow hips, long pale hair, elbows raised as he braced against the scarves knotted at his wrists.

A stray thought grazed my mind: a wish that he had darker hair, and more of it on his torso. But it was only momentary, a twist in the rising surge of my appetite. I clenched my muscles and moved to make him gasp. Every time I ground against him a wave of heat seemed to billow up from the point where we were joined, filling me to bursting. My vision grew blurred. I tugged at my nipples, grinding them between my fingers. Ben bucked beneath me, thrusting upward, trying to fill the need he saw in me—but without the slightest idea of how great and hollow and ancient was that void in my soul.

For a moment, I didn't see Ben or the bed. I saw a great slab of rock, and a man without a name, and my wails seemed to echo back from stone walls as I slammed down upon him, burning with the ferocity of my orgasm, my face distorted with pain.

"Whoa," he said. "Jesus, Milja."

I burst into tears and struck at him, howling, over and over again. He couldn't even shield his face.

Poor Ben freaked out then. He told me that I had *serious fucking issues, you crazy bitch*. And that was it, for that relationship.

Vera was pleased when I told her the engagement was off, though she tried to show sympathy.

Oh, how I tried my best not to think about the prisoner after that, as I studied and made new friends and, after graduation, buried myself in my new job. What would be the point, when Father would not let me go home—not until I was safely married? And to be honest it wasn't too hard to forget, most days, because in Boston it all seemed entirely unreal: not just the cavern and the bound man isolated in darkness, but the silent little church and the mountain village. It seemed like a story, something from a movie I'd watched as a child. America was loud and roaring with life, and its steel and glass and crowds and wide horizons filled me to the brim, leaving no room for memories. I loved my new world and I tried my hardest to fit in—as much as any shy, bookish foreigner can fit in.

But I dreamed about him at night. I dreamed about him stretched out, shifting hopelessly the few inches permitted by his bonds in a desperate attempt to relieve his locked muscles. I dreamed he stared into the darkness and stretched back his head and called my name, and that he told me everything about himself: secrets always forgotten when I woke. I dreamed him shivering under the snow of our brutal winters, and choking in the flash floods of spring. I dreamed his body under my hands. And every morning for five years I woke with my pillow wet with the tears I'd cried in my sleep.

Then one day I received a phone call.

"Hello, *Nana* Vera." I said, cradling the flat plastic slip awkwardly between jaw and shoulder as I tried to wrestle papers back into a folder, and hearing the shutter sound effect that told me I'd accidentally taken a photo of my ear *again*. "What's up?"

I was desperately hoping she wasn't in one of her chatty moods. My boss could see me across the open-plan office and we weren't supposed to take personal calls during work time. I'd told Vera that, several times, but she was under the impression that the rules didn't apply to her.

"Milja. I'm so sorry, honey. I've got bad news."

"What?" I dumped the files on my desk and took a proper grip on the phone. "What's happened?"

14

"It's your father. He's been taken ill. You have to go home straight-away."

Home. For a moment the shiny modern office around me flooded with shadows, and I smelled damp stone and church incense. On my tongue was the greasy taste of mutton, and under my feet was the bounce of wild thyme.

"Milja? Did you hear me? Are you still there?"

"Father is ill?" I repeated, faintly. Far away, I heard the screech of the mountain eagle, high and cold and cruel.

Chapter two

EGAN

We flew out of Logan International together. Vera was old enough to be my mother, and I had no one else to take that role. It was a comfort to have her with me, though at the same time we seemed to be driving each other crazy. My cousin worried and tutted the whole way from my apartment to the airport—about the taxi being late, about the way everyone else was driving, about the cost of the last-minute tickets, about the clothes I'd chosen to travel in and the airline luggage allowance and the rudeness of people nowadays, all pushing and grousing at the terminal entrance. We elbowed our way through the press with the best of them, and trundled our wheeled suitcases down the interminable ranks of desks to our designated check-in.

That was where I discovered that I didn't have my passport on me anymore.

The gush of panic made me feel sick. I knew I'd had it with me in the taxi, because I'd checked for the fourth or fifth time, at Vera's insistence. I'd slipped it into my jacket pocket, I'd thought—but the pockets weren't very deep. Now they were inarguably empty.

"What were you thinking of, you silly girl?" Vera asked, her voice rising. "One thing I ask you to do, and look what happens! We'll miss the flight now!"

I could see the people in the queue behind us starting to stare. "Ring the cab company and ask them to get the driver to check, *Nana*," I suggested desperately. "And I'll go back and look. It might have fallen on the floor." I wanted to get away from Vera for a moment, just so my ears could stop ringing. My cousin was five-foot-nothing when she took her spike heels off, but she had the voice projection of an opera singer.

I left my suitcase with her, waiting resentfully to one side of the desk while the next customer checked in, and I headed back down the long, long hall of the terminal, scanning the scuffed floor for my passport. The thought that we might miss our plane, that we might not be able to fly, that we might not reach my father for another day or perhaps at all—it made my throat swell and my eyes burn. Hundreds of feet passed back and forth under my frantic gaze. Knots of people clustered everywhere, waiting for their desk announcements—could they have parked their overstuffed baggage on my fallen passport without realizing? I wanted to shout at them all to get out of the way. I wanted to beg them for help.

I was nearly back at the entrance door when a man stepped in front of me, blocking my path. I sidestepped; he stepped too. I went left, but he moved to bar my way with his leather shoes and his chinos and his casual suit jacket. I lifted my gaze to glare at him, feeling unwise words burn upon my tongue.

"Milja Petak?" He looked down at the open passport in his hand, and then into my face again, and smiled. "It's really not such a good likeness. You look like a kid in this."

Hope slammed me in the breastbone. "Where did you get that?" I blurted, snatching it out of his hand.

"Sure, you're welcome. It was on the floor just over there." He gestured toward the doors. He had a square face and square shoulders: sandy-blondish hair, sandy-blondish eyebrows, pale eyes.

Cute, said my hindbrain.

"You should have handed it in!" I snapped, which wasn't fair at all because I hadn't gone to the information counter myself. But I was too wound up and my mouth was running well ahead of my brain. I double-checked that it really, truly was my passport photo there on the back page, relief making my temples pound.

"Sorry," he said mildly. He had a slightly non-American accent.

"Right," I huffed.

"You okay, then?"

I glowered at him, too addled to think straight. His mouth twisted at one side, suggesting concern. "Okay," I said, since nothing else came to mind except a feeling I should thank him, and I didn't *want* to thank him or anyone because I was mad as hell. "Okay, then."

Then I turned on my heel and stalked back to Vera, my head held high.

We made it onto the transatlantic flight to Zurich, almost at the front of the queue. Vera's red-dyed hair, short at the back and sides and curly on top, bobbed down the aisle in front of me all the way to economy class, but she didn't want the window seat. "I don't like to see the ground when we take off. It's bad enough, that feeling in the stomach. You sit by the window."

Taller than her by some way, I loaded our carry-on bags into the overhead lockers and slid into the window seat. Vera took the middle one of the row of three, and immediately started complaining; "Ach! Look at this! There's no legroom!"

She had no cause to bitch, I thought, trying to arrange my rather longer legs into a comfortable position for the flight. "Put your blanket under the seat in front and you'll have more space."

"And these seats are tiny! Whoever designed this economy class must have an ass like a clothespin! How do they expect us to put up with this for six hours?"

"Excuse me."

That was the moment I looked up and saw the man waiting to take the aisle seat as soon as Vera removed her magazine and MP3 player and bag of toffees. It was *him*—my sandy-haired passport retriever. I went crimson. He smiled, tentatively.

I couldn't help noticing more about him this time round—the way his hair was cut to stick forward in a cute ruff, for example. And his full lower lip. And that he really was pretty handsome.

Vera gave a sigh of pure resentment and gave up her claim to annexing his seat. As our new neighbor settled in I looked out of the window. Well, I could hardly start a conversation with him across Vera's generous bust...

I just wished she'd stop her stream of niggling complaints, which were no longer just irritating but now embarrassing. And she kept up the sniping through preflight announcements and all the way to altitude, with only a brief break, eyes screwed shut, for the actual takeoff.

It was the second most acute feeling of relief I'd experienced all day, when the flight attendant approached, turned her lipstick grin on Vera and said, "Compliments of the captain, madam. Would you care to be upgraded to business class?"

I don't know whether everyone around us shared my relief, or just resented her luck. But the squeaky wheel gets the oil, I guess. Vera patted my hand and went off forward in the stewardess's wake, promising she'd swap over and let me take a turn in the comfortable seat after she'd had a drink and a nap.

I took a deep breath and turned to my neighbor. "I am really sorry," I said in a low voice. "I was very rude before. I should have thanked you. I wasn't mad with you: I was mad with me."

"Ah, that's okay," he said, showing his teeth in a little grin. "I figured you were feeling stressed. You looked...really upset."

His gentleness, and the personal comment, slipped past my defenses. I felt my eyes fill up and I blinked hard, looking away. Not fast enough though: a tear escaped and splashed on the back of my hand. Suddenly I found myself scrabbling through my pockets.

"Here." He held out a packet of travel tissues. I took them gratefully, mopped my eyes, sniffed shamefully and apologized several times over.

"I'm not having a good week," I admitted, my voice wobbling a little still. "I shouldn't...it's my father...I'm worried..."

"Your father? Is he on the flight?"

"He's back home in Montenegro—we're flying out to see him—he's really ill—" My Kleenex knight got the whole tale and listened seriously all the while, leaning in over the empty seat between us so that I wouldn't have to share my story with the whole cabin. Father's collapse during the Divine Liturgy—

"Sorry: your father is a *priest*?"

"Serbian Orthodox. They're allowed to marry."

"Oh—I see."

—and his confinement to bed in the village. No, he hadn't been taken to hospital, which was miles away over rough roads; it sounded like he was still talking and capable of sitting up, with help; it was hard to tell how much danger he was in or what had happened, but Cousin Vera was always great in a crisis, like when I got glandular fever, and she'd be able to help. Please God it wasn't a stroke or a heart attack. I was his only daughter and he didn't have any close family left in the country and I felt terrible not being there when he needed me. I hadn't seen him in five years. It felt like a lifetime.

I felt drained by the time I stopped talking. He nodded at me sympathetically, drawing his teeth over his top lip. "Ah now, you've told me all that, before I even told you my name." He put out his hand. "I'm Egan, by the way."

"Hi, Egan. Sorry for bending your ear." I took his hand, but it was more like a gentle squeeze than a shake that passed between us. It was nice though, a warm and empathic mini-hug, even if it came from a stranger.

It was just nice.

"Okay, you can stop apologizing now. You've caught up."

I nodded, abashed but somehow not minding.

"You're transferring on to Podgorica from Zurich, then, I'm guessing?"

"Uh-huh," I said, though he'd messed up the pronunciation of the city name.

Egan reached into the pouch before his knees and extracted a paperback travel guide to Serbia, Croatia and Montenegro. "We're going to be plane buddies all the way, then."

I raised my brows. "Really? What are you going out there for?"

"Um. Business." A glance downward indicated the white shirt beneath his jacket. "I'm in security systems."

"Uh...?"

"I.T., mostly. For a bank."

"That sounds..." I got stuck for a polite adjective.

"Awful, right?"

"Yeah."

"But at least I get to see a new country in my lunch breaks." He fished inside his jacket. "Perhaps you can help me... This is the place I'm staying at." He showed me a business card printed in Montenegrin script. "I can't actually pronounce the words for the taxi driver at the airport. It's like half the vowels are missing. And there are all these little marks…"

Smiling, I read the address, which was full of accented letters that didn't exist in the American alphabet, and then I read it out for him, line by line. He repeated it after me until he was happy. "So that's a *TS* not a *C*?"

"Yep. And that one sounds like a *J* even though it looks like a *D*."

"Ah grand. I can see this is going to be fun. Still, at least it's not in Cyrillic—that was what I was really scared of."

"You'll still find the Cyrillic alphabet in churches. But not out in the streets these days. Things are changing." That's what I'd been told, anyway. It'd been five long years since I'd seen for myself. The reminder made me uncomfortable. "Are you from Newfoundland, by any chance?" I asked, changing the subject. I'd had a Newfie roommate at college.

Egan shook his head. "Good guess, but no, I'm not. My mother's Irish—that's the accent you're hearing. American father, though." He smiled self-deprecatingly. "Dual nationality."

"So which country do you live in?"

"Uh, well, I grew up in Ireland. But I've been based in the States since. I try to travel on whichever passport gets the friendly reception at a given national border." He rolled his eyes. "Which, when I'm working in England, is neither."

We spent some of the rest of the trip looking through his tourist book, and I taught him a few helpful phrases and told him what useful details I could remember about my native country—which was sadly little, when it came down to it, even though Montenegro is only about the size of Connecticut and has less than a fifth of the population. A tiny place, relative to the States, but I'd experienced firsthand only my own small village, a few summer visits to Žabljac—which wasn't that much bigger—and that one trip to the capital Podgorica when I'd been put on the plane out to Boston. Everything else was hearsay, acquired from Father. But I liked talking to Egan; it took my mind off my own anxieties. And it was easy. He wasn't pushy or weird or anything. We stopped talking only when they dimmed the cabin lights to encourage us all to sleep. Vera never came back from business class, but I didn't mind at all.

When we touched down in Zurich we walked through to the transfer lounge together. Egan wheeled Vera's suitcase for her, which delighted my cousin even though it didn't stop her throwing me sharp little glances of warning.

We compared tickets for the flight onward, but this time we weren't sitting anywhere near each other. I shrugged and smiled, but felt a real pang of disappointment.

"Here," he told me, as the call for boarding came over the public address system and we rose, a little wearily, to face the next leg of the journey. Whipping a pen from his inside pocket, he scrawled on the back of the business card he'd shown me earlier. "I hope your father's going to be okay, but if there's anything I can do to help...call me."

I looked at his name, *Egan Kansky*, and the cell phone number beneath. "Don't you need the card to get to your lodgings?" I asked.

"Not anymore." He grinned. His eyes under the airport strip lighting were gray blue, broken up by little flecks of gold. "I've had expert tutoring."

After landing in Podgorica, our journey was only half over. We took a bus out north from the capital, spent the night dozing over a table in a cafe in Nikšić before changing to another local bus, and drove uphill for several hours—along good roads, but through increasingly wild country where the sheer limestone crags and their clinging black pines looked like something from an eighteenth-century Romantic etching. At the tiny town of Šavnik we hired the nearest they had to a taxi service, bouncing along an unpaved track in the back of a truck, up a nothing road into the Durmitor mountains, beneath beetling cliffs. I was glad it was summer; the upland meadows were a riot of Alpine wildflowers, but in winter the road to the village becomes impassable.

It was so strange to see the familiar landscape with fresh eyes. It looked incongruously *Heidi* in parts, cute little haystacks and all. And I realized how much I had missed the mountains, with their great green flanks and their jagged bare peaks and their deep sudden gorges cut by rivers. Patches of snow clung to the shadowed places by the road, even now in August when the direct sunlight felt scorching hot. It was a beautiful land, but cruel too. There were miles and miles of rock and grass and *nothing* else. We were nearly scraping the bright-blue sky overhead, it felt. And once above the tree line, the lush wildflowers gave way to thin sheep-cropped turf through which the white limestone jutted everywhere, like bones through peeling skin. This terrain was something other than picturesque—to me it had a quality of terror, as if the secrets it hid were unspeakable.

The village itself had changed, I thought, as we dropped into the valley and drove into what passed for the central square and the dogs ran around barking with excitement. There were more abandoned houses, and the ones that were still occupied had huge satellite dishes on the corrugated metal roofs that had replaced the old wooden shingles. But I had changed far more than Stijenjarac. I could see it reflected in the stares of the others as I climbed down from the vehicle: me with my tight jeans and my makeup, with my sunglasses and my looped plastic necklace. Even Vera, with her short red-dyed hair and her bright pink Versace handbag, looked out of place here, though she waved and strutted and called out to people as if she'd last seen them only a few weeks and not decades ago.

The place reeked of sheep. I'd forgotten that particular detail.

The old women clad in headscarves took us indoors, tutting at me and muttering to each other just as if I couldn't understand the things they said. I cast one last look up the mountainside to the distant white blob that was our church, before following them.

Father wasn't even in his own bed: he had collapsed in the village and it had been impossible to take him up the long climb to our isolated house. Now he occupied a borrowed sofa in someone's back room, under twin pictures of St. Sava and His Holiness the Patriarch. Father had changed too: his big black beard was gray now, his face thin and bony. I was shocked: he was only sixty, but in this country he was an old man.

I cried when I saw him. I buried my hands under his thin ones and kissed his cheek, horrified that we had lost so much time between us. His skin felt loose on his bones.

"Milja," he said, squeezing my hand with a ghostly echo of his old strength. "Look at you, little chick. You are so grown up. You are an American beauty queen now!"

"Papa," I chided him, "what are you thinking of, scaring me like this? You said you would tell me if you weren't feeling well!"

"I was fine, just fine. A little fall, that's all, and now all these women have got me tied up in their shawls and I'm not allowed to get out of bed.

I miss my house. They cook bean soup for me but, ach, they do not do it properly. I want to make my own soup."

"Don't worry, *Adzo*," said Vera. "I will cook for you from now on: the proper old recipe my mother taught me." She shot the attending beldames a hard look, as if their hospitality was an imposition. There was a sound of offended huffs.

"Milja." Father's grip tightened. I could see the worry in his eyes, and I leaned in closer. "I left...I left a lamp burning up there."

I frowned. "That's all right, Papa—it will have burned itself out."

His voice had sunk almost to a whisper. "In the passageway, you understand. Someone should go up and check."

I nodded to show that I understood. "Don't worry. I'll go make sure everything is okay."

"She will not," Vera said firmly. "Not on her own. She'll have to wait until I have time to come up with her."

"It's my house!" I glared at my cousin, but she was at least as stubborn as me by nature and had had far more practice.

"It is not right for you to go up there by yourself," she said, holding my gaze. "Not on your own."

We'd never spoken to each other about the family secret—not a word— but for the first time I realized that she *knew*—about the man in the cave, and about my disgrace. I couldn't help flushing, and I could only hope she took it for anger. I dropped my eyes. One thing at a time, and Father most urgent of all.

We wanted to take him to a hospital in Podgorica straightaway, but he was hugely reluctant, and to be honest it wasn't clear that he was strong enough to travel. Vera appointed herself head nurse, infuriating all the old women, and tried to rally his strength. I don't want to remember those days. I felt as though every fiber in my body was screaming from the strain. We took lodgings in the house across the street, and while Vera saw to his material needs I sat with my father and read to him from old magazines, and tried to get him to eat despite his birdlike appetite.

It was a strange, frustrating time. My father's condition worried me desperately. Probably because of the high mountains around us, my cell phone had no connectivity; I was cut off from my job, my friends and all but my two relatives. It seemed likely that my fledgling career had taken a serious blow. I thought about Suzana, my roommate, and wondered if she was looking after our cat Senka properly, and whether Senka missed me. Suzana was off to the Burning Man festival this year and wanted me to be home in time to cat-sit, though she'd tried not to hint too broadly. I thought about the New England Aquarium on the Boston harbor front, which I always made a habit of visiting in the last week of August, just like the first year I'd arrived in the States. It looked like I'd miss it this year. I'd been fascinated by the dark tanks in particular: the hypnotic dance of the jellyfish in the UV glow, and the terrible patience of the long-legged crabs under their crushing columns of water, down there in the dark, so cut off from the world of light.

Now it was my turn to feel cut off from the world, suspended between everyday life and the black depths inside the mountain so close by. I kicked around the village when I wasn't needed, aware of the stares of people I half remembered but who were more than half strangers now. There were no children in evidence and the room we'd used for a schoolhouse in my youth had reverted to being a storage shed: all the young people had moved out to Žabljac to work in the ski-resort hotels, or down to the lowland cities. I couldn't sit with the men in the tavern, and the women made it clear I was not approved of. Somehow, at twenty-three, they managed to make me feel like an outcast teenager again, sulky and uncertain. Only the village dogs were pleased to see me, perhaps because I bribed them with bread crusts. The lonely little church on the hillside beckoned, but I didn't quite dare defy Vera and head up there on my own, and she showed no eagerness to walk several kilometers and climb the two hundred steep steps, muttering about her sciatica whenever I suggested an ascent.

After four days Father agreed he was able to go for medical treatment—but Vera swept out of the room triumphantly to organize transport before he revealed his one condition. "Someone," he whispered to me, plucking at the sheet over his chest, "someone... Come closer, Milja." He looked around the room, as if he was worried a spy had crept in among the shadows.

"It's all right, Papa. We're alone. You can talk." My heart was beating uncomfortably fast.

"Someone from the family must stay and guard *him*. It is our holy duty."

So, I thought, it wasn't all just something I'd imagined. It was *real*. "He's...still there?" I said hoarsely.

Father's watery eyes sharpened for a moment, his brows drawing together in consternation. "Of course. Nothing has changed. Except that...Milja, you are not a child anymore. You know you must do what is right."

"What is right, Papa? What do I do?"

"You must stay until I come back. If you have to leave...if I am kept in hospital... I have wired the cave with explosive. The switch is in the passage. You must bring the walls down upon him."

chapter three

OUT OF THE DEPTHS

It was not until my father was driven away safely in a hired car with Vera that I made the climb up to our old house.

"I don't like it," my cousin told me, holding on to the passenger-side door as we stood in the square, preparing to part. She spoke in English, not just because she was more used to the tongue after years abroad, but because we were being watched, quite openly, by knots of villagers. It was highly unlikely anyone could follow our exchange, but still we kept it down to a low and urgent undertone. "I've spoken to your Uncle Josif; he is flying out tonight from Boston."

"What? How did he get away from his business?" I didn't ever remember Uncle Josif—he was accorded the title by dint of his comparative age and status, though he was my cousin's husband—taking a day off from the construction company he owned, except for the highest holy days of Christmas and Easter.

"Never you mind. He will be here in a couple of days, so you will not be on your own with these…peasants."

I cringed. Those *peasants* had flatly refused any financial remuneration for lodging, feeding and caring for us or for my father. "*Nana* Vera! Don't call them that!"

"Why not? They are peasants—they know nothing. You mustn't let them into the church, Milja. They will rob the place; a church without a priest is nothing to them. And if they found *him*..."

Like some ghost, her meaning hovered between us. I swallowed. "You've seen him, then?"

You believe? I might have added.

She nodded curtly. "Once. You remember when we came to visit, when you were ten? Then. Horrible."

Did she mean that he was horrible, or that his situation was? Her expression of disgust could have meant either. Was I alone in hating what we'd done to our prisoner?

"Don't go near him on your own," she commanded, her eyes narrowing to slits as if she could read my mind. "Wait until your Uncle Josif gets here."

"Uncle Josif isn't family," I reminded her. He'd met Vera when she was working in a tourist hotel on the Gulf of Kotor, and his own family originally came from Cetinje. "He shouldn't be involved. *Tell no one else*: that's the rule, remember?"

"Don't you tell me what we have to do, Milja. We are running out of menfolk. If you'd married..."

"Don't start!"

"You want your father to die before seeing you a bride? Because that's the way you're going."

"He is not going to die!" I snapped, and for a moment we stood scowling at each other. Vera had the grace to look abashed.

"Of course he's not, honey," she muttered.

"Milja." My father's croaky voice came from the backseat of the car. I leaned in to see him, and he touched my head gently as if giving me a blessing. "You must bring the money from the house. It is under the slab in front of the window, you know the one."

"Yes, I know."

"Hospitals are expensive: I can't have your cousin paying for me to lie in bed. Bring some of the old statues too, from the passage, when you come to see me. We can sell those."

"Yes, Papa."

"Don't forget what I told you, little chick. The switch..."

"No, Papa. Don't worry. I will do what you said."

Then they left me.

* * *

Everything was familiar, and yet everything was strange. I was seeing now with the eyes of a foreigner: the cramped little buildings wedged under the brow of the cliff, with the domestic rooms crammed against the church in peculiar proximity. Even the steps themselves—two hundred rock-cut rises at the end of a dusty track. When I was young I had run up and down them every day without a thought, but now I was ashamed to find that my thighs ached and my breath came short.

I couldn't face the church and what lay beneath it straightaway, so I went into the house first, using the key Father had left me. Nothing had changed, and yet...everything had. I knew the pattern on the rug before the fireplace and the contents of the dresser drawer on the left and every one of the books in Father's study; I knew the shabby winter coat hanging behind the door and the chipped ewer in the center of the table (I'd dropped it when I was thirteen and we'd never found that piece of the lip). But my old room was empty and smelled of plaster dust, and the quilted coverlet on the bed, which I remembered as a vibrant patchwork of flower shapes, looked faded and cheap. I couldn't have grown much taller since eighteen, but the roof felt lower.

I hadn't realized we were so *poor*. My friends in America would hardly believe anyone could live like this, without Internet or a washing machine or cable. Forget dishwashers; our house didn't even have piped hot water— we collected rain in a cistern up in the cliff face. Down in the village at least they had electricity and solar panels and television. Up on our crag here we were still lighting kerosene lamps and cooking in a log-fired oven.

I wandered around the house, touching things at random. I wound the clock and set it to the time specified by my otherwise-useless phone. I put the single plate on the table away in the cupboard. There was a covered pot on the stove-top, but when I lifted the lid the smell of rotted beans turned my stomach. So I sat down at the table and gripped my hands together. This was my home, but I did not feel at home here. The dissonance made my head ache: inside, I was a happy child and an aching teenager and a grown woman of twenty-three, all at the same time. I was part of this place, and I was a foreigner. I had returned to the home I loved, and yet I was an intruder.

My gaze shifted to the spines of the books in the case. Even from here

I was sure I could recognize and name each one, just from their colors and shapes. As a game, I began to work my way across a shelf: *Modern Engineering Principles and Practices...The Homilies of St. Macarius... The Mountains of Serbia...First Steps in English* (from which Father had taught me: British English, not American English, taps not faucets)... *The Child's Encyclopedia* volumes Two, Three and Four (but not One, which I'd dropped being chased home from school one day and never recovered)...a Bible...the *Book of Enoch*...

Cover him with darkness, that he may remain there forever.

Forever. Down there in the mountain behind me, bound hand and foot. Had he noticed that the priest had stopped visiting? Did he realize that he'd been abandoned by the man now, just as the girl had abandoned him years ago? Had he called out, unheard, with only the echoes standing in witness to his pleas? Had he missed the food and the drink that I no longer brought him, the touch of my hands, those tiny mercies in an eternity of suffering? Had I made it *worse* by offering him ease, then depriving him again just as he learned to hope?

The sun-patch thrown on the flagstones by the small kitchen window had disappeared, as the shadow of the cliff above shifted. I shook myself from my trance and rose from the chair.

Fear was no longer an excuse.

If the house had felt strange, the soot-blackened interior of the tiny church, with its icons so darkened by age that only their gilt halos could be made out clearly, was like something from another era; something medieval and now distinctly unwelcoming. St. Michael, patron saint of our family, stood over the recumbent Devil still, and watched me with mournful disapproval as I retrieved from under the floor tile the key to the narrow padlocked door behind the altar. My hands were unsteady as I probed the lock, but I remembered the old trick of jiggling the key against the teeth to persuade it to turn. I stepped into the passage beyond for the first time in years.

An arm's length behind the wooden door was something new: a metal door I'd never seen before. Nonplussed, I looked it over. It had deep lintels and jambs, also steel, and no lock but two heavy bracing bars. It was, I worked out, a homemade blast door, welded from many sections. Father must have fitted it himself, when he decided to prepare the world's last line of defense against the prisoner below.

It took the weight of my shoulder to move the steel door on its hinges.

Down I went, into the dark, the first person in weeks to tread this path. I carried only a two-liter bottle of water and a flashlight. The church's lingering scent of frankincense gave way to a cellar smell of damp stone. From the niches to either side, the nameless statues of forgotten gods watched me pass.

Down, down, my feet scuffing the stone on which no dust settled. My fingers spread, brushing the rock.

The passage opened out into the cavern. Daylight filtered in from the broken roof far above. Great slabs of limestone lay spilled across the path of my flashlight.

There. There he was. Just as I remembered. My nightmares were all real. I felt my heart pound against my ribs like it would smash them.

Dear God.

I was seeing *him* with adult eyes too. He didn't look like a titan, or a demon, or a god. He looked like a man: perhaps in his early thirties, swarthy, with an athletic build and really dark lashes and hair going prematurely gray. Tall, but not inhumanly so. Dirty; naked; abused. His exposed armpits and crotch were exclamation marks of vulnerability. I picked my way over to the slab and knelt over him. His face was just the same as it had been five and more years ago: stubbled, haggard with pain but handsome despite that. Breathtakingly so, like the agonized beauty of certain icons.

I touched his face. He opened his eyes. "Milja."

I began to cry.

His voice was hoarse. "You...came...back."

I was shocked: he'd never addressed me before. The words "I'm sorry!" spilled from my lips along with my sobs; "Oh God, oh God—I'm sorry! Papa sent me away! I didn't want to go, I didn't—"

My tears were dripping on his face. I wiped clumsily at them, smearing the dirt. "What's your name?" I begged.

He didn't answer.

"Who are you?"

He tried to moisten his lips. "I...don't remember."

31

Bending forward, I pressed my wet cheek to his. Did I believe him? I don't know. He could be Loki or Prometheus or Azazel; I know I didn't care anymore. When I sat up I reached to the nape of my neck and undid my necklace. The sheath of bright blue plastic peeled off to reveal a supple length of steel-toothed metal: a wire saw.

This was it. The moment of choice.

The moment I betray my family, I thought. *My father, who has trusted me even after last time. The whole line of my blood. All those people over all the centuries, who have stayed here, slaves to this prisoner, because it was their duty. Because they were keeping the world safe. Because they were obeying the will of God.*

I cut through his bonds, one by one. It took a long time. The leather resisted even the titanium-tipped saw-teeth, and I wondered what the hell it was. I thought about Loki's son, slaughtered by the Æsir so that his body parts might be used as rope—for only a god might bind a god. The thought was foul and I tried to push it aside.

As I cut, his breathing grew louder and louder, sucking great lungfuls of the flat cavern air as if he were building up to a fearful effort.

When I freed his second ankle, he rolled onto one hip. For a moment he lay without moving, groaning a little under his breath.

I touched the back of his hand. "Take your time," I whispered, wondering if I would have to pull him to his feet. That wouldn't go well; he was far too heavy for me.

But then, with a heave and a grunt, he sat up, pulled the severed ends of his tethers loose and rubbed at his leg. The skin beneath his bonds was sticky-raw: I saw how he had to pull the leather off to free his wrists and feet. His breath came harsh and shallow, and I think the change in posture was as agonizing as the removal of the binding. When he opened his screwed-up eyes I passed him the water bottle.

He didn't know how to open it. He had no idea about screw-top caps.

"Here." Quickly I remedied the situation. The water escaped down his throat and chest as he glugged it back, cutting runnels in the dirt there.

I was wearing a long skirt that day to mollify the old women; I wet the hem while he was getting his breath back and tried to gently clean his face with the cloth.

That was rash. He caught my wrist in one hand; I felt the fingers of his other on my bare calf. Our eyes locked, and I felt time hang, breathless—before he moved to cover my mouth with his, and I tasted blood and stone and darkness in his kiss.

There were no words. There had never been adequate words for his pain and need, or for my hunger. All these years my guilt and my loneliness had pulled me back to this place, and to this moment: this kiss. I grasped his shoulder and felt the play of his muscles as we moved together; beneath my fingertips there was grit stuck to his skin that might have been there for centuries. I yielded to his cold lips and his arms and the press of his torso, repudiating my yesterdays and throwing away all my tomorrows in the rush of this moment, this ache. He had already taken my heart: now he stole my breath and my senses.

The only thing that kept me from rapture was his grip on my wrist, tight and growing tighter. I could feel the bones of my wrist grinding together; in the discomfort I felt a dim echo of his agony—and because of that I welcomed it. But the hurt grew and at last I broke the kiss with a gasp.

I heard him growl.

"Please—not so tight!" I begged.

He looked down at his hand as if he'd never seen it before, and abruptly he released me. I cradled my wrist, rubbing it, and stared up at him through my lashes. I was half-afraid, half-enchanted, and dizzy with uncertainty and arousal.

For a moment he took my face lightly in his hands, thumbs limning the bones of my cheeks. In the half-light I saw the slow shake of his head. "My star of the morning," he breathed, "come to lead me to the day."

I didn't understand.

"Is there a sun shining still?" he whispered. "And snow upon the high peaks?"

I nodded inside the cage of his fingers.

"Is there grass?" he pressed me, brushing my lips with his. His skin was warm now. "Do trees still lift their arms to the sky?"

"Of course."

With all the muscular uncoiling of a snake he rose up on his knees over me. I saw his skin gleaming with perspiration. Maybe he was no titan, but he was far taller than I was; he loomed like a wave about to fall. For a moment then, I admit, I thought that he was about to seize me and press his naked body down upon me—but instead he put his head back and stretched, flexing each joint, and just by watching I understood the inexpressible pleasure of being able to move and twist and ease every muscle: the visceral joy of freedom.

He laughed disbelievingly, low in his throat. "Show me."

"Show you?"

"Which way is out?" he asked, reaching to pull me to my feet as he rose up himself. My legs were weak and I tipped against him, dizzy.

Oh God. His naked body, here, now, against mine. I can feel his…

"Okay. I'll take you." I was blushing with shame for what had not happened.

And that was how I came to release the prisoner of eons. The act itself had been so abrupt—so sudden—that now it felt utterly unreal. Even the throb of my flesh and the quiver in my legs made it seem all a part of my fantasy.

I led him to the tunnel mouth, but he wasn't content to follow and he pushed ahead, drawing me by the hand. He didn't spare the icons and the votive offerings a single glance: his attention was fixed upon escape. As the first breath of warmer air came to us he released me and hurried forward, fending off the walls as he stumbled because his legs were still a little uncertain beneath him.

I felt then the clutch of fear. He didn't look back to see if I was following. He didn't seem to remember me. All his focus was on what lay before him and, as I hurried to keep up, every straining inch of the distance between us tore at me.

Was he going to abandon me, now that I'd freed him?

The door to the church was standing open. He surged out into the room, searching for an exit. I wondered for a moment whether he would be able to cross holy ground, but he didn't even seem to notice his surroundings: he had eyes for nothing but the outer door, its ancient planks outlined by the sun. He wrenched it open and the blazing glow of the afternoon poured in upon him, lapping his naked flesh, haloing him in light. A human would have flinched and shielded his eyes: even where I stood, at the back of the chamber, I was half blinded. Tears swelled my eyes and my throat. He only lifted his chin, staring.

Beneath my feet, the ground trembled. It lasted perhaps a second or two—almost as if the Earth itself shivered.

The breath stopped in my breast as I waited for what would happen next—for him to burn to ash perhaps, or for an eagle to swoop down upon him from the heavens. Or for him to unfurl demon wings and vanish with a clap of sulfurous thunder. I didn't even have his name to call out in my terror.

None of those things happened. It was just an earth tremor, one among many we suffer yearly. A little dust fell from the arched ceiling. My companion didn't even seem to notice. Instead he looked back into the room, toward me, and stretched out his hand, pleading. I moved to lay my fingers in his and he pulled me against him, holding me tight. I could feel his strong, hard body trembling. Without words we stood holding each other, looking out upon the valley and the village below, with its fields and its brown-and-red tin roofs and the snow-capped peaks of the Durmitor range beyond: the terrifying open vistas of freedom.

He wouldn't come out of the sun. It was impossible to blame him for that, but I did try to persuade him, worried that he would be seen from below. He only looked at me with mild curiosity, as if I were singing some pretty tune in a language he didn't understand. Going right to the lip of the rock shelf, he sat down bare-assed upon the warm stone, his feet swinging in space, and stared off into the distance like he would never tire of the view.

Lean and naked and as filthy as road crew, every pore stippled with dirt.

Well, it wasn't like I could *drag* him indoors.

Eventually I left him there with the water bottle and went into the kitchen to find him food. It was all I could think of doing; my imagination had extended no farther than his release. In fact the situation seemed to have robbed me of all my wits. I stood in the middle of the room, my hand on my breastbone, feeling the pressure build in my lungs as my breath came fast and shallow. What had happened in the cave seemed unreal; what sat outside was impossible; what awaited in the future was unthinkable.

It's not real. How can it be real? If it is real, how can I have done it?

"Papa," I whispered. "You told me not to. But I did. What do I do now?"

Part of me wanted to rush out again and check that he was still there, and to feast my gaze on those dark eyes and those long hard muscles, the unself-conscious nakedness of his body. Another part of me wanted to hide in my bed with the quilt over my head. Maybe he'd just go away, and the thump of my heart and the tingle in my flesh would be the only evidence left.

I pulled a helpless face. I'd come in here to feed him.

He must be starving.

It took some time for muscle memory to come to my rescue. In five years I'd grown used to such a different way of living. There wasn't anything fresh in the larder that hadn't spoiled, of course, but I lit the wood stove and pumped water by hand from the cistern, into pans that I set upon the hob top. Boiling up rice and dried lentils, I fried onion and garlic and the very last of the withered apples from the pantry, found a ham wrapped in linen and carved off slices to add to the mess. Dishing up a plateful, I carried it outside.

With every step my nervousness grew.

He'd gone.

Oh, I thought, my heart swooping into my belly: *Oh*. The cliff edge was empty.

Had he melted away into the sunlight? And yet the sheer griminess of his skin had convinced me that he was solid flesh and blood. I'd touched that. I'd *felt* him. He was a *man*.

Maybe he'd set off down the steps toward the village. I hurried to the head of the rock stair, but there was no one visible on the flight, and no untoward disturbance in the village below.

Surely, if he's down there, they'd be going crazy? I'd hear the dogs at least.

He put his hands on my shoulders from behind me.

I convulsed with shock, and the plate of food in my hands slipped and shattered on the rock, sending the pottage splattering. "Oh!" I yelped.

"Do I frighten you?" He put a hand on my hair—and perhaps it was meant to be soothing but I felt a hot wet flow sink down through my whole body from head to core.

"I'm sorry! Oh God, I've ruined it," I panicked. I tried to stoop and pick up the broken pottery, but his hand tightened on my shoulder, just enough to hold me in place. If I wanted to escape his grip, I'd have to make a point of wrenching free. So I froze.

"It doesn't matter," he said.

My heart was rocketing—not from the silly surprise, but from a deeper fear. I wondered if anyone was looking up from the village—and if they were, could they tell that there were *two* figures in front of the church?

"You must be so hungry," I protested.

"I am."

He let me turn in his grasp to look up at him. That was a mistake on my part. I was inches from his naked flesh. *Don't look, Milja: don't look.*

I looked into his face instead.

Oh crap. How had I ever thought his eyes were black? They were *silver.* Not just gray, no, but metallic silver like the molded garments adorning icons of the Holy Family. They caught the light and they threw it back. His contracted pupils were almost lost in the shine, and—weirdly—it made him look blind.

I licked my dry lips, trying to hide my shock. "There's more in the pan. I'll just…"

"It's kind of you. But there's no need."

"You need to eat…"

"But not beans." His chuckle was soft and dark, like soot. His eyelashes were sooty dark too, I noticed, and long—the sort of lashes that made women weak at the knees, that let a man get away with murder. But it was his words, and the undisguised intent behind them, that made me blush and drop my gaze to the hand on my shoulder. I noticed then that his wrists—which had been scoured raw by the tight bonds, I knew that, I'd *seen* the bleeding flesh—were whole and uninjured. It made my own skin creep, just a little.

I swear the pounding of my heart was audible.

"Where are we?" he asked, mercifully. "What's that city down there called?"

"Uh. Stijenjarac. It's not a city. It's a…it's just a village." I dared lift my gaze to his again. "It's nowhere. No one's ever heard of it."

He lifted one eyebrow.

"Things have changed while you were…" I swallowed. "A lot."

"It seems so."

"How long? I mean…do you know how long it's been?"

His mouth made a half smile that had no humor in it. "How could I count?"

"What are you going to do?" I whispered.

His eerie eyes never left mine. I was starting to think that he didn't blink, ever, and that was more unnerving than I cared to admit. "I don't know, yet," he answered, whispering too. He might almost have been mocking me. I couldn't tell.

"You'll need clothes. You can't go down there naked. I'll find you some…spare pants."

He took the hint and let me go.

My hands were trembling as I walked away, and my clothes felt too hot and too damp and too tight.

It felt horribly wrong going into Father's bedroom to get him clothes, but I had little choice. I found clean black drawstring trousers and a black shirt folded in a bottom drawer—the pants would be too short in the leg, and the shirt would hang upon his torso like a sack—and I brought them into the kitchen. I hooked down the tin bath from its place on the wall and filled it with water from the stove-top and the cold cistern. There was no point in putting him into clean clothes, I told myself, if he was as filthy as a coal miner beneath.

The heat was going out of the day as I went out to fetch him. But not even the golden afternoon light could touch the dark of his unkempt obsidian hair. That gave me pause; I could have sworn that he'd been graying, when I saw him underground.

"I've drawn you a bath," I said awkwardly, standing well back. "Please…please come in and wash."

He was hunkered on the cliff edge this time: a bird of prey waiting to swoop on the land below. Every ropy muscle of his body stood out stark, like an artist's drawing in charcoal. He glanced one last time into the sun, full-on, without blinking, and then rose from his perch to go with me. Already his movements were stronger and more assured.

Oh, beautiful. Oh God, he's so beautiful it's crazy. It's not natural. I can't deal with this. I am so out of my depth.

I looked away quickly. Then I preceded him into the kitchen, feeling his gaze upon me. That evoked memories of his mouth and his hands that made me feel even clumsier in comparison. And it was so hard not to look at his crotch.

"Are you sure you don't want food?"

He shook his head, with a half smile.

I pointed at the bathtub. "Well, there you go."

He barely glanced at it; his attention was already on the other fittings of the room. He walked about, frowned at the stove—I was ready to yell a warning if he made to touch the hot surface—ran his hand over the stone sink and the handle of the pump, circled to a wall and looked closely at two framed photographs that hung there. One was a formal one of my father, beardless in those days and clutching his university graduation scroll. The other was of Father and me. I must have been eleven or so when it was taken; my hair was worn in bunches back then and I'd had big goofy teeth. I was so pleased now to have grown out of both.

He ran his fingers across the picture glass. "How is this done?" he asked. "It's no painting. A true likeness."

"Um...light-sensitive chemicals." Once again I caught a glimpse of the depths of his ignorance, and it made me dizzy. "It's complicated. I can explain sometime."

"Such wonders." He glanced along the wall and his gaze fell on the bookcase next. He tilted his head. "Those...those are all books?"

"Yes." *So how does he know what printed and bound books are, then?*

"I saw them in your dreams," he said as if answering my unspoken question.

I startled, not knowing whether to be more worried about what he'd just said or the fact that he'd known to say it.

"So many." He reached out and touched the spines gently, almost with reverence. I felt a twinge of pity.

"No. These are very few; we have more in the other room. And there are millions and millions of books in the world. In every language. For children, for adults... Books about *everything*."

He looked sideways at me. "Which one of them is the most important? Which should I start with?"

"Huh. Um, well...my father would say that one." I pointed at the Bible. "It's our holy book."

He reached out to take it off the shelf and I found myself going suddenly tense, as if something terrible were about to happen. But he only opened it and leafed through the thin, densely printed pages toward the beginning. I saw pleasure dawn in his face.

"Such perfect, tiny script!"

"It's printed, not handwritten. By machines. Ah. I'll... You've got a lot to catch up on. Don't worry about it yet."

"What language is this in?"

"Serbian. The script is Cyrillic." *Which, of course, you've never seen in your life.*

"Ah yes," he said, as if at a casual reminder. His gaze drifted across the text. Then he read out from the second page—early in Genesis, of course: *"And the Lord God said, Behold, the man is become as one of us, to know good and evil; and now lest he put forth his hand, and take also of the tree of life, and eat, and live forever: Therefore the Lord God sent him forth from the garden of Eden."*

There was a pause. He blinked heavily—the first time I'd seen him do that—and when he looked at me again there was a very strange look on his face. I found myself stepping backward.

"You should bathe before the water gets cold," I said, nervously. There was suddenly something horribly ominous about this tall, naked, filthy man standing in my kitchen. The late afternoon light through the window behind him cast his face into shadow. He hadn't moved, but he seemed to *loom*, somehow.

What have I done?

He nodded slowly, as if he were listening to a different voice altogether, and slotted the Bible back into the shelf. Then he turned to the tin tub—and hesitated. "What do I do?" he asked.

The question was so unexpected, so gauche, that I laughed out loud—and then covered my mouth in embarrassment. But he smiled too, hitching one angled brow.

Oh hell but he was handsome, despite the dirt. Far too handsome to be safe. I could feel my cheeks glowing pink.

"Sit in the tub," I suggested, and tried not to watch too intrusively

40

as he complied, folding his long legs and settling into the warm water. I busied myself preparing soap and washcloth and rinsing cup.

"Soap," I said helpfully, handing it to him. He looked at the green bar, sniffed it cautiously, and then looked back at me with a quizzical expression.

Of course, I told myself. *Even soap probably wasn't invented when he was...he was...*

I couldn't even imagine how long ago that was. I chose to concentrate on something a little less nerve-racking. "Okay," I said, kneeling beside the tub, taking the bar from his hand and dunking it in the water. "Like this."

I started on his shoulders and back, lathering up and stripping the dirt off. It wasn't, I reasoned, like he could reach his own back anyway—he needed a helping hand. I wasn't trying to be provocative, honestly, any more than he was trying to be provocative by sitting there naked. It just... moved that way. His shoulders were hard and muscled, and warm to my hand. He moved under my massaging fingers, reacting with little stretches and grunted exhalations of pleasure as I worked down the knotted muscles of his spine. The skin revealed beneath the grime looked sallow now, but as if it would brown easily if it had the chance to spend time under the sun. His head was turned, watching me.

Silver, hot-metal eyes. I felt like I could feel his gaze, as if it were a tangible thing, lingering on my hips and thighs and breasts.

If he knew how wet I am down there...

When I'd finished with his back, I came round and started on his chest. I had no excuse for that, and I did not meet his eye. Maybe I was hoping he wouldn't notice. But my hands were just so hungry for him, burning to explore the hard lines of collar and breastbone and the rough, dark hair drawn like ink lines down his torso. For most of my life his body had resided in the deep places of my mind; it had dominated my dreams and burned in my fantasies. Now it was out in the light, a chiaroscuro no longer but a sculpture in three dimensions. My hands blurred across his form, learning its shapes and textures, turning memory into actuality. It was like I needed to make him real.

But anyone who'd ever bathed a dog, or a child, knows that you can't keep your own clothes dry. It just doesn't work that way. I was aware that my blouse and skirt were clinging to me in soapy damp patches. I was aware that he was looking at those. I got about as far down his torso as his diaphragm when he lifted a wet hand from the bath and trailed his fingertips across my cheek, then dropped it to cup my right breast. Drips of water slipped from my blushing face like tears. His hand burned a dark print on the cotton of my top.

My breast fitted perfectly into his palm, I noticed, as he squeezed me softly. A nervous little noise escaped my lips.

"Milja," he said, a hoarse edge to his voice. "In the darkness, you were a light to me. Light and hope and sustenance."

I used you, I thought. *I used you for my own needs, selfishly, like a child using a toy.* But I couldn't say that. "I'm so sorry," I whispered.

"You keep saying that."

"I didn't mean to abandon you. I never forgot, I thought of you all those years..."

"I know."

That made me tremble. "Forgive us. Father was so afraid you would harm me, that's why he sent me away."

His brows drew together. "How could I harm you?" His calloused thumb, slipping beneath the layers of my clothes, played with my puckering nipple. "I was bound fast."

"Spiritually, I mean," I whispered, my eyes fluttering as sensation raced like fire across my skin from the point of my breast.

"Hm." He released my nipple, only to take my soap-lathered hand from where it pressed against his chest and push it into the bath water, down between his thighs. "Like this?"

"Oh," I squeaked, my eyes widening. I don't know why I should have felt surprised. I'd held what waited there in my hands before, eagerly—but as I found in its surging rise how very little patience it possessed in waiting, I was taken aback at my own reaction. My slippery fingers seemed to have a mind of their own. As they wrapped about his length I felt it thicken.

"But you are not afraid, are you Milja?" he growled, his lips brushing mine.

He was crediting me with more courage than I thought I possessed. In truth I didn't understand how my hand was so bold when my heart was racing with fear. I squeezed him tighter, awed by his utter solidity. And

42

that was when I saw it in his eyes: the change. It was like…it was like watching the pilot light on a domestic furnace just as it catches the gas and goes from a single point of intense heat to a roaring blue conflagration. Something in him changed like that; an elemental ignition from interest to implacable intent.

He rose to his feet in the bath in one long fluid motion, water streaming down his body, every muscle limned and glistening. I wanted to touch the scars hacked into his hard flat stomach; I wanted to trace them with my tongue. From miles above, or so it seemed, his face looked down upon me, ominous as Judgment. Since I was still kneeling upon the floor, his stance put me face-to-face with the dark object of all my secret fantasies and all my father's fears.

And I wanted to kiss it, like a pagan woman giving worship to her idol hewn from wood or stone, just as the Prophets condemned over and over again in the Old Testament. I wanted to draw his length into my embrace as if I could take his pain into me. But I was too scared.

He filled his lungs in a great breath that seemed to go on forever. I felt his hands on my head, fingers entwining in my hair. When they tightened, the sweet sharp pain ran through me in flash, from scalp to core. Suddenly I was drenched with heat, and I quivered as if I'd been slapped.

I hadn't known anything about this. I'd never guessed that I'd react to having my hair pulled like that—in many ways I was still so inexperienced. But *he* felt it: he knew. One hand in my hair, he lifted me to my feet. Then he stepped out of the bath, looming over me, and pushed me back across the room. There was absolutely no mistaking his intention now.

My rear met the heavy wooden table and my retreat stopped abruptly. I looked up into his face, wide-eyed. He pressed up against me, his arousal painfully evident, and all but bore me over as he kissed my open lips. I'd have lost my balance if he hadn't had me pinned against the wood, and gripped me by the hair.

"Milja," he said, and it really was a growl this time. My hands were on his wet bare body and I could feel the flame burning beneath his skin, threatening to set me on fire. He bit my lower lip, pulling it between his teeth, making me whimper. My whole body seemed to be dissolving, everything wet and slippery as if I were the one who'd been soaped up, all the strength ebbing out of me even as his strength grew. His fire, my water.

Oh God but I could feel that strength, and feel myself at its mercy. His need was overwhelming—and it made him clumsy and abrupt. He pushed my blouse up to my armpits and—clearly having no clue what to do with my bra—shoved that out of the way in similar fashion so that he could bury his face in my bare breasts. His kisses were ravenous; I could feel him shaking under my hands. My nipples, wet from his mouth, hardened like gemstones. He crouched to mouth all the way down my stomach as if he were devouring me alive, filling his tongue and nose with my scent and my warmth, gasping between kisses. Then he bunched my skirt up at my waist and caressed my legs, his hands strong and forceful, yanking the wisp of lace between my thighs aside so that he could sink his face into my sex. I fell back upon the tabletop, my elbows knocking the wood. His stubble rasped on my skin. As his tongue settled over me I spasmed and arched, twisting away from him and thrusting into him all at the same time, overwhelmed by his mouth. He pinned me, and I yielded joyfully. His fingers spread me as he kissed and sucked and licked. My whimpers of pleasure became frantic, and his attentions grew even more desperate; I was being eaten by a starving man.

Soaring on the storm of my arousal, I wrapped my fingers in his ragged hair. "Please...oh God, please!" I had no other name to cry out.

Oh. This was what I had been dreaming of. Five years of dreams.

Braced on his arms, wrapped in my legs, he ate me like a wild beast devouring his prey. Release took me and I wailed without words, and I heard his throaty grunts under my cries as he pinned my bucking hips and wrung out every last drop of ecstasy from my flesh.

I wanted to collapse into his embrace. I wanted to stroke his face and kiss his lips.

But that wasn't what he had in mind at all. Abruptly, he stood and stepped back enough to flip me, folding me facedown over the table. After all his sweet attentions, that wasn't what I'd expected and I think I resisted a little, without thinking—but he put a hand on my back and pushed me down hard, pinning me. The breath went out of my lungs.

His intent was primal, all animalistic lust, and he didn't even pretend to be apologetic about that.

I shut my eyes, feeling him gather my long skirt again and throw it over my hips, baring my ass. His hands took possession of that like Joshua marching into the Promised Land: he caught hold of my lacy little panties and this time he just tore them to bits between his hands.

Oh God, I mouthed. I'd never had to deal with *anything* like this; it frightened me, and it turned me on. I was wet and puffy already, from the ministrations of his mouth and from my own shameless arousal. I was very glad of that readiness when he pressed up against me, hard as rock, bulling his way into my sex. My eyes flashed open.

I was staring straight across the kitchen at the family photos on the wall.

"No, please!" I gasped. "Not here!"

All the breath was sucked out of my lungs. For a moment I couldn't breathe, couldn't see, couldn't think—it was like I was falling through hard vacuum.

Then there was daylight. And grass under my feet. And I was standing—sort of, because I was bent over a great oak table that *wasn't there anymore* and only the man's hard hands on my hips were stopping me pitching forward onto my face—and I was looking down a mountain-side at a village in a valley far below.

I screamed, when I got my breath back. That took long enough that some part of my brain did recognize that it was *my* village, that I was somehow standing on the familiar mountain shoulder an hour's hike above our church, that the sun was starting to set, and the roofs were on fire with the evening light, and we were *outdoors...how had that happened—?*

OH GOD, WHAT IS HE?

He let me pitch forward onto my hands and knees in the sheep-bitten grass. But that was the extent of his mercy. He reached out and took a grip of the hair at the back of my scalp, pulling my head up and drawing my throat taut. Wet heat ran through me. His thighs were hard and rough against the bare skin of my exposed bottom.

"Oh God, oh God, oh God," I sobbed as he entered me again, all the way. He felt more solid than the mountain beneath my knees; the only real thing in a world that seemed capable of vanishing in a trice. I was grateful for the implacable grip and the inexorable impalement. I was grateful for the hot brief pain—and more so when he slipped a hand around to the front of my sex to caress that pain away. Ass in the air, fingers clawing at the turf, I felt him start to move inside me, fierce and urgent. I let go then of any sense of self, any right to a rational understanding, and yielded to him entirely, my mind an empty hollow thing, my body nothing but an open vessel vibrating to his punishing rhythm.

I wasn't expecting pleasure, but then I had given up expecting anything. My spasm, when it came, took me by surprise—and my cries made him roar. He was so deep in me when he came that I felt like I was being split in two.

I came back to consciousness when he laughed in my ear.

"I remember."

My face mashed into the grass, I couldn't even breathe properly, much less answer him. Only when he withdrew from me did I tip over and roll onto my back, my heart thundering. He stood over me, silhouetted against a red western sky and the bare rock of the high mountain peak.

"I remember now," he repeated, stretching up his arms and staring at his spread fingers as if he'd never seen them before, "who I am."

The sunset had found its way into his eyes, somehow: they gleamed like live coals.

"Who?" I asked. The sky and the mountain were wrinkling up around him, like a plastic backdrop exposed to a heat gun. Reality shrank and warped, the stress lines radiating in threads from behind his shoulders.

It almost looked like he wore great blurred wings.

"Azazel," he said, his bared teeth white against the black scruff of his stubbled jaw. "Right arm of the Serpent: commander of the Egrigoroi: of highest standing amongst the Watchers: scapegoat for the world: fallen and most loathly son of Almighty God."

The misshapen fabric of the universe snapped and gushed light, blinding me. The mountainside vibrated like the skin of a drum, making rocks dance and slide and tumble. I flung an arm over my face and screwed my eyes shut.

When I opened them again, he was gone.

chapter four

FORGOTTEN GODS

For a long time I sat there on the mountainside, hugging myself and shaking with shock. My damp clothes didn't keep out the breeze. The light turned to pure sunset red, and then the sun dipped behind the peak to the west, and shadow slipped over the rocks and the grass and wrapped me in its clammy hand. I started to shiver from the cold then.

I waited, but he didn't come back. Eventually I admitted I was losing the light, and that if I didn't get down off the mountainside, I'd be trapped up there all night. Stiff and stooped, my thighs cramping, I set off.

The descent was nightmarish. Not so much at first—I had enough light to see where I was putting my feet, and where the cliff edges were on the narrow shepherds' path—but as the day turned to dusk and then darkness, with no moon yet risen, I found myself stumbling and slipping and creeping along with one hand on the rock face. I barked my shins and wrenched my muscles. I started to cry, too scared and angry to hold it in any longer. My tears scalded my cheeks. By the end, in my despair, I was even cursing him out loud.

Him: Azazel; angel then and demon now; a Prince of Darkness. I must have been crazy to call him the names I did.

But it didn't make any difference. He didn't return, either to rescue me or to rain hellfire upon me. I'd been abandoned.

I made the last and steepest part of the descent on hands and ass, sliding my bruised rear over the rocks one bump at a time, desperately trying to work out where the cliff face to my right ended and the drop began.

I don't know how long it took. It felt like forever. By the time I stumbled to my front door I felt utterly exhausted. I crawled into my narrow bed with my clothes still on, not bothering to make up any sheets on the bare mattress. Pulling the faded quilt over my head, I was still sobbing as I lost consciousness.

When I woke up the next morning, the tears were all gone. In their place was a scarred hollow, cold with guilt.

I knew what I'd done. I stood face-to-face with it as I looked into the mirror at my wide eyes shadowed with black rings, and my hair hanging loose about my pinched face. I spread my hands across my pale belly, touching the bruises Azazel's fingers had left upon my hips. He'd kissed those breasts, that stomach, that dark fleece. He'd bitten that swollen mouth, and rooted like an animal between those narrow thighs. Even now my body remembered his, with a mutinous glow I tried to ignore.

I had betrayed *everyone*. I had given my love, over years—and my body in a few wild moments—to something whose evil I couldn't even start to imagine.

My whole life was a lie.

How could I confess this enormity to anyone? How would it be possible to even *ask* for forgiveness? Did God forgive this sort of crime?

I took my flashlight and went down into the cavern. I'd done a module on demolition at college, and the course had included three years of geology. Father had laid the explosive well, I thought: if it detonated as planned then it should bring the whole hollow in on itself. I took a duffle bag and filled it with the icons and idols from the rock-cut passage until I could only just hoist it onto my back. I wanted to pack Father's favorite books too, but I couldn't carry them, so I took the two framed photographs off the kitchen wall.

I pulled down my father's copy of the *Book of Enoch* though, and leafed through it as it lay open on the table. The words were like an accusation aimed straight at me: *And Azâzêl taught men to make swords,*

48

and knives, and shields, and breastplates, and made known to them the metals of the earth and the art of working them, and bracelets, and ornaments, and the use of antimony, and the beautifying of the eyelids, and all kinds of costly stones, and all coloring tinctures. And there arose much godlessness, and they committed fornication, and they were led astray, and became corrupt in all their ways.

I put the book back on the shelf. Then I returned to close and bar the blast door in the passage. I set the timer, thumbed the ignition and walked out of the church.

I was halfway down the two hundred steps when I heard the crack and thud of the explosive. It was more muffled than I'd expected, but after the first detonations the great gruff sound of falling rocks seemed to go on for an age. Tiny pebbles danced as the ground vibrated around my feet.

I didn't look back.

In the village, the dogs that used to follow me about now barked at me and howled in distress. The earthquake the night before had cracked several walls and collapsed the dome on the tower of the church, but at least no one had been hurt. I paid American dollars, the bulk of my own cash, for a beat-up Zaštava that must have rolled off the auto-line back when Marshal Tito was in power, along with a tankful of gas.

That automobile got me all the way to Podgorica, though it shed its exhaust muffler en route.

I didn't dare look back. Not once.

Father had been put in a private room in the hospital, on the same corridor as the chapel so that he might go and pray there when he felt strong enough. The room was bare and ugly, like the rest of the hospital, but it was quiet and I was grateful: the public wards with their mumbling old men and their smell of urine and despair—never quite masked by the chemical reek of bleach—made my heart ache. How was my strong, wise father with his love of machinery and his pure baritone reduced to this pitiful state? What had gone wrong in the world that this was the end for us all?

"His heart is under a lot of strain," the doctor told me as Father slept. "We are running tests but it looks like his whole system...his kidneys aren't working properly. We'd be looking at a transplant...if we could find a donor."

"I'll donate one of mine," I said. "I only need one, don't I?"

The doctor tilted his head. He looked tired, I thought, even though it wasn't yet midnight. "Don't be too hasty. We will certainly run tests. Tissue compatibility, you understand?"

"I'm his daughter, aren't I?" The hope of being able to do *something* to fix this terrible situation made me loud.

"But even if you are a suitable donor, it's not at all clear that he's strong enough for surgery of that magnitude at the moment. I'd need to be happier with his overall condition before agreeing to that."

"But he might get worse while we wait!"

He sighed. "For the moment we need to be patient."

Left alone, I circled to the bed. Vera and Uncle Josif had gone to the hotel room she'd found across the street, once I'd promised I'd stay the night. I sat myself in the lumpy leatherette chair by the head of the bed and took my father's hand.

"Little chick." His voice was no louder than a murmur but his smile was sweet. I saw the glint of his eyes under half-raised lids.

"Did I wake you? Go back to sleep, Papa; it's okay."

"I could always hear your voice, even with a whole school of children shouting."

I thought I'd been mousy-quiet at school. I squeezed his hand reprovingly. "You'd better not have been listening in just now."

"Of course not. I didn't hear a word."

"Good!" I kissed his temple, hard.

"Milja...why are you here?"

I took a deep breath. "Some men from the village...they came up and wanted to come into the church. I didn't trust them. I was afraid." It was hard to lie to my father, but much easier than confessing my true guilt. "I did what you said, Papa. The switch in the passage. I brought down the roof of the cave."

"He's buried then?"

"Gone. Forever." My heart was beating so loud that I was sure he must be able to hear it.

My father sighed. Perhaps if he'd felt stronger he would have been more agitated, but he just looked at me sadly, his eyes wet. "Well then. It is done. Our family is free of its obligation."

I nodded, biting my lip. For a long time there was silence. My father's eyes closed and I started to think he was asleep again.

"Milja."

My head jerked up, my whole body startling as only someone with a guilty conscience does. "Papa?"

"This room...the hospital bills. You need to take an icon or two to Branko."

"How do I find him?"

"You brought the money from under the window stone?"

"Yes."

"And the book that was there too?"

He meant the tiny black address book bound about with elastic bands. I nodded. "Yes."

"Branko is here in Podgorica. His phone number is on the first page, but you must add two to each digit written. He will buy off you."

I'd stashed the duffle bag in a lockup at the public station, paying for a month's rent. "No problem."

"Milja..."

"What?"

"Be careful."

Podgorica is not a pretty tourist-trade city. Its old buildings were bombed almost flat in the War Against Fascism, and its modern architecture cannot dream of matching the high-rise glass-and-steel majesty of Boston, though there's a lot of building work going on right now. I insisted on meeting Branko in a public space, one of my own choosing, and I chose a park that was shaded by scruffy trees and surrounded by ugly pastel-painted apartment blocks. I was grateful the sky was partly overcast and lazily threatening a summer downpour. Summer in the capital wasn't humid, not like the Boston I'd left behind, but I'd heard it could be insanely hot. Even now I stuck to the shade.

As I walked across the worn earth in the dusty shadow of the plane trees I remembered the story Father had told me of King Xerxes, who on his way to invade Greece had fallen hopelessly in love with a plane tree and bedecked it like a royal bride in gold ornaments. Strange to think of a man conceiving a passion for a tree, I thought—but then at least both were creatures of the Earth, bound by their material nature. Wasn't it more unnatural for a denizen of the highest Heaven, a being of pure spirit, to take on flesh and indulge the basest human appetites?

The comparison—and the memories it roused—made heat rise to my cheeks. I stuffed the thoughts back down in my mind, out of sight.

I was nervous. The unlicensed selling of antiquities was strictly illegal of course, not to mention the small factor that the objects from the cave did not, strictly speaking, belong to my family. They were property of the Church itself, I supposed, if only the Church knew. It was too late now to feel the prick of conscience—my emigration and college fees had been paid by these black-market transactions—but it did make me walk cautiously, looking around for policemen. I hadn't been able to shake off the feeling, since blowing up the cave, that I was being watched.

So I'd been cautious in my dealings with Branko. I'd bought a local SIM off a street vendor for my phone, taken pictures of my chosen artifact (an icon of St. Stefan) and sent them for inspection. Branko had sounded wary at first about dealing with me instead of Father. But he'd made an offer that seemed to me to be reasonable—not that I really had any idea how much such things were worth, but it was a gratifying number of euros—and we'd agreed to meet. I'd bought a plastic bag of oranges and the palm-sized picture, wrapped in newspaper, now nested among them.

I reached the central fountain, which wasn't playing at that time and didn't even have any water in the basin, and glanced around, trying to look as casual as if I were only expecting to meet some boyfriend. Children skateboarded on the concrete slopes and old people sat in the sun. Three priests sat on a bench and threw bread to the pigeons, talking earnestly to one another.

I thought of the red-brick church I'd passed on the road to the park. I'd wondered whether to go in and make confession, but I hadn't dared. It was funny really—brought up in a priestly family, I'd simply assumed throughout my childhood that I was included among the sheep rather than the goats. Faith had never seemed something that needed a lot of work and sin never seemed a burden; not even my furtive visits to the prisoner, which I'd privately counted as acts of compassion. In America I'd gone to church when Vera took me, without either resentment or pleasure. Now—oh *now*—I knew what guilt felt like at last, and uncertainty too.

My place among the saved could no longer be taken for granted. I needed to make sure I was forgiven, but I balked at the thought. What confessor would believe me if I told him the whole truth? He'd assume I was out of my mind.

I looked away from the priests, shivering. I was alone, without the sympathy of either God or man. My transgression, in fact, must be entirely unique. Nobody else in human history had screwed up quite the same way I had.

A man was looking at me from the other side of the fountain. He was bald and middle-aged and wore a jacket over a stripy sweater-vest. Was that what a black-market antiques dealer looked like? I double-looped the plastic bag around my wrist and fished my phone out of my jeans pocket.

Here waiting, I texted Branko.

The man looked at his own phone, got up from his bench and sauntered over to me. I could feel the plastic bag growing clammy against my hand.

"Miss Milja?" he asked. He didn't know my surname. Father had used a nom de guerre.

"Uh-huh."

"Branko. You've got the picture?"

I nodded. He looked fussy and down-in-the-mouth, and there was something so tawdry and dull about him that it was hard to believe we were doing anything criminal.

"Come over here, and let's have a look at it." He touched me on the shoulder, steering me around the basin of the fountain.

"Come where?"

"Just over here out of the way."

I followed him a few paces, then stopped. I liked it right here in the middle of the park, where there were lots of witnesses. He wasn't a big man, but he was bigger than me. "This is fine," I said, teeth gritted.

He sighed down his nose. "You think I should hand over a stack of notes where anyone could be watching?"

Personally I preferred *anyone* to *nobody*, but I got his point. "On the wall there," I suggested, pointing my chin at the fountain. "There's no one close by."

He shrugged and we found a point on the low wall where we could turn our backs to the world. Drifts of litter stared up at us from the tiled basin. "Want an orange?" I asked, opening the bag.

He smirked. I passed him the small square parcel.

"Have a cigarette," he told me, offering a pack from his jacket pocket.

"I don't smoke."

"Have," he said, "a *cigarette*. You don't have to inhale, eh? Make like a president."

I accepted the cigarette and a lighter and lit the one clumsily from the other while he unwrapped the little wooden icon and looked it over critically.

"Keep the pack," he said. I looked down to see a little wodge of colored euro notes folded inside the cigarette packet, and I realized that I'd been expecting a brown paper envelope like in the movies.

"Thanks," I muttered.

He slipped the painting into his inside pocket where the cigarettes had rested. I bowed my head as I tried to casually pocket my own pack. A shadow came between me and the sun.

"Selling Church property is a grievous sin," said a voice.

When I looked around, the three priests from the park bench were lined up behind us.

With an uneasy smile, Branko sidled out of their direct line of attention.

"Good afternoon, Miss Milja," said the one in the middle. They were all bearded, of course, and all wearing black cassocks, but he was the oldest and the slightest, his long gray hair tied back in a ponytail. The other two were big—one with a rufous beard, one with a badger-striped black one—and I realized that they both looked a lot like they'd been brought along for their muscle.

My heart and my stomach collided with a clang.

"There's no need to worry," said the one with the gray hair and the spectacles, seeing the look of panic that widened my eyes. "We just want to talk to you about this photograph." Reaching into the leather bag that hung at his shoulder, he held out a black-and-white print. "My name is Father Velimir," he said pleasantly. "What's yours?"

"Milja," I said numbly, my brain a blank. It was a picture of some sort of statuette, but I was mostly wondering what sort of awful trouble I was in and how to get out of it. Screaming at the top of my lungs seemed an option.

"I meant your surname, of course. Your father's name. We know you're working on behalf of your father. Why didn't he come himself, this time?"

I opened my mouth, looked him in the face—and said nothing. His expression hardened for a moment, then relaxed. "Look at the picture, Milja," he said gently, as if talking to a simpleton—which was probably the impression I'd managed to give him. "Do you recognize it?"

It was a crudely worked female form, very pale and with almond-shaped eyes, cupping its breasts for the viewer. Her pubic area was nothing more than a hatched triangle. There was no scale in the picture but the lack of detail made me think it was quite small. I shook my head, reasonably truthfully. There'd been several similar idols in the tunnel, before I looted them out, but I didn't recognize this one in particular.

"Your father sold this one to Branko here a year ago. It's not the first item he's sold, is it?"

I bit my lip and kept silent.

"He must have uncovered quite a cache. But this one found its way into my hands. Do you see the writing on the pedestal, Milja?"

I risked a slow nod. There were letters of some sort scratched into the base beneath the statue's feet.

"Do you know what language they're in?"

"No," I answered in a small voice.

"It's a very old one called Proto-Canaanite. It's the script that eventually gave rise to the first form of Hebrew. That means it's a particularly ancient statue, Milja. And not many people can read that writing. Not many people at all. Do you understand me?"

"Yes, father."

"But I can. And it says something very strange."

"What?"

"That doesn't matter, child—it's a prayer. To a heathen goddess. So, it's nonsense, of course. What I want to know is, where did this come from? Where did your father find it?"

I shook my head and whispered, "I don't know."

"Really? What about this one? And this one? And this?" He drew more blown-up photographic prints from his bag: a potbellied Egyptian dwarf; a multi-breasted Diana of the Ephesians; an ivory crucifix; a golden mother and baby that might be the Virgin Mary Theotokos...or again, might not. "Where is your father stealing them from?"

"He's not stealing them," I said, knowing I was lying but unable to think of a better excuse.

"Where's he *getting* them from, child?"

"I don't know."

"Well then, I think you should take me to see him, and he can tell me himself." With a twitch of his head Father Velimir signaled to the priest with the red beard, who reached out a heavy hand and took hold of my arm.

I didn't stop to think. I stabbed my lit cigarette into his long beard, and the moment he let go of me to beat in instinctive panic at the smoldering hair, I jumped backward onto the wall and into the basin of the fountain, dashing for the far side. Chip packets skidded under my feet. I didn't hear anyone pursuing, and as I scrambled over onto the concrete beyond the fountain I risked a glance back. Father Velimir and his sidekicks, looking flustered, were stomping around the circle in my direction but without any great speed. The gap between us was already considerable.

I grinned to myself, knowing there was no way a priest would shame the cloth by chasing me through a public park.

Unfortunately, it turned out that they didn't need to. Father Velimir pointed at me and shouted at the top of his voice, "Thief! Pickpocket! She's stolen my wallet! Stop her!"

Heads turned. A man in a T-shirt rose from his bench and began to lumber in my direction. So I fled. Under the plane trees, across the scorched grass, right through a shrubbery, my heart so high in my throat I could hardly breathe to keep my legs pounding beneath me. The blasted bag of oranges was looped so tightly around my wrist that it was cutting off the blood to my hand, but I couldn't pause to unwind it. I put everything I had into running.

But it wasn't enough. The good citizen caught up with me as I was almost at the park gate, grabbing my shoulder and whirling me round.

"Got you!"

His grip was harsh enough to hurt. Someone nearby was shouting in English.

"Get off me!" I squealed, and swung the bag of oranges at my captor's head. He staggered, swore—and then slapped my face hard enough to make me see stars.

"Bitch!"

chapter five

THE FALL

H ey—hey—HEY!" There was a man, *another* man, running in. "Stop
that!" he yelled as he rushed up to us, forcing me and the righteous
guy apart. "What the hell do you think you're doing!"

I was shocked to recognize Egan.

And my assailant was surprised enough by the sudden intervention to
let go and step back a little. "She's a thief! A dirty Gypsy pickpocket!" he
snarled in Montenegrin.

"You don't do that! You don't do that to a woman!" Egan was
shouting—in English, of course.

"She stole a wallet! I saw her!" His imagination might be getting the
better of him, but it hardly mattered—my white knight of course did not
understand a word of his language.

"Leave her alone!" Egan was coldly furious, one arm thrust out before
him to fend the guy off at chest height. "She's with me!"

"Yes," I joined in, in English, as inspiration hit me. "Leave me alone!
This is my boyfriend! We will call the police!"

My fellow countryman did a double take as his grasp of the situation
turned to sand in his hands. He obviously didn't expect to have come
across a dirty *English* pickpocket. I reinforced the message by grabbing
Egan's shirt-sleeve and clinging to him.

"Go away and leave us alone!"

The guy looked totally confused.

Egan swept an arm around my shoulders protectively. "You heard her. We'll call the police!"

The language barrier was too much. Mutual incomprehension made his heroic arrest of a sneak thief farcical. He scrunched up his face in disgust. "Fucking Americans!" he growled, then spat on the floor at our feet and slouched away.

"What did he say?" Egan asked under his breath.

"Um. He said '*Welcome to our beautiful country.*'"

"I bet he did." The Irishman looked down at me. I could not imagine anything I wanted to see more at that moment than his too-cute spiky crop and his cautious smile. Even the pressure of his arm around my shoulders felt just perfect, as he squeezed me gently. "You okay?"

"Yeah." I touched my slapped face, testing the tender skin, and then giggled unsteadily as I felt the incongruous weight still dangling from my wrist. "D'you want an orange?"

He took me three streets away to a cafe with a vine-shaded yard. It was, after all, his lunch hour, he explained as he ordered us *punjene paprike*: he'd been taking a short cut through the park when he saw me. "What are you doing in Podgorica, Milja? I thought you were out in the sticks somewhere?"

"I was." I took a sip of the chilled Nikšićko beer the waiter had plunked down in front of us both. "My father's been transferred to hospital here."

Egan asked the right questions and listened sympathetically as I brought him up to date on Father's medical condition. He passed me a paper napkin when I got teary and squeezed my hand, before withdrawing his own as if embarrassed by its boldness.

"I shouldn't be dumping all this on you," I mumbled. "It's not fair, really...I'm just this girl you bumped into and I keep offloading all my crap. I'm—"

"Don't you dare say you're sorry! It's no problem at all. I like... listening."

"You're good at it."

59

"Thank you. Are you still sure we shouldn't go talk to the police?"

"Absolutely sure."

He looked unhappy, but nodded. "So what was going on in the park, with your man there?"

I sniffed wetly, ashamed. "Nothing. Just a stupid misunderstanding."

"Ah now." Egan narrowed his lips. "He *hit* you. That's not nothing."

"Yeah well, that's just my luck with men. And you're lucky he didn't hit *you*. This is a land with a fine tradition of machismo and blood feuds, remember." I balled up the damp tissue paper. "Thank you, for coming to my rescue. That was really good of you."

He laughed. "I'm glad I was there."

"So am I." I dabbed again at my eyes as my throat swelled up, and managed only to mumble, "Oh, screw it all."

"What do you mean?"

"I'm not doing anything right at the moment. Oh—I just wish I was back home in Boston." I waved my hands helplessly. "I'm sorry...I miss my own place, and my cat and my friends and everything. This doesn't feel like my country...I mean, I've never lived in this city before. I only saw it on the way through to the airport. I wish Father was better."

"He will be soon, I'm sure. You'll be able to take him home."

I shook my head. "I don't want to go back to the village either. I *can't*." The vehemence of that last word startled even me, and I looked at Egan in sudden embarrassment.

"Can't?"

"It's...oh, it's complicated."

"Ah." He raised his blond eyebrows and looked meek. "A bloke, I'm guessing?"

The word was unfamiliar. "Bloke?"

"Uh... Fellow. *Dude.*" He pulled a wry face. "Two nations divided by a common language, eh? Sure, when a woman says 'It's complicated,' it usually means there's a man."

I managed a lopsided half smile. "Yeah."

"Want to talk about it?"

I looked down at my hands. I couldn't go to confession in a church, but I desperately wanted to offload some small part of my burden. My head filled with stone and shadows again. My voice came out husky. "There's this...man, back in the village. I grew up with him around. We had a relationship...sort of...when I was eighteen. But when I went back this time...it all went really wrong."

Egan frowned. "Are you all right?"

He meant *Were you assaulted?* I realized. For a moment I relived the bruisingly fierce intercourse on the mountaintop. But though Azazel had been rough, there was no doubt that I'd wanted it, fear or not. "No," I answered. "No, it's nothing like that. It was just...not what I'd pictured."

"Ah, well." He looked sympathetic but relieved. "People do change, over the years."

"No, it wasn't that." My tears were threatening to spill again and I hated that, hated my weakness. It made me harsh in my self-condemnation. "He hadn't changed *at all,* that's the thing—it was just I'd never seen what he was really like. How bad he was. My father had warned me all along, but I never listened. I was a stupid teenager and I thought I knew better than everyone else, and I was *wrong.*"

"Ah: *with the ancient is wisdom; and in length of days understanding,*" he said ruefully, and with the unmistakable air of someone quoting a higher authority.

I swallowed my tears, glad of the distraction. "Who said that?"

"Er...it's something biblical." He looked nervous, all of a sudden. Quoting the Bible is a sure way of making most young women run for the hills, I guess. "Book of Job, maybe," he admitted.

"Well, yeah, there you go. I was young and *really* stupid. Bottom of the class."

"I don't know. You strike me as pretty smart."

"You don't know how dumb teenage girls can be."

"Dumber than teenage boys?" He lifted a brow. "Oh, I doubt that."

That was a challenge. I sniffed and gave him a narrow look. "So what's the worst thing you ever did as a boy?"

"Me?" Egan's eyes widened a little in alarm and he drummed his fingers on the table before answering with a sickly grin. "Sure, my bad habit was mooning after gorgeous girls who already had much older, cooler boyfriends. With cars."

I shook my head sympathetically, trying not to laugh.

"They never even knew I was there," he sighed. "I spent...no, I'm not going to talk about it: it'd just sound too stalkerish. Believe me, I made a total arse of myself."

"That's the pits."

"It is."

I shook myself inwardly, trying to gather my shredded dignity. "Still, I suppose the only way from the pits is upward."

"*Ready to mount to the stars.*" He smiled, clearly relieved I hadn't fled after the first one. For an I.T. guy, he certainly liked his classical quotations, I thought.

"And that's from Job too?"

"Uh, no. That's Dante. *The Divine Comedy.*"

Yeah, I said to myself, suppressing a shiver. *It's a comedy all right. Hear me laughing.*

By the time I left Egan, feeling much the better, I had a stomach full of food and yet more insistences that I should call him if I needed help, any help at all. I smiled to myself as I walked back to the hospital.

He was nice, I thought, a little wistfully. Really nice. And cute, in a totally normal, not-like-a-fallen-angel way. You could pass him in the street and idly think *Hmm, yeah that's fine.* Azazel was more like...*Oh God I want to lick him and feel my tongue burn.*

Just the thought was enough to evaporate my new sensation of peace and make me pensive. I hurried my pace and trotted up to the hospital door, into the fug of antiseptic and down the corridor, the bag of oranges swinging in my hand.

And I turned a corner—and there he was: Azazel. Slap in the middle of the passageway, as darkly beautiful as I remembered and half a head taller than anyone who shuffled or queued or strode past him—even though Montenegrins are among the tallest people in Europe. Looking straight at me with those shivery inhuman eyes. A half smile twisted one corner of his mouth. He was clothed, for a change, which should perhaps have been some source of relief—he wore black pants and a white sweater of fine knit that hung loosely from his otherwise bare shoulders—and in the second that I stood there, gaping, I entertained an incongruous image of him wandering naked through a department store, oblivious to the outrage of respectable shoppers as he chose his garments. He clearly hadn't got as far as the shoe department though; his feet were bare on the scuffed hospital linoleum.

I shook my head, feeling terror crash in my veins. "No," I mouthed, tears burning in my eyes. Then I turned my back on him, urging my legs to a stumbling run.

The corridor darkened, light leaching from the day, and everything went deathly quiet. To my inexpressible horror I saw the human figures scattered down its length slow, as if freezing on the spot. Eyes stared, unblinking. Feet hovered mid-step. A fumbled plastic cup hung from the fingertips of an irritated-looking nurse, the water within bulging out in midair like melted glass.

Time seemed to stand still.

But not for me. In that unnatural silence I could hear my pulse thudding in my ears. Sweat slicked my thighs.

I ran. The bag of oranges struck the floor behind me. I didn't sprint, because there seemed to be no strength in my legs, but I lurched away and kept going. I headed for the chapel, because it was the only place I could imagine offering sanctuary.

Bursting through the double doors, I found myself in a square room with a false dome and garish modernist frescoes; even the iconostasis screen before the altar looked like a garden trellis. There were no windows, just some wall lamps pretending to be stained glass. No way out, and no one in the chamber. I whirled to face the doors and backed off into the center of the chapel.

The doors were pushed back. Azazel stalked in. From the corridor beyond I heard a brief hubbub of human sound, muted again as the doors swung shut behind him; clearly the world was being allowed to carry on as normal. But here in the chapel, nothing was normal, nothing natural.

He looked much cleaner now, and less gaunt, but he hadn't bothered to shave or cut his hair. To my eyes his smile had grown, if anything, more wolfish.

"Stop it stop it stop it," I gabbled, holding up my hands to ward him off as he walked toward me. "You can't come in here. This is holy ground."

He did pause on receiving that news, and glanced toward the altar.

"Lord Jesus Christ, deliver me also from every influence of unclean spirits," I pleaded, crossing myself.

Azazel's expression was one of mild amusement. "I never met the

63

man," he said. "He was…after my time. Though to be fair, the same goes for anything after Genesis."

Two more steps brought him so close to me that my hands were pushing against his chest. I recoiled and backed away as far as I could, nearly tripping over my own feet, ending up pressed against the flimsy screen separating notional sanctuary from notional nave.

"Are you scared of me, Milja?" he asked softly.

I didn't answer. Under those silver eyes I was like a deer transfixed by truck headlamps.

"Why are you scared?" He reached out and touched my cheek, and I flinched.

"What do you want?"

"Huh. Isn't that obvious?" His caress was gentle; incongruously so, after the uninhibited roughness of his attentions on the mountainside.

"No!" I said, as his fingertips grazed my throat and breastbone and then circled my nipple. He was so close that I could smell his skin—earth and sweat no longer, but a peppery warmth that was far from unpleasant. "Go away! Please!"

For a moment he looked taken aback. Then he shook his head. "Are you trying to tease? Your desire is like a beacon on a hilltop, Milja. I can see you burning."

Maybe he could. What did I know of his perceptions? I tried to shrink from his grasp but he cupped my breast, hefting its softness. "I don't want you!" I cried.

He laughed. "Don't lie to me." His hand seemed to kindle a fire in my flesh. He stooped and brushed his lips across my averted cheek, his breath warm. I shuddered from head to toe.

"I'm not lying," I said desperately: "you're not listening. *Please*."

"I can hear your pulse," he growled, his teeth tickling my ear. "I can smell your need."

Desire ran through me like melted wax, pouring through my breasts and belly and pooling in my swollen sex. It took my breath away, and my dignity, and my caution.

"You piece of shit!" I sobbed.

Well, *that* worked. I guess not many girls had ever spoken to him like that. He stepped back—and as all the lights in the room shrank to tiny glows, the darkness grew and thickened, crowding in around him. His white sweater seemed to glow with phosphorescence. There was no amusement in his face anymore, just red pinpoints where his pupils should be.

"All right," he said softly. "I'm listening now."

I wet my dry lips. "You left me on the mountain. You *fucked* me and you left me on the mountain in the night. I could have broken a leg. I could have *died* out there. I had to crawl home in the dark. You fucked me and you dumped me and you're a *goddamn demon*—" I broke off suddenly in panic, covering my face with my hands.

He looked away. I heard the fierce intake of his breath and then a long exhalation before he could bring himself to answer. Slowly the room lights reasserted themselves. "It was not done well," he growled. "I...I was overwhelmed. My mind was full of old thoughts awoken." He straightened his shoulders. "I will apologize. You will forgive me."

If he'd been human I would have laughed. Hysterically. "Forgive you?" I repeated, in a whisper.

"Yes." He put his open palm between my breasts to feel my pounding heart. "I forget sometimes how fragile you are."

"Us...humans?"

"Yes."

He meant it. He really meant it.

"You're a rebel angel. Like in the *Book of Enoch*. Like in the Bible. It's real, isn't it? All of it?" My face was doing strange things, muscles twisting all awry. "Heaven and Hell and the Garden of Eden and Noah's Ark and Jonah's whale and all that? It's all real? The Last Judgment? Eternal damnation? All of it?"

Azazel opened his mouth as if to reply, and then hesitated. Something shifted in his quicksilver eyes. "So you believe everything you read, then?" he asked.

"I believe...in one God, the Father Almighty, Maker of Heaven and Earth," I started, the words of the Creed rising to my lips with easy familiarity even though I hadn't given my actual faith much thought in years; "and of all things, visible and invisible—"

"Shh." Azazel put a finger on my mouth to still it, shaking his head gently. "Don't be like that. I'm not going to hurt you. You believe in angels and demons, don't you?"

"I do now!"

"And what is it that you think we do?"

"Drag me to Hell?"

He shook his head, the merest twitch. The little smile was back, battered and a bit uncertain now, but back. "Not right now. I've no interest in your"—he laughed under his breath—"immortal soul."

"Then what?"

"This." He caught my chin and bent to kiss me—not the full-blooded kiss of a movie hero, but a soft, slow brush of his lips across mine. It was like being touched by a burning ember: it set me on fire. For a moment I couldn't breathe. "This," he repeated, his hands moving over my breasts, circling my waist. "This," he whispered, cupping the curve of my ass and pushing his long fingers down into places of shivering, shameful delight.

I couldn't help it—I quivered against him and let slip a moan, half fear and half something else altogether. And yet somehow I managed to writhe out of his kiss. He looked into my eyes from inches away.

"You said you were fallen," I whispered.

A tilt of his eyes acknowledged that, even as his hands slid over my hips. "We did not fall: we leaped."

"Has God forgiven you?"

He curled his lip. "That seems most unlikely."

"So you're damned." It was taking all my strength not to yield to the ache and the need in my own flesh.

Azazel breathed out a humorless laugh. "Oh yes."

"In league with Satan."

That seemed to rankle. "Leave him out of it. I am one of the Egrigoroi." The word sounded Greek, but the press of his body was a sharp reminder that theology wasn't his only concern, and that another matter was growing more urgent.

"You're pure evil."

"So you say." He was working my blouse open now.

I pushed his face away. "Please. I can't do this. I can't do this with you."

"It's what you've wanted all your life." Azazel sounded breathless. I couldn't contradict his words, not directly. They were all true.

"It's wrong."

66

"It's what you ache for."

"It's against the will of God!"

"*Fuck Him!*" Azazel snarled, catching my hair and pulling my head back so sharply that I saw stars. "Five thousand years of torture—do you think I'll crawl back to the foot of the Throne now?"

Tears sprang up in my eyes, a physical reaction to the hair-pulling as much as anything. "But He's *my* God," I cried.

He had me pinned. His face loomed over mine. There was mutinous rage in it, but he kept his voice low. "No, He's not," he whispered. "You belong to me now."

I don't know if it was his words or his body or the way he'd pulled my hair, but despite my fear my body was responding with more than tears. I didn't dare think about it; I certainly didn't dare let him know. "I didn't agree to that!" I whined—and his response was chilling.

"What makes you think you have a choice?"

And to that I had no answer. I was speechless with fear. I looked into his burning eyes—and even in my terror I thought of his millennia of impotent rage and humiliation. Tears brimmed out onto my cheeks and ran down my face.

For a long moment he held me. Then, without warning, he thrust me away. I staggered. "You need to calm down," he growled. "It must be a shock to you, I realize. You'll see more clearly in time. I will return when you're in a better mood."

Stepping away from him felt like stepping from a warm room into a cold night. Shivers crawled up and down my back. I pressed my knuckles to my lips and sniffed back the tears as I watched him turn and march toward the doors.

Then those doors opened inward, and a wheelchair pushed through. Sitting in the chair, bundled in a blanket and dressing gown, was my father. Steering it from behind was my cousin Vera.

For a long moment everyone froze. I watched the blood ebb from my father's face as recognition sank in, leaving him gray as a corpse. I saw Vera turn wide eyes toward me in utter disbelief. I couldn't see Azazel's face from where I stood—but the lights in the room flickered and shuddered, shrank to nothing and then flared up like torches.

He took a single stride to the wheelchair, grabbed my father by the front of the dressing gown, and lifted him one-handed until they were nose to nose and my father's feet kicked the air. I wondered wildly if Azazel had grown taller; he seemed to tower over them both.

"I should kill you," said the demon, "*very* slowly."

"Azazel," I gasped, moving in, my feet like lead, all the air burned from my empty lungs. I don't even know if I made an audible sound. All that came out of my mouth was a wheeze. "Please—no!"

He cast me a glare over his shoulder. "But it's only proper to respect one's father-in-law," he said coldly. Then he dumped the limp frame of my father back in the wheelchair and strode from the chapel.

Everything after that was blurred, for a long time. I couldn't recall many of the details afterward. There was shouting and crying, and me kneeling over my father, and Vera running out into the corridor. And then they came to take Papa away in a stretcher, and we followed and then we were thrown out and there was more shouting and Vera screaming in my face and everything was black, and white, and black, and white.

You whore, she screamed at me.

Look what you've done.

And Uncle Josif was there too and he pushed me all across the room.

Look what you've done, they said.

You've killed your father.

You whore, you lying murderous slut.

Then at some point the doctors came and said, *He is resting, he is out of the woods for the moment.* And I wanted to go in and see him but they wouldn't let me, and Vera said, *You will never set eyes on him again, he would die of shame if he saw his filthy diseased whore-daughter who lies with animals and worse than animals.* And I was screaming that I would see him, he was my father, I had to see him, they had to let me. And all the while the nurses were trying to get us to keep our voices down and saying, *You must be quiet, you cannot upset him.*

So I said, *I will be quiet, just let me be with him.*

Then they said, *Take these, and if you are quiet we will let you in but you must be quiet and if you take these they will help you calm down.*

So I took the pills and after that everything got quiet like they said, really quiet and blurry and far away, and they let me see Father, lying on his bed, sleeping, looking so white and frail like a man of sticks, and I cried and kissed his hands and sat by his bed and then I don't remember what happened after that.

Except that I woke up again and it was like trying to lift my head from under a bag of wet sand. I was lying in a corridor and there were three men going in through the door opposite me. And one of them turned and looked down at me in passing and it was the priest with the silver beard and the glasses, and he looked at me like I didn't matter at all, and then the wet sand covered me up again and I don't remember anything else.

When I woke, it was broad daylight. I was lying on my side across two chairs in the corridor outside my father's room. The door was closed. There was no one nearby.

I sat up slowly. I felt terrible—weak, and floaty, and everything felt faraway and overexposed. It was hard to keep my eyes open without squinting. My mouth felt as dry as the Sahara.

I went into Father's room. The bed was empty and made up, the sheets starch-stiff and so white I couldn't look at them. The curtains were wide open. Vera and Josif sat in chairs in the corner of the room, hands on knees, silent.

"*Adzo? Nana?* Where is he?" I asked, my voice barely able to rasp from my dry throat.

Vera lifted her head. She looked gray and slack, like all the muscle in her face had collapsed overnight and everything had slid downward. "He died last night. A heart attack. They took him down to surgery but he died on the table."

I blinked. I wanted to ask why they hadn't woken me. But I felt too weak to speak.

"No tears?" Vera asked.

No tears. I was dry and empty, like a bone left for years on a hillside. There was nothing in me but a great hollow of exhaustion.

"In the old days," she said, softly, softly, "we would have taken you out to a place of curses, and cut your throat and buried you facedown at a crossroads. And we would never have spoken your name again. That is how we would have cleansed our family honor."

She was exhausted too, I saw—worn out by worry and work and

lack of sleep, trying to care for my father. Her eyes were sunken in dark hollows. She had been beautiful once, in the pictures she'd shown me of her wedding day: petite and vivacious. Now she looked like a hag.

"You killed your father," said Josif. "Have you nothing to say now?"

I swallowed, trying in vain to moisten my throat. "I didn't kill him," I said, in a voice like a dried-up wisp of grass blowing across the floor. "The priests came...I saw them...they were looking for him..."

"Shut up, you lying bitch," spat Vera. "You don't even feel contrition, do you? Get out."

"I want to see him."

"You will *never* see him."

I looked down, trying to marshal my broken thoughts. "He's my father—"

"He's not your father, as you were no daughter to him. This family disowns you and forgets your name. Get out of here, and go to Hell where your demon master lives. You can ask him to call you 'daughter,' as you spread your legs for him again."

My throat closed up, tight and dry. I knew there were no words left. I turned away. But as I reached for the door handle, I heard Josif's voice once more.

"Don't think you're getting away with it, girl. The evil thing you did will not be unavenged. Vera's uncle may have left no male kin to cleanse his family name, but there are other ways."

I looked back over my shoulder. I wished I hadn't.

"We will tell them." Vera rose to her feet. "We will go to the Church and tell them the secret that was kept so long. Josif has relatives among the bishops. They will listen. They will know what to do to wipe this stain of evil from the face of God's green Earth—and to take you with it. You will pay."

I walked out of the room.

I walked out of the hospital.

I walked three blocks before I reached a junction. There was a Communist-era statue there commemorating some ancient political victory—the winning of our freedom from the Austrians, perhaps, or the Turks, or the Fascists. It showed a huge bronze eagle hovering over a stone crag, a broken chain dangling from one foot.

That stopped me in my tracks. I thought of the eagle tearing at Prometheus's liver, day after day. I thought of the fallen angel rising after centuries from his place of torment. I thought of Azazel, somewhere, waiting to swoop and collect me for his prey. I thought of the Church—with all its ancient machinery of control and punishment—turning toward me like a creaking bronze titan woken from slumber.

I reached into my pocket and found my phone and a card with a number scrawled upon it.

"Egan," I rasped as the connection clicked through. "It's Milja. Please. I need you to help me. Right now. Please."

chapter six

SANCTUARY

E gan drove round to pick me up in a taxicab. He found me standing by
the roadside, and I suppose I must have looked utterly forlorn because
he jumped out as the cab parked up and he hurried over.

"Milja—what's happened?"

"My father's dead," I said in a flat voice.

He put his hands on my shoulders. "I'm so sorry."

"They say it's my fault."

"*What?*" His hands tightened.

I liked that grip of his—it felt like I was going to blow away among the
litter without something to anchor me. "I need to get away from here," I
told him.

"All right so. Okay. Get in."

He opened the curbside back door for me and then went round to
the other side. The taxi driver looked at us both in the rearview mirror,
and I hoped Egan wouldn't ask me what had happened. Not in front of a
stranger.

"Where do you want to go?" Egan asked me. "Have you got a hotel?"

I shook my head. I'd spent the last two nights sleeping on chairs in the
hospital. No wonder I ached all over.

"Friends?"

"No." I shook my empty, useless head, feeling my shoulders drop as I added, knowing it sounded childish but unable to stop myself, "I want to go home to Boston."

"Okay." Egan sounded dubious. "I'll take you to the airport if that's what you want. Have you got your passport on you? An air ticket?"

I shut my eyes, wanting to sink into the darkness. "My cousin Vera has my passport," I said. She'd put it in her hotel safe with her own, because she thought it wasn't secure with me walking around with it in my shoulder bag.

"Ah now, that's a problem." Egan's voice was gentle. "Milja, you don't look at all well. Let's get you somewhere quiet."

He gave an address to the driver. I didn't object. I didn't care anymore. I looked at the streets sliding past. Egan said nothing, though I could feel him watching me. I didn't cry: I had cried over Azazel and cried over my father, all in vain, and I had no tears left. But I slept, unexpectedly, falling into a doze without even realizing it. I only knew when the car stopped and Egan opened the door for me.

"Come on," he said, offering me his hand as if I were a little kid.

I looked around vacantly as he helped me to my feet, seeing tall white-painted walls with bright fuchsia bougainvillea sprawling over the tops, and no other traffic. It looked like a back road in an affluent suburb.

"This is the house my employers are putting me up in," he told me, leading me to an anonymous gate of black metal and pulling a key from his pocket.

"The bank?"

"Uh, yes." He touched me lightly on the shoulder to usher me inside. "It won't be problem."

There was a tiny courtyard beyond the gate, and inner doors, and walls of stone. An old building, I thought vaguely, behind the modern facade. Inside, the floors were tiled and the rooms austere, smelling of polish. I saw big, plain furniture that looked antique; a single rug in the center of the living room was the only concession to softness. There were no pictures on the walls and no ornaments, except for a small wooden crucifix as we entered and a wooden statue of Mary and the Holy Child on a far sideboard, cracked with age and still bearing traces of gilt and paint. There was no indication whether this was intended as a shrine or an art statement.

"Have a seat, Milja, and I'll get you a drink," said Egan, as a door opened and out came a woman; an old woman wearing a headscarf. She looked at us with an expression of surprise.

"Ah, Milja—this is the housekeeper, Dejana."

"*Dobro jutro*," I said, automatically, though I had no idea if it was still morning or not.

"Dejana, this is Milja who will be our guest. She needs looking after. Can you find her some…orange juice?" He looked at me for confirmation.

"Yes," I said, gratefully.

"Orange juice," he repeated for Dejana's benefit, miming lifting a glass and drinking from it. She nodded, turned back and disappeared into the room she'd come from.

"Dejana doesn't talk, but she understands what you say." Egan had that nervous look tourists get when they're worried they sound like patronizing foreigners. "Anything you need, just ask her." He sat down in an armchair opposite me and looked into my eyes. "Are you in trouble, Milja?"

I nodded.

"Do you need the police, or a doctor?"

"No."

"Can you tell me about it?"

I looked down at my hands. I wanted to. I meant to. But I opened my mouth and no words came out. Egan waited.

"It's all right," he said at last. "Just rest. You're safe here. In fact, there are several guest bedrooms here and no one else but me staying right now. So how about you lie down for a couple of hours? You look like you need it."

"Okay." I'd been asleep in a drugged stupor all night and then some, but I still felt exhausted.

"Sure, well, I have to go out just for a little while. You took me out of work early, that's all. We'll talk when I get back, shall we? In the meantime, the bathroom's over there if you need it." He pointed across the main room. "It's shared I'm afraid, but there's a bolt on the door. Come on—let's find you a bedroom."

He led me down a short corridor and opened a door into a bedchamber that matched the living room for style: plain, heavyweight furniture and a crucifix as the only adornment on the whitewashed walls. It made me horribly aware that I possessed nothing but the clothes I stood up in, my phone, my credit cards and a crushed cigarette packet of euros. Everything meaningful and comforting and familiar had been taken away.

"That'll do, won't it? My room's at the end of the corridor there. The others are all empty."

"Great. Thank you." I made myself meet his eyes and smile. I don't think it was convincing.

"Try and get some sleep."

Alone, I inspected my room. A single window looked out onto an enclosed garden. The bed was only sized for a single occupant, but was made up with clean sheets. In fact there was a guest welcome pack in sealed plastic on the bedside table: toothbrush, toothpaste, soap, shampoo, a three-pack of disposable razors. Nothing feminine. There was a large bottle of water too, which I opened eagerly. Only when I'd knocked back about a liter did I spot the pajamas: brand-new, still in their sealed packet, old-fashioned, striped-cotton male pajamas.

Weird, I thought, in that vague emotionless way that I seemed to have acquired. They seemed to be anticipating only single men as guests here. I wondered if Egan wore matching attire at night, and though the thought didn't exactly make me smile it was a moment of lightness.

There was no bolt or lock on the bedroom door. *Weird*, I thought, again.

I went back out into the public room, and found Dejana setting a large glass of juice on the table in the dining niche, along with a plate of sweet *potika* pastries and some smoked ham. She nodded at me when I thanked her, but pursed her lips and dropped her eyes when I asked, "Have you been here long?" Conversation, even in mime, was clearly not encouraged.

I ate slowly, more because I felt my body needed it than from appetite. I thought about Father—not the shrunken, frail man of this last week but the big hale Papa of my childhood, always ready to fix things mechanical, always humming to himself as he worked, always prepared to stop whatever he was doing and talk to me and patiently explain this or that. But still the tears would not come.

I shut my eyes. In this warm, silent room it was easy to picture my father, easy to imagine him sitting opposite me. I could almost hear his breathing. I could picture his broad face with his spectacles slipping down his nose, and his dark eyes watching me with gentle concern.

"Papa," I said, sliding my hand across the table toward him.

A warm touch brushed the back of my hand. A feathery brush of fingers. I shivered and opened my eyes—but there was no one there. Just the warm afternoon light and an empty chair and a fugitive scent that might have been church incense.

I wanted to weep. It would have been such a relief. But I couldn't.

Afterward, I went to my room, shrugged out of my clothes, put on the top half of the pajamas—the shirt hung down to mid-thigh on me—and climbed into the bed. I thought I'd just curl up and nurse the hollow in my chest, but I passed into sleep almost at once.

I closed the door of my apartment, dropped the keys in their bowl and walked through to the kitchen, where Suzana sat cuddling Senka the cat.

"Hey," I said. "How was your day? Bet it wasn't as bad as mine. A *three-hour* meeting called at five o'clock—can you believe it? I'm dead on my feet."

"Your boyfriend's in the living room," she said to my back, as I rooted around in the refrigerator for pepperoni and celery sticks.

"What?" Her words didn't make sense to me at all.

"Your *Turkish* boyfriend." Her cold disapproval was audible even with my back to her. "He's waiting for you."

"He's not Turkish," I said as I turned, but now I knew exactly who she meant.

"He looks Turkish, and he says his name's Aziz."

Senka chose this moment to dig her claws in and Suzana's attention abruptly transferred from me to the cat, who escaped at high speed through the door into the living room. "Ow!"

"Oh crap," said I, following.

Azazel was sitting on the back of the sofa, his bare feet on the cushions, petting the cat—who was practically climbing on him in order to butt her head underneath his chin. He inclined his neck so that they could rub cheek to cheek and ran his hand down her spine. Senka dipped and arched and let out an ecstatic yowl.

"Senka likes you," I observed. Just the sight of his inky lashes against his cheek made me clench inside.

He opened one eye. "I like cats," he said. "Free spirits."

Senka proved this by jumping down from the sofa-back and bouncing away across the floorboards to another chair where she could wash herself. Azazel straightened and consoled himself by looking me up and down with a smirk of undisguised appetite.

"Aziz, huh?" I said.

"Aziz el-Diren. *Warrior of the Resistance.* Like it?"

"Witty. You've picked up some modern languages then?"

"Some? All of them."

I blinked, discomforted by such excessive ability.

"Languages fascinate me. There are so many of them, these days, and they carry such complex histories wrapped in tiny words." He spread one hand. "I've been traveling about a lot."

"Nice."

"And surfing your Internet. A truly astonishing thing."

"Eeeeek." I pulled a face, my alarm genuine. "You know, you mustn't take everything you see on the web seriously. Really. Especially the porn."

"The porn was very interesting," he said, deadpan.

"Or *anything* in a comments section. People say stuff, but they don't act like that in real life."

"A good thing too. Any species possessed of that much hatred would surely wipe itself out." He glanced at Senka, amused. "Though you all seem to like cats."

I bit my lip, gathering myself.

"How have you been, Milja?"

I took a deep breath. "My father's dead."

His smile did not waver. "Should I offer condolences?"

"You killed him."

"I did not. But he was an old man, and very ill. When I held him here"—he mimed a clutching hand—"I could feel his heart stumbling."

"Don't."

"Old men die, Milja. Even more easily than young ones."

I wanted to hit him. "Say you're sorry," I whispered.

"Why?"

"He was my father," *you bastard*. "And he always felt sorry for you!"

But the second that was out of my mouth I knew what a stupid *stupid* thing it was to say, and I flushed.

Azazel, eyes narrowed behind silky lashes, waited until he saw my shame before he answered, very quietly: "And oh, that helped me so much."

I put my hand over my face, hiding my eyes. Of course, nothing looked the same from his perspective. He had every right to hate his prison guards as much as he hated the Architect of his torment.

"Don't cry," he said. For a moment I was surprised, until he ruined it by adding, "You are much less attractive when you cry."

Rage spiked in my breast, petty though it was. "I *can't* cry," I snarled, and then was surprised when he laughed.

"Oh, it has begun already!"

"What has?"

"You'll find out." Stepping down from the sofa, he held his hand out to me. "Come outside."

I briefly considered refusing the invitation, but then what would that achieve? Taking the very tips of his fingers in mine, I let him lead me out onto our apartment balcony.

Outside, it was a sunny day downtown. Skyscrapers of glittering tinted glass soared overhead. We were standing on a roof terrace, in a restaurant I didn't recognize, although—yeah, probably *because*—it looked very upmarket. Waiters in white dinner jackets flitted between tables where the well dressed drank wine and nibbled fiddly looking hors d'oeuvres.

Of course there wasn't really a restaurant on my balcony. Not in real life.

"Oh," I said with relief, "it's just a *dream*."

"Of course it is."

"Luckily for you," I pointed out snippily as he led me between the tables. "They usually insist on guests wearing shoes at places like this."

I also took the opportunity to look down at myself. I was wearing a light figure-skimming sleeveless dress, very short—it barely covered the essentials—which I'd never seen before and was definitely not what I'd thought I'd worn to the office. And I was sure I was wearing no bra or panties beneath it.

That made me look to see if others had taken any notice of our arrival. There were a few people staring, certainly. The men looked curious. The faces of the women watching my companion expressed a less guarded interest—simultaneously disparaging and avid.

Azazel glanced at me over his shoulder and bestowed a dark smile. "Am I embarrassing you, Milja?" he asked, drawing me closer so that he could nip at my ear.

"That's not the word I'd pick." Since it was only a dream, I figured, I didn't have to be so careful about provoking him. But he only laughed again and pushed me gently to the wall of the terrace, so that I could look over the parapet at the giddy perspective of the avenue many stories below, and the traffic crawling by.

"See this," he said, slipping his arms around me. "I love this view. Look at it. All around. Only a few thousand years ago you learned to smelt copper. And now—all this. Incredible. You are wonderful!"

"Wonderful?" I was taken aback at his enthusiasm, and terribly distracted by the way he pressed up against my ass.

"Don't you see that? Great cities of glass and steel, and vehicles that cross continents and the space between worlds. Electrical power that makes day out of night and does the work of uncountable hands. Your science—your art and architecture, literature and music. Computers and the Internet. Wonderful, what you have made. Beyond words!"

This wasn't entirely what I'd expected. He'd been, well, so grim and cynical until now—though with good reason. At this moment, beholding all the kingdoms of the world like, I thought, Satan bestriding the High Places, he was positively ebullient.

"And pollution and war and climate change, and Big Brother and cyber-bullying," I said, testing him.

He shrugged, looking out over my head. "You will overcome those things in time, I suppose, with enough thought and imagination."

"Maybe. We've got technology at our fingertips but Stone Age emotions."

"You take such a short-term view. I'm more optimistic, Milja."

I turned, staring up into his face. "I thought you hated us all?"

"Hate? Me?"

"You're…" I looked around at the diners and dropped my voice, which was ridiculous. I know. It was, after all, a dream. "You're a demon. The enemy of mankind."

He shook his head, eyes narrowing. "An enemy? Is that what you think?"

"Well. Aren't you?"

He shook his head, as if in disbelief at my ignorance. "For tens of thousands of years we cared for you, right from the Ash Winter when your species was brought to the edge. That was our remit—our holy duty. We were the Watchers—shepherds of those last helpless, naked, toothless hominids with their lumpen rock tools and their wildfires. Your kind was *this* close to extinction...but we stood about you and guarded you from the beasts and the darkness and the cold; we led you to clean water and new sources of food. We made sure you survived. And as we watched over you, slowly we taught you and nurtured your potential. Art. Music. Tool-making. Fishing. Sewing. Pottery. Look it up, Milja: it was all our doing. No, our crime was never caring too little."

"Then what was it?"

His eyes were like pools of moonlight. I could become trapped in there, I thought, and drown.

"We got too involved. We interfered."

"With women?"

He chuckled. "In the Divine Plan."

"And what is that?"

Azazel lifted an eyebrow, making no pretense of being inclined to answer. It was hard not to bristle under the insult. I remembered the quote about weapons from the *Book of Enoch*. "Metalworking...was that you then? Is that what you taught us?"

"And look what wonders you've wrought."

"Look at how many people *died*."

He put his lips to my ear for a moment. "Everybody dies," he whispered, as if it were a secret. "*Everybody*."

"But they died under the weapons you made."

"I showed you the working of metal, that's all. What you did with it is your own affair."

"The wars, the massacres...doesn't it bother you?"

"Why should it?"

80

"I thought you said we were wonderful?"

He shrugged. "As a species."

I felt gooseflesh prickle me from head to toe. "And as individuals?"

"Some of you are wonderful. A very few, I'd say." He put his finger on my breastbone and traced it down the inner curve of my breast, making me shiver. "You, for example."

The cold thrill of fear he evoked in me focused down from the generalized to the very specific. I knew what he wanted. My voice quivered, as the sensation of his touch trickled all the way down through my belly, and lower still.

"I'm nothing special." Was I reduced to begging to be overlooked?

"You are now. You're mine. You are my wife."

That's what he said to Father.

"No. I'm not." It was hard to contradict him, but I forced the words out. My nipples were so stiff from his teasing that they ached.

"What?"

I tried to push his hand away but it didn't work, so I just kept talking as he picked me up and sat me on the lip of the parapet, spreading my thighs so that he could stand between them, and I felt the canyon of the street yawn open behind me. "I'm not your wife. The human race has moved on a bit since you were last around. Marriage isn't just a question of grabbing any woman who takes your fancy anymore. Or buying her off her father for a couple of goats."

That made him chuckle again. "What is it, then?"

"Partnership. Love. Commitment. Free consent. Given under law, which grants equal rights on both sides, without duress. I am *not* your wife."

He cocked an eyebrow. "Would you prefer I used another term then? Lover? Paramour? Concubine?" He grinned, almost nose to nose with me. It was hard to see, but I suspected it wasn't a very pleasant grin. "*Pet?*"

I swallowed hard. "At least you're being honest now."

"Madam, please." A waiter had appeared at Azazel's elbow. "You mustn't sit there. It's not safe."

"She sits there because I want her to sit there," said my companion, not looking at him. "And she is as safe as I choose." He hooked his hand around the back of my head and took a grip in my hair. Then he pushed me backward, almost to the horizontal, over twenty stories of empty air.

Fear was like a vise; it made me wrap my thighs tight about his hips.

"See?"

I was cradled at the end of his arm by his hard hand and nothing else. My stomach muscles ached. My throat hurt with the effort of my breathing.

It's all a dream. If I fall, I'll just wake up.

"Do you trust me, Milja?" he whispered. Then he pulled me back to the upright position again. My heart was pounding like it wanted to break out of my rib cage.

"Sir, sir." The waiter was wringing his hands. "Please, take a seat at your table. The sommelier is ready to take your order. Anything you require, sir, compliments of the house."

"Go away," Azazel growled, and kissed me. My blood was on fire with wild terror and gratitude, and a knowledge of my helplessness that was so dark and primal that it drowned my rage. When his fingers sneaked beneath the tiny skirt of my dress and slid between us, they found me wet with arousal.

I moaned breathily.

"What, Milja?" Azazel whispered, as I wrapped my arms about his neck to stop him flinging me from the heights. "In front of all these people? That's hardly proper." His fingertips danced and it felt like it was my soul he was touching.

It's a dream, I told myself, blocking out the turned heads and round eyes of the diners. *Just a dream.*

There were no clothes between us, not where it mattered—I guess that was part of the dream too—just the great hot hardness of him pushing against me. I lifted my legs like I was raising a portcullis and he made his entry: all bulk, all slick, all pent breath and biting kisses and shuddering fire.

When he leaned into me it tilted me back over the void. I felt his hands tight on my hips as he uttered a groaning laugh into my mouth. I felt it all—the terror and the vertigo and the surrender and my burning burning need of him. He was slow and then he was strong and then he was moving like a man who could no longer help himself, his muscles locked in a rhythm of intent. All my weight was on his neck, but my arms no longer felt strong enough to hold myself.

If I fall he will not let go, I told myself. *He wants me. He won't let go.*

So I let my hands slip, and I fell back, and the whole world swung upside down as my back arched; the skyscrapers plunging like silver spears from heaven and the screams of the diners a pandemonium beneath my feet, and the blare of the gridlocked traffic like the sound of trumpets above.

He did not let go.

He held me in place on the parapet, filling me as my upper body hung upside down over the drop and the blood rushed to my head and the heat broke between my open legs.

He did not let me go, but fell with me, and in falling we burned like lightning.

Orgasm shocked me awake, and for a while I just lay there, washed in the after-quakes and recalling my surroundings.

Egan's place.

The erotic dream had been so vivid that it was almost a disappointment to find myself back in the strange house in the suburbs. True, the dream had been dirty and upsetting…but it wasn't the fear that lingered. My body hummed with pleasure and it wanted more.

But though I shut my eyes I was no longer able to fall back into sleep. My mind was too alert now, and the blankets felt too warm. If I didn't get up soon I'd need to touch myself in order to recapture the escape into sexual bliss.

It was just a dream.

Of course I'd been having nightmares about our prisoner for years. This one was different though: this one I remembered in every detail.

I got up. It was still daylight, and the drinks I'd consumed had completed their journey and were nagging my bladder. I grabbed the toiletries bag from the nightstand. There was a folded bath towel placed on the foot of my bed that hadn't been there before, and I wondered if it was Dejana who'd come in and left it for me while I slept, or Egan. The latter possibility did not creep me out as much as it should have.

Only then did I notice my discarded clothing, now laundered and pressed and stacked neatly on a chair. I gathered the pile into the crook of my arm, frowning. It was nice to have clean clothes for a change—it was wonderful—but the implications were disconcerting.

I padded out barefoot into the living area, heading for the bathroom. Egan was sitting in an armchair, sipping from a coffee cup and reading the screen of his phone. His mouth fell open as he saw me, then he sprang to his feet and moved to stare out of the window, his turned back like a shield.

I was surprised, and then embarrassed, and then amused. I was so used to wandering around my own apartment in my night-clothes that I hadn't thought twice. And—I looked down to check—honestly, all I had on display were my legs. The oversized pajama jacket hid everything else. Egan must see as much on any high street in summer, and a whole lot more on any bathing beach.

"Morning," he said, looking obstinately into the little courtyard.

"Heya," I answered, warmed by his chivalry. And, if I was honest with myself, still tingling from the effects of my dream. Part of me wouldn't have minded him turning to look.

Then his choice of word registered.

"Morning?"

"Sure. You slept right through the night."

"Oh God, *no*." Was it the after-effects of the pills they'd plied me with, or just exhaustion?

"It's all right. It's Saturday now. I'll ask Dejana to bring you breakfast."

He was wearing a long-sleeved T-shirt, not a work jacket, I registered. Saturday, right. I'd lost track of days. "I'd...better go get dressed."

I hurried into the bathroom—austere and masculine just like the rest of the place—and in less than twenty minutes I was showered and dressed and so grateful for my clean clothes and hair and teeth that I could have kissed someone. I would have lingered, enjoying the hot water...but its touch brought back the sensuality of my dream only too clearly and I could sense the slippery slope beckoning. I turned the dream over in my head as I toweled my damp hair, a little appalled at my exhibitionist sexual submission but trying to be clear-eyed. So, I'd had a dirty dream. Didn't that happen to everyone, some time or other? It had been Azazel's dominance that had turned me on—in fact *dominance* did not begin to describe it. His *possession* of me, as a man owns an object—and his flagrant demonstration of that ownership. No more furtive sneaking about in shadows; no more secrecy. Public claiming of what he wanted, without shame.

It was just a dream. But I am so worn out by keeping secrets.

Egan was still by the window, but now talking on his cell phone. "I'll ring you back later," he said when he saw me. "Coffee, Milja?"

He poured as I nibbled at scrambled eggs and piles of toast. My body still felt like it glowed from within.

"Do you feel like talking?" he asked, sitting down opposite me.

I didn't know where to start, but I owed him an explanation. So I told him...some of the truth. I told him my father had suffered a cardiac arrest. I told him that Father had for years been selling off the forgotten antiquities stashed in his church—"Not for money, not for himself, he never used a penny—I swear it. He used it to get me to America and pay for a good college. He was just trying to look after me. I was his only child and he was afraid of what would happen if I stayed in the village"—and then I told him about the incident in the park. "I screwed that up. I just needed the money to pay the hospital fees, but the Church...the Church had noticed this stuff turning up on the black market and the dealer betrayed us. And they followed me back to the hospital. They must have, somehow. They found Father."

"You're saying they *killed* him?"

"No." I sank my head in my hands. "But it wouldn't have taken much, just the shock of seeing them there, of being accused. Father was so frail. They wouldn't harm him deliberately, no, of course not."

And I hope to God that's true.

"That's awful, Milja. I am sorry."

"Vera and Josif blame me. And they're right, but it wasn't deliberate. I wouldn't hurt my father!"

No, but I disobeyed him and betrayed his trust and he died thinking me a demon's slut. No: not just thinking—knowing.

"Of course not." Egan squeezed my hand. "They will realize that, when they get over the first shock of their loss. They won't blame you."

"That's not true. You don't understand." I bit my lip, unable to say more, and finished weakly: "You don't understand this country. This isn't America. They won't forgive me."

"Can't you talk to your cousin?"

I shook my head. "I just want to go back home to Boston."

"To be sure. Well, how about I go see Vera for you, and maybe pass on the money for the hospital fees, and ask her for your passport back?"

"No." My response was swift and vehement. "You mustn't go near her! If she sees you she'll remember you from the plane, and she knows your name and she'll be able to find us."

Egan frowned. "Are they Mafia or something?"

"No." The word was out a split second before I thought *Damn, that would have made a good excuse, why didn't I say yes?* I looked down at the table between us, groping for explanations that weren't actually lies. I didn't want to lie to Egan. "The Church wants their stuff back," I mumbled. "But it's too late."

"Ah now, you're saying you think the *Church* is after you?" There was an odd tone in Egan's voice. I was examining the breakfast crumbs intently, so I couldn't read his expression, but I could imagine how it sounded to an outsider and how he must be thinking I was a paranoid wacko.

"They're very important here. And powerful. I'm in bad trouble. They'd lock me up for a long time."

Not thousands of years, perhaps, but long enough.

I couldn't tell Egan about Azazel—how on earth could I? It wasn't something any normal person would believe if he hadn't seen for himself. So I'd mentioned not one word about our prisoner or my awful guilty part in the events. But it made me jumpy and angry with myself. "I shouldn't be dumping this on you, it's not like it's anything to do with you. I mean… why are you helping me? Why are you being so nice?"

It came out sounding a lot more accusatory than I'd intended. Egan blinked and looked away, embarrassed. He even flushed a little.

"I don't know…I just thought you looked like you needed someone."

And I'm a girl. I'm a girl on my own, in trouble, and you can't resist. Chivalry is only the desire to save the damsel from everyone but yourself. It suddenly felt like my head had cleared, and I was looking at him from a cold distance. *Would you have still come to my rescue if I'd told you I wasn't single, Egan? Oh no, hold on, Milja—you're thinking like a village girl now. A big nasty boyfriend would just be fuel to the fire for his type.*

And then another voice in my head, a gentler one that could almost have been my father's, said, *And you know that he likes you; you saw it from the start, and you've been taking advantage of that, Milja. If anything, you've been using him.*

All of a sudden I felt ashamed. Ashamed of judging him so cynically, and of my own dishonesty. I wasn't going to—I couldn't—tell him about my demon lover. But I'd thrown myself on his mercy, and now he was all I had. It felt like I needed him. Did I even have the strength to go it alone?

"You're a nice guy," I said apologetically.

He pulled a face. "That's usually an insult."

"No, I mean it. I'm grateful. You've been really good to me, Egan, and I don't deserve it."

"Don't you?" His eyes told me he didn't believe my words.

"No, I don't." I felt my resolve harden. I pushed back my chair and rose. I was frightened, but I tried not to let it show. "I'm not getting you any deeper into this mess. It's my problem, not yours. Thank you for all your help."

He sat back. "Sit down," he said softly.

I hesitated.

"Sit down and don't be an eejit." His accent grew stronger for a second. "I'm not kicking you out on your own, Milja. I'm not going to abandon you. Just...no. We can sort this thing out. Somehow or other. You're not on your own."

I sat. I was so relieved that I gave a sort of hiccup and then went crimson with embarrassment. Egan grinned and patted my hand.

"So, now...let's think. If you want to fly back you need your passport. Do you know where it is right now?"

"Last time I saw it, it was in Vera's room-safe at the Hotel Mimosa."

"So if that's beyond reach, I suppose you could report it stolen and apply for a new one?"

"I suppose." I'd need more than a bare passport to get back into the States, I suspected. What about my visas and stuff? "It'll take weeks."

"Do you know how to make the application?"

"No—Father did all that last time."

"Well, we can look it up online. You'll need to submit photos for a start, won't you?"

"Yes."

"We can begin there. There's a chemist's about a mile away that has a photo booth, I think."

"A chemist's?"

"Drugstore. You Yankee."

I smiled. "*Apoteka*," I told him. "You foreigner."

We drove out to the mini-mall. Egan, it turned out, had had the foresight to hire a car the day before, and I was glad to see that he drove with assurance.

I didn't like the fact that a big silver SUV slid out into the main road behind us and followed all the way to the store, but it passed when we parked and I didn't say anything to Egan.

You're being paranoid, Milja.

The mall was fairly upmarket, in keeping with the genteel neighborhood, and there weren't crowds of people around. A small dog was tied up outside the door to the drugstore—something beige colored and fluffy—and it wagged its tail in greeting whenever anyone came in or out. But when I approached it took one look and flattened itself to the ground, beating the tip of its tail in appeasement whilst whimpering. A thin stream of urine ran out from beneath its belly across the concrete.

I stared at the dog, feeling sick. Could it tell what I'd done?

Egan wasn't looking, luckily.

It was a big store, and it did have an automated photo booth at the back. I took two sets of passport snaps, just to be sure, and then wandered up and down the aisles, filling a basket with deodorant and moisturizer and all the useful things I didn't have anymore.

When I looked up from a packet of dental floss, there were three men watching me from the top end of the aisle. They were informally dressed, fairly rough looking, and they weren't carrying baskets.

I dropped the floss into my stash and walked casually in the other direction, toward the back of the store. Rounding the end of the aisle, I spotted Egan in the parallel row staring at the shelves with the pained frown of someone trying to work out which product was what purely from the packaging pictures.

"I think we might have to go," I told him as I hurried up.

"What's wrong?"

He followed the line of my gaze back down the aisle, just as three men rounded the corner. Two were a couple of those nondescript guys I'd already spotted. The third, leading them, was my Uncle Josif.

"That's her," said he, pointing.

chapter seven

CONFESSION

O
h crap," I said, backing off.

"Okay..." muttered Egan, and as he started to retreat after me I turned tail, dropping my basket as I scurried up the aisle.

That was the moment that the missing third stranger stepped out at the top end, cutting off our exit route to the tills and the door.

"Milja!" said Josif loudly behind me. "Come here!"

No way was I obeying, but I didn't see a way out. I looked wildly up and down the lane as the men started to close from either end. The lone man was nearly on top of us.

Then Egan stepped in front of me, brandishing a mop from a display stand of Wonder Cleaning Products, and he swung it and smashed it with all his strength across the side of the man's knee. The guy folded with a hoarse scream. Egan reached out, grabbed me and practically threw me up the aisle in front of him; I only kept my feet by running. I piled through the queue at the till, shoving people left and right. A glance behind told me Egan was on my heels, still brandishing the mop and taking rearguard action, so I belted across the parking lot in the direction of our rental car.

There was an odd cracking noise.

"Run!" Egan roared, appearing to my right and pointing the remote key. The car sidelights flashed twice. I could hear Uncle Josif shouting too, though I couldn't take in the words. I bundled into the passenger side and Egan gunned the engine before I even pulled the door shut, and we lurched forward. I thought we were going to hit a post for one heart-stopping moment, but he wrenched the wheel right and we spun away, scraping against some innocent's rear spoiler.

"Ah!" I howled, trying to hold myself down on my seat as we hurtled out into the traffic lane. The Orthodox prayer for beginning a journey leaped into my mouth; "Oh Savior who hast journeyed with Luke and Cleopas to Emmaus, journey with thy servants as they now set out upon their way, and defend them from all evil!"

"Amen," Egan growled, spinning us abruptly through ninety degrees and down a side street that was far too narrow for the speed he was accelerating to. A child on a bicycle barely made it out of our way.

"What're you doing, you lunatic!"

"They're following us."

I looked over my shoulder and saw the silver SUV through the rear window—but I only got a glimpse because Egan grabbed my head and shoved it down into his lap. "Head down!"

"What!" I wailed, my face bouncing off his hard thigh and then the steering wheel.

"Get down in the seat well!"

I shoved myself back onto my own side and crouched in front of my seat, knees jammed against the dash. We were going down a long straight slope; I could see a lot of sky and the tops of buildings and a distant set of traffic lights over the middle of a big junction. They were lit red.

"Ah, shite," said Egan grimly.

Go green, go green, I thought. *Let us through!*

They went green. Egan jerked the car over a lane and we shot past a queue of traffic, underneath the lights and back into lane. I shut my eyes and tried not to get impaled on the gearshift.

Three minutes and several switchback junctions later, Egan slowed the car. "We've lost them."

"What, what, what," I mumbled stupidly. "What the hell? You could have killed us both!"

"Who were those men?" he countered.

"I don't know! I mean...one was my Uncle Josif. I've never seen the others before."

"They shot at you." Egan's eyes were still alternating between the road and the rearview mirrors: for once there was no gentleness in his face. "Didn't you hear it?"

"*What?*"

"Your man who recognized you—he called them off, I think. But there were at least two shots. So yeah—what the hell? Good question, Milja. They wanted you bad."

I crawled back onto my seat and stared around us, but the roads looked peaceful and nonthreatening. I didn't know what to think. "Where are we headed?"

"Back to the house."

"No!" I grabbed his arm. "They followed us from there—they know where we're staying—God knows how—the taxi driver I suppose—" Words tumbled out as the thoughts spilled through my mind. "We can't go back there: they'll be waiting for us!"

He flicked a look at me sideways. "That's grand," he said, turning into the lane for the city center.

"What? What's happening?"

"If they're waiting at the house, we'll head for the Hotel Mimosa. This is our best chance to get your passport when there's no one around. Do you remember the combination to the safe lock?"

"Uh. Yes. If she hasn't changed it."

"You're such a pessimist, Milja."

He was the second man to accuse me of that today. I opened my mouth, shut it again and went quiet. The city scenery hummed and beeped and growled past us. I sat watching, but my mind wasn't on what was in front of my eyes. In my head I replayed the events in the drugstore, trying to make sense of the chaos.

I hadn't seen much. It all seemed unreal, except for the feeling of panic and nausea. Nothing much was clear—except the absolute lack of hesitation with which Egan had smashed that man's knee. I saw that over and over again.

"What the hell was that with the mop?" I said as we turned in front of the hospital and pulled up in front of the hotel.

"Pardon?"

"You broke his leg. I saw. You broke it. Just like that!"

Egan pulled a face. "Ah, well...you see, I grew up playing hurling."

"What's hurling?"

"It's a game for men with iron balls and no teeth," he muttered, squinting up at the hotel's multistory facade. "Come on."

We walked round to the back and then into the hotel via the service parking lot and the swimming pool area. No one stopped us; no one so much as glanced at us. As we crossed the lobby I tried to see if Vera's key was hanging on the board behind the desk, but I couldn't be sure.

"They might have checked out," I warned Egan as we climbed the stairs to the third floor. He'd refused to take the elevator.

"Well they certainly haven't left the city yet."

He insisted on taking the lead as we emerged into the corridor, but there was no one in sight. We padded down the carpeted hall to room 312.

"What's Montenegrin for *room service*?" he whispered.

I told him, and he knocked and made a reasonable go of reproducing the syllables. But there was no answer. He tried again, and pushed the handle, in vain.

My shoulders drooped a little. My next plan was to go back down to the check-in desk, ask for the key and hope that the receptionist remembered me accompanying Vera.

I didn't get the chance, as it turned out. Egan stepped back and looked the door up and down. It wasn't an upscale hotel, and the doors on this floor were faced in cheap veneer and carried an old-fashioned lock. Without warning, he slammed his boot sole hard into the wood. The noise made me cringe. He had a kick like a mule: on the second blow the jamb splintered and the door flew inward.

That was the moment I really stopped pigeonholing him as a "nice I.T. guy."

And when he stalked into the room I followed, praying that we had the right occupants and that nobody else had heard.

We got half of what I asked for, anyway.

Inside, the hotel room stank of incense and hot wax. The curtains were drawn tight, so that it took us a while for our eyes to adjust, because apart from the open door the only illumination came from ranks of candles weeping wax all over a dressing table loaded with icons. My cousin Vera knelt at the foot of the bed, her face buried in the quilt cover, her shoulders shaking.

My feet felt like they were made of lead.

Egan scanned the visible area, went to check that the en-suite bathroom was empty and then said to me, very softly, "The safe?"

Wide-eyed, I jerked my head to indicate the built-in wardrobe. He pointed a finger at me, and then at Vera, his expression grave. As he went for the cupboard, I took a deep breath and closed on her hunched form.

"*Nana*? Are you all right?"

I'm not sure what I expected her response to be. To ignore me, probably, or perhaps to fly at my face in fury. She didn't do either. She lifted her head from the bed, and I glimpsed the big dark stain she'd left on the duvet. Then she turned her face toward me and I saw where it had come from; there were encrustations all over her lips and lower jaw that looked black in this dim light but that I knew, with a sickening lurch, should be red.

Her eyes were sticky and swollen half-shut.

"Oh my God, Vera, what did they do to you?" I gasped.

"She did it to herself," said the man behind me in the doorway. Silhouetted against the lit corridor, he was nothing but a bulky shadow. "She took a knife to her tongue in horror and repentance at the things she had to confess to us. Such foul secrets and such black sins. A burden unbearable."

I stared as he closed the room door behind him and came forward into the circle of candlelight. It was the big priest with the gray-and-black striped beard, the one I'd seen with Father Velimir, and I could only think *Don't look at Egan, Milja, don't give him away.*

Hidden behind the open wardrobe door, in the half dark, Egan was momentarily unnoticed as the newcomer entered the room. The priest's attention was all on me, hunkered down over my shaking cousin.

"Now we have you, witch," he said lifting his hands.

Egan stepped out—and the cupboard door creaked. The priest moved faster than I'd have expected, turning to the new threat—and then he took a step back, face slack with fear.

"Is that *him?*" he asked, starting to cross himself. "Jesus Christ have—"

Egan took that advantage. He kicked the priest in the gut, grabbed his beard as he folded, and punched him in the side of the head. The big man went down like a stone, without another word but nearly taking Egan with him.

What the—? I thought.

"Get the light!" my companion hissed.

I scrambled for the switch by the bed. The electric light dispelled some of the claustrophobic ecclesiastical atmosphere, though it didn't make the scene any less crazy. I stared as Egan used a dressing-gown belt to tie the priest's hands behind his back.

"Don't just stand there!" he told me. "The safe's locked—get it open."

I had to climb over the bed to reach the wardrobe without trampling people. But once I was there I hesitated, unable not to look at the priest laid out alongside the bed.

"He's fine," said Egan, checking the pulse at his throat to demonstrate. "Hurry up, Milja."

I took his word for it. What else could I do? Vera made a horrible moaning noise as she watched us, and I wanted to echo the sentiment. I felt sick with confusion and horror. The four-digit code I punched in on the safe keys winked redly at me from the interior of the wardrobe, like the eyes of a devil.

The safe did not unlock.

I tried again. I tried a different combination of the numbers, in case I'd misremembered. It made no difference. I turned to Egan, standing astride the unconscious priest, and shook my head.

He went over to Vera and knelt down to face her. Just for a second I felt a scream of protest rise in my throat—but it was the normal, familiar Egan who looked her in the eye. His expression was mild and when he spoke his voice was soft and sympathetic.

"We need Milja's passport. Where is it?"

Vera shot me a venomous look and a red trickle ran from the corner of her mouth. She shook her head.

"Will you open the safe for us?"

He was so cute and warm and gentle. Any middle-aged woman would trust him on sight.

Vera looked him in the eye and bared bloody teeth in a snarl.

"Please, just open the safe. We'll go, and you'll never see us again."

She spat full in his face. I saw the crimson splatter across his cheek.

Egan's expression didn't change. He reached out and put a hand on her shoulder though, and I saw the weight of it press her down.

"No!" I cried, launching myself across the bed. "Egan, don't! Don't!" I grabbed his shirt and pulled at him wildly. "Stop it! Just leave her alone!"

He glanced up at me. I couldn't read his face at all; I was just hypnotized by the patina of blood flecks. "You need that passport."

"And what are you going to do—beat her up? You can't! For God's sake Egan, she's my cousin!"

"She'll open it if we make her."

"No, she won't!" I could see the rage in Vera's eyes and I knew she'd rather die. She'd always had a thing for the Holy Martyrs. "And you're not going to try!"

He stood up. "Your choice, Milja." His voice was still mild, but there was a gravity to it. "You know what it means. Your choice."

It meant I would be trapped in the country with an armed gang after me and no route out. I shook my head. "Just leave her alone. Let's go. Let's go."

He stooped and reached for Vera again. For a moment my heart was in my mouth, but he only snagged the lace handkerchief she always carried in the pocket of her cardigan. Taking my arm, he helped me off the bed. He was wiping his face as he headed for the door.

Vera made a noise behind us as we left: a noise of pain and pure hatred.

"Quickly." It was the only word Egan said to me as we clattered down the stairs. Until we got almost to the front door and, looking out through the glass, saw a man lounging against our rental car, smoking.

"Oh hell. Is that—is that one of them?"

"Out the back," Egan announced. He had hold of my elbow and he wasn't letting go. We marched back through the lobby and the bar and out through the pool area. There was no one waiting out the back so we hustled down a side road and hailed a cab.

"I don't think you're getting your rental deposit back," I said shakily.

"Huh." He shrugged, opening the door for me. "It's on the business account."

We took the taxicab right to the busiest part of the town center, paid it off and went for a long, random walk. We hardly spoke. Everything I felt when I looked at Egan was so conflicted—gratitude and anxiety and guilt all mixed up together—that I didn't know where to start.

"We should go to church," he said, suddenly.

That shook me from the dumb contemplation of the hot dog in my hand. I realized I hadn't been tasting it anyway. "What?"

"If it's priests that are after you, like you say, then where's the last place they'll expect us to hide?" He pointed across the street at a church facade where people were drifting in and out, then added, "And we need a place to talk."

I clenched my jaw, girding myself inwardly. It would not, I imagined, be a very pleasant conversation.

It made me nervous to approach the church, to ascend the stairs past the beggars and slip inside. Once upon a time the brightly painted interior with its lush frescoes and warm banks of candle-glow and its gleam of gold would have felt embracing, like entering bodily into a familiar story-book from childhood. It would have closed out the outside world with all its rush and complexity and grime, and instantly put me in a place of serenity. Not anymore.

I steered us to the first and most obvious icon near the door and kissed the picture of St. Basil. "Cross yourself," I muttered to Egan. He followed my example clumsily and I winced. "Wrong way round—*right to left*," I hissed. "And *three fingers*."

"Oops." He did it again, properly this time.

We were lucky—this was an Orthodox church that had pews, some-thing I hadn't seen before outside the States. Traditionally the people of my faith stand for services. Egan and I settled ourselves in at the back, well away from the iconostasis screen before the altar. I tried not to look around us too suspiciously. And I kept my voice as low as possible as I spoke.

"Who do you really work for, Egan?"

He was pulling up the knees of his jeans to get more comfortable; he stopped moving as my words sank in. "What do you mean?"

"This stuff you do. The kicking in doors and the evasive driving and the *beating people up* at the drop of a hat. Don't tell me you learned to do that by playing too much *Call of Duty*."

"Well, no." Egan wrinkled his nose sheepishly. "I haven't always had a desk job, you know." He sighed. "I went into the armed forces straight from school."

I glowered at him. "In Ireland?"

"Ah..."

"Are you going to tell me about it?"

"I am not."

"I see."

He smiled, to mollify me. "But I do work for a bank now, honest."

"Would you have hurt Vera?"

His eyebrows met in the center as he looked pained. "No, of course not. I might have...scared her, that's all."

I wondered if I believed him. I really wanted to.

He shook his head, ruefully. "It would have solved a lot of your problems, getting that passport back. Now we're stuck looking for alternatives."

There was a tap on the bench beside me and I jumped.

Proot said the tiniest voice. A fuzzy gray kitten stood on the pew at my side, looking up at me with big amber eyes. I'd never seen a cat allowed inside a church before, but I'm a sucker for them in any situation. I put my hand out to pet it and it wound itself enthusiastically in circles, starting to purr. I could feel its small bones under the soft fur and I wondered if Suzana was feeding Senka properly.

"I'm assuming you *don't* have an alternative plan right now," Egan said, recalling me to the matter at hand.

"No."

"Right, well then, before we go any farther, are you going to be honest with me?"

I felt cold creep along my spine. I kept my head down, watching the kitten. "What do you mean?"

"There's something you're not telling me about this."

"What makes you think that?"

"The priest. He said, when he saw me, *'Is that him?'* And I swear he nearly peed his pants."

I shook my head. "No... He said *'Who is that?'*"

"Milja, I've picked up enough Serbo-Croat to know that's just not true."

"Don't call it Serbo-Croat," I muttered. "We don't use that term anymore."

"Fine. Montenegrin." Egan cleared his throat pointedly and waited for a real answer, and when I kept quiet he pressed on; "What did he mean? Who did he think I was?"

The kitten hopped up into my lap and lay down, staring up at Egan as I stroked its furry back and chewed my lip. It was a fair question, I admitted. Egan had the right to ask what sort of trouble he was getting involved in. For all he knew it could be drugs or people-trafficking or some organized-crime vendetta.

"I... There's this..." My brain felt like it had flatlined. "I don't know how to explain."

"Well, start at the beginning."

"I can't. You won't believe me."

"How do you know that?"

"Because you're...sensible." I looked helplessly toward the altar. "Really really sensible. And normal. And not from round here. And I wouldn't believe it if I were you, and you were me."

"Okay...that's some buildup. Should I be flattered by the *sensible* bit, then?"

"Oh yes."

"You make it sound like I'm a turnip farmer."

I snorted, covering my nose. The kitten dug tiny claws into my lap.

"Just take it bit by bit."

"The antiquities I told you about..." I started, realized that was a dead end and then began groping for some sort of agnostic gloss on the story. "The priests...think...that I've done something really bad."

"Uh-huh?"

"They think there was something kept in the church in our village.

Some*one*. Like, a prisoner." I paused, waited for Egan's response, whether encouraging or derisory, but he made not a sound and did not stir, and I didn't dare look at him so I blurted, in a rush, "An angel. A fallen one. They think I let it out."

The silence was excruciating. I made myself look at him at last. He was staring down the nave as if he hadn't heard me, his face expressionless, but when I turned my gaze to him he met it.

"And what do you think, Milja?"

I felt myself crumbling inside. "What do you mean?"

"Do you believe they've got it right? Did you see an angel? Did you let it out?" His voice was so gentle that I wanted to cry, but there was a bead of sweat on his temple that caught the candlelight like gold.

He thought I was delusional.

I wanted to deny it. I wanted to tell him, *Oh no, it's just some crazy local superstition and this old man Father Velimir has taken it way too seriously, but how do I prove that?* Yet the thought of lying to Egan made me ache. I'd already lied by omission, over and over again. It weighed on me like slabs of rock.

I looked away. "Am I a crazy-ass religious nutcase then?"

"I don't think so. That's not the impression you've given so far."

He had his cautious, sensible voice on again, and all of a sudden, quite perversely, I wanted to break that. "There was an angel," I said flatly. "Tied up in a cave. He'd been there five thousand years, he said. I let him go free."

Egan kept quiet this time.

I started to count, wondering how long it would be before he laughed, or stood up and walked out. *One...two...three...four...five...*

"Why?"

"Huh?"

"Why did you let him go?"

I blinked. "I felt sorry for him." That was so woefully inadequate that I had to follow it up. "He was in pain, and it was so cruel, and so unfair..." I broke off abruptly. Where was he leading me in this?

Egan was sitting with his hands steepled together before his face, fingers pressed against his mouth, frowning at me.

"Do you believe me then?"

He tapped his fingertips against his lips, thoughtfully. "I don't think you're lying. And those priests believe it, presumably." *Tap, tap.* "I'll tell you something else..."

"What?"

"They're trying to take you alive."

I pulled a face, uncomprehending.

"If they'd been trying to execute you as some sort of act of revenge, or punishment, they'd have had you shot in the drugstore, without hesitation. And it'd only take one man to do it. Or they'd have shot out our tires at speed afterward and killed us both in the crash. They're trying to bring you in alive. Why do you think that is?"

"I don't know!" My voice rose a little too loudly and the kitten needled me again. "To put me on trial? To punish me more?"

"Maybe. It's interesting, don't you think?"

"*Interesting?*"

"Ah now, I'm sorry...that was a bit thoughtless of me." He smiled in self-deprecation. "Look, Milja, I think I need to make a phone call."

"Who to?"

"I have...contacts who might be able to get us out of the country. Through unofficial channels. I think we might need them."

Army people? Special Forces? CIA? Irish Republican terrorists? Maybe I really was going crazy.

"I can't ring from in here. You just stay for a moment, Milja."

"No!" I grabbed his arm. "Don't leave me!"

"I'm not leaving you." His hand on mine was firm. "Not ever. I will keep you safe, I promise, Milja. But you need to stay out of sight. I will be five minutes, no more."

I looked into his eyes and I believed him. I stayed, with the gray kitten nestled on my lap, and I tried to pray. But the traditional words were like dead leaves on my tongue and the only prayer in my heart was *Please keep him safe. Please don't let him leave without me.*

There was a creak as someone sat on the pew in front of me.

"Hello."

My eyes flashed open. If it had been anybody I recognized as a pursuer, I think I would have screamed my head off, but it was someone totally unknown to me. An older man: little lines creased around his eyes as he smiled. Silver hair, but black brows that denied he was truly aged. Deep-set, hauntingly wonderful blue eyes. A bit George Clooney. But better looking.

"Ohhh," I said, as the kitten dug all twenty claws into my thighs.

"It's a pleasure to meet you. Milja, isn't it?" He extended a hand for me to shake over the back of the pew. As the kitten rose up on four agonizing paws, arched its back and spat at him, he glanced briefly at it and withdrew his hand. "I'm Uriel," he said urbanely, as if nothing had happened.

"Uriel?" I said through gritted teeth. "Like in 'the Archangel Uriel'?"

"Yes." He looked pleased. "That's right. *Exactly* like in the Archangel Uriel."

chapter eight

GHOSTS

It would be nice to report that I said something wise or memorable. I didn't. I didn't get any farther than thinking, *Oh no. Oh no no no.*

"How are you enjoying this church?" he asked cheerily. "There was a lot of fuss when they decided to put in the pews. The traditionalists don't like it at all, and I've got to say I think it makes the place a bit cluttered."

"Um. It's nice to have a place to just sit. And think."

"And pray, I trust?"

"Yes."

"There's an icon of me up near the Bishop's Chair." He winked. "I hope you'll go light a candle later."

"Right." It came out as a squeak.

"Don't be shy. You're a remarkable young woman, in your way," he said. "The first person ever to release one of the Watchers from their prison—did you know that?"

"Really?" My voice was tiny.

He hooked up the side of his mouth. There was something about his eyes that was truly disquieting. "I somehow imagined you might be... prettier. And with bigger breasts. I mean, his last wife... You should have seen her. Wow."

I clenched my jaw. "Sorry to disappoint."

"Oh, I'm used to disappointment. I wouldn't know where I was without it, to be honest. Sex, was it? Some kind of infatuation?" He rolled his eyes, addressing himself as much as me. "Of course it was. And I thought the bonobos were risible."

I blushed. The kitten withdrew its claws from my skin, but remained fluffed up with outrage as it let out a grumbling yowl.

"Don't blame yourself, Milja. It was probably bound to happen sooner or later, given the setup."

"The setup?"

"You think it was bread crusts and rainwater that kept your Azazel alive for three hundred generations? He's one of the Sons of God, girl—created and sustained by the Living Presence. Cut him off from that, bury him in a mountain and forget him, and he dies. Slowly. But surely."

"I don't understand."

"Of course you don't. To sustain the Egrigoroi, to eke out their torment for eons, they were given guardians. Human watchmen who would feel responsibility and pity and—who knows?—desire. *That's* what keeps them alive. It's a piss-poor substitute for the infinite love of the Almighty, but it suffices."

"That's..." I struggled to express my feelings. "That's horrible."

"The Lord of Hosts certainly has a sense of irony." He shook his head. "Of course the weakness in the plan is that one of you might love...too much. *Quis custodiet ipsos custodes*, heh?"

"What?"

"Who watches the watchers?"

"That's just disgusting," I whispered. "To use compassion like that..."

Uriel lifted a finger and wagged it at me gently. "Careful, girl. Sin of Job. Don't go there."

"Job?" I remembered my Bible stories reasonably well I thought, even if I hadn't read them in years. "Job was an upright man, without sin. That was the point."

"But he questioned the justice of God. That was his sin, to be repented in dust and ashes."

I stuck my lower lip out, feeling the heat rising in my chest. "Then it's already too late for me. And I don't repent it."

Uriel's eyes widened. In the shadowy nave they looked like they had a pale bluish glow. "Really?"

I floundered through my hot thoughts. I regretted the consequences of what I'd done, of course: my whole world had been torn apart. But I did not, could not, repent or disown the feelings that had made me cut Azazel's bonds. "Yeah," I answered, like a stubborn child glowering before a teacher. "Really."

"You will," he said.

Then he rose and walked out.

"Milja, we've got a place."

I jumped as Egan's hand fell on my shoulder. The kitten sprang from my lap and ran away under the pews.

"You okay?" he asked.

I nodded. For a moment I considered telling him what had just happened, but the impulse passed. I'd somehow garnered a sort of qualified acceptance for my story from Egan, and I didn't want to blow that by talking of archangels paying a visit the moment he wasn't looking. "Where are we going?"

"For the moment, a safe place. Just someone's house, I think. But I'm trying to arrange a way across the border. I'll let you know as soon as I hear the details."

"But what about your stuff? Your job? You're just going to walk out on them?"

He touched his pocket. "It's all covered. I've spoken to them, and I've got clearance."

I bit my lip, humbled and a little horrified by his willingness to drop everything and throw his life into chaos.

For me.

He led me out into the sunshine and we walked down an avenue of sycamores to a corner opposite a bar, where a vehicle waited for us. Not a taxi, but a beat-up minivan with a back made of slats, the kind that takes agricultural workers to the fields and then heads to the market loaded with boxes of vegetables. There were even kale leaves scattered across the corrugated metal floor. Egan made me wait in a doorway as he approached the driver, had a brief chat and then signaled me to climb into the back.

"Who's the driver?" I asked as we set off, rattling over every pothole. I wasn't really expecting an open answer.

"Just a guy who works for some people I know."

I pulled a face. "Why can't you tell me?"

"I will, later. It's just that now...well, we're not exactly in friendly territory here."

I squinted between the planks. It looked like we were heading south, toward the outskirts of town.

"What's he like?" Egan asked.

"Who?"

"This escaped angel of yours. Did he tell you his name?"

"Azazel."

Egan sucked in his lips.

"You can look him up online, if you like. The *Book of Enoch*—this really crazy apocryphal book that never made it into the proper Bible. It's all about the fall of the angels."

"What's he like?" he repeated.

The answer to that was so huge I didn't know where to start. All my life I'd kept quiet about our family secret. I hadn't even mentioned it to Ben, in college, and reticence had become an ingrained habit. I made a face as I tasted the words. "Angry," I said, slowly. "Resentful. Horny. Pretty much like you'd expect to be...if you'd been tied up for five thousand years."

Egan's eyes were hooded. "Except I'd be dead after that long."

"Yeah, well. He's not."

"Horny, you say? So, have you two...?"

The van jolted on a cracked slab of road and I grabbed at the metal frame. I wished he weren't staring at me so intensely. It wasn't like I wanted to talk to Egan about my demonic lover. It made me feel really self-conscious. But I wasn't going to lie. Not anymore.

"Yeah." Was it my fault it came out sounding defiant? "But I didn't know who he was, at the time."

"So, that story you told me. About your man you had a thing with when you were eighteen. That was him?"

"Uh-huh." Why was he looking at me like that? Why did I need to justify my love life?

"He forced you?"

"No."

"Tricked you?"

Was this some sort of interrogation? "Not exactly. I don't think so, anyway."

Egan bounced his knee in counterpoint to the bumps of the road. "He's handsome, then, I guess? No horns or bat-wings like in the pictures, I'm assuming?"

"Well he wouldn't stand out in a room full of international models. He's human looking. But yeah...compared to ordinary people, he's... noticeable."

Egan's pale eyes held mine. "I suppose you're not to be blamed for falling for him, then."

"No I'm not!" My hurt was audible.

Egan looked away briefly. It wasn't an apology, but it was a retreat. He took a deep breath. "Do you know where he's gone?"

"No."

"Do you know what he's planning to do?"

I shook my head. "No. And I don't want to."

It was a room full of international models. The women looked that way anyway, and I was sure that some of their faces were familiar from magazines. The men mostly just looked incredibly well-heeled and pleased with themselves. Both genders stood around holding cocktail glasses and laughing as they talked. Photographers prowled the crowd armed with oversized flashbulbs. Through open doors I could see an azure sea, but inside the room were full-sized palm trees and a colossal aquarium two stories high, in which sharks swam among brightly colored corals.

It looked like the champagne party of the year.

I walked through slowly, looking left and right. My own dress was bright scarlet and nearly floor-length, though it left my arms and a deep V of cleavage bare. The material was soft and clung to my thighs like silk kisses.

Azazel just didn't do underwear, I was forced to accept.

I found him sitting in a leather armchair, talking to a group of people around a small table. He hadn't bothered to get dressed up at all, but looked exactly as he had last time—which was enough to make my blood race. He beckoned me over, but there was no space for me to sit so he patted his knee. I perched obediently, and he drew me into his lap.

"Where are we?" I asked. Sitting like this, our heads were just about on a level. He slipped one hand over the small of my back, caressing me, and my spine arched like a cat's.

"I've no idea. Some party. I thought you might like to try this very very expensive drink."

It came in a fluted glass and looked like champagne with little flakes of gold in it. It tasted like sunlight and went straight to my head with the first sip.

"Nice?"

"Yes. Azazel...why me? Why do you want me?"

Just for a moment he took his attention off my body and looked me in the face. "What a strange thing to ask."

"I mean, look at you. Look at you! You could have practically any woman here that you wanted, even without threatening to massacre her family or reduce her country to ash or whatever your usual chat-up line is. Really *beautiful*, clever women. Why me?"

"You think me devoid of all sentiment? You were there. You fed me. You freed me."

I recalled only too well what Uriel had said about me feeding him. I wet my lips.

"What was your last girlfriend like?"

He watched my expression, smiling slightly. "A little shorter than you. Long red hair. Mismatched eyes—one brown, one green."

"Big boobs?"

There was a glint of teeth beneath his lip. "Are you jealous of a woman dead five thousand years, Milja?"

"Hell no. I just...wondered."

"She was an oracle, in a village on the edge of a great river. She would breathe the fumes of certain leaves and tell people what futures lay before them, and she would dance under the moon to call the wild ibex down from the steppe. I was...very fond of her."

I wondered what the hesitation hid. He looked a lot calmer in this new dream, I thought, though his right hand was stroking my back and his left caressing my thigh in a way it was hard to ignore. I thought of his wild-dancing Pythia and asked, "Did you have any children?"

The light went out of his eyes. "We had three."

That shook me, for some reason. "What happened to them?"

"The boys were killed. The girl...I don't know. I hope her mother hid her." He put his face to my hair and inhaled. "Talk about something else."

"I'm sorry."

His fingers slid into the valley of my breasts and he kissed my temple.

"I met Uriel." It was the only conversation topic that I could bring to mind. Between neckline and navel my scarlet dress was held closed by loops of golden wire snagged over filigree toggles. Azazel was fiddling with the top one. For a moment he went still.

"Be careful of him." His whisper was warm on my ear, but I couldn't see his face. "He's not your friend."

"I worked that one out."

The first loop fell open, revealing a little more of my cleavage. Azazel had me sat semi-facing the other people round the table. I wasn't remotely interested in them, but I wondered if they were watching. A glance from under my lowered lashes told me they were, sort of, though carrying on their own conversations.

"Will he come after you?"

"What?" Azazel's voice was lazy and full of husky tones that made me shiver. His lips brushed the whorls of my ear.

"Will the archangels come to lock you away again?"

"They might. Would you be sorry?"

I shuddered. There were hot and cold flashes running up and down my body, and I could feel the tight points of my breasts poking against the sheer fabric of the dress. A second loop slipped, and now my neckline was not just low but plunging.

Azazel celebrated by touching my nipple through the cloth and tracing a circle that made me whimper under my breath.

"You like being watched," he said.

"That's not true." My mouth had gone dry.

"You like me touching you in public."

I was sweating lightly. *It's shame*, I told myself, as he returned to the toggles and slipped a third. *It's shame, not excitement*. The men around the table had mostly stopped talking now, their conversation stumbling to a halt. A woman giggled.

"Please," I whispered, closing my eyes.

"I own you," he said. "You are mine. These are mine. If I want to...I will bare you in front of everyone, Milja. And you will let me."

He tugged the slash of my dress open—just a little, not enough to be obscene—and slipped a hand beneath to play with my breast. Just fingertips. My nipple felt like a blazing sun as he traced orbits.

"What're you doing, man?" someone said weakly. "That's not right."

"Azazel!" I whimpered.

"Do you want them to see, Milja?" His voice, thick with lust now, was hot against my ear. "Do you want them all to see how you belong to me? I will let them look at your breasts. Then I will pull up your dress and put my hand between your legs and make you come. You won't be able to stop me. You won't be able to stop yourself. All these people will see."

"Smile everyone!" A burst of light went off beyond my closed lids.

I looked. I couldn't help it. The little cluster of socialites at the table were blinking and staring and didn't know where to put themselves. Two photographers stood before us, and another flash went off capturing the whole group.

"Hey," said one of the paparazzi, realizing what was going on under his nose and suddenly focusing in on Azazel and me in our big armchair. "We have seen."

I didn't have the wits left to wonder at his odd phrasing.

"You're mine," the fallen angel growled. Then he let his fingers drift out from their nest, catching the cloth as they went. He revealed my left breast in full, my nipple haloed in pink like a rising sun.

Flashguns exploded.

He took the loose cloth at my shoulders and drew my open dress off, baring me from throat to waist. Back straight, eyes lowered, blushing and shuddering, I sat upon his lap and knew myself owned.

Bang went the cameras: *bang, bang, bang!*

Bang!

The rut in the road pitched me simultaneously out of sleep and forward onto my face, crashing into Egan. He had to grab me to stop me flopping onto the floor with legs and arms flailing.

"Ah!" I yelped.

"Wakey wakey," he laughed, propping me back onto the seat. "You all right?"

I looked around wildly. The van was climbing an unpaved farm track. We were right out in the countryside. I clutched at Egan's arm to stop myself sliding down the metal bench and clear out of the tailgate.

"I can't believe you slept the whole way, Milja."

"I...I've been sleeping a lot lately." My whole body throbbed with arousal. My breasts were tingling, and under the scratchy lace of my bra I could feel my nipples hard as bullets. My panties were soaked. "I don't know why."

I desperately wanted Egan to grab my breasts.

"Well we're nearly there now, I think." He wedged his leg across the width of the van, fencing me safely in as the vehicle dipped and bounced. I held on tight to his arm and guiltily breathed the scent of his clothes—and wondered what the hell was happening to me.

Our destination was more than just a house, it turned out—and less. Perched on a knoll of rock, with a sharp drop to one side and an orchard and vegetable garden on the other, it was—or had been once—a small fortress. One tower still stood, bushes growing like stubble on the crumbled battlements, but most of the building seemed in ruins. The bottom floor still looked occupied though; there were plastic chairs outside under a grape trellis, and a satellite dish bolted to the ancient stonework.

Egan paid off the driver. "Don't talk to them about who we are or where we're going," he told me as a middle-aged couple emerged from the door and approached us.

I didn't *know* where we were going, I said to myself.

The householders were Petar and Jelena. They welcomed us, smiling, and took us round to the terrace at the back for dinner. Their dog took one look at me and fled into a back room, which made my heart sink. But the cats liked me. In fact, by the time we had finished eating there were six cats lined up on the wall separating us from the valley, two under the table rubbing against my ankles, and one in my lap.

When I'd done with my bean soup, I went to use the outhouse (there was no indoor plumbing, we were warned, which made me think wistfully of my father's house) and took a walk along the ridge of the rocky little hill. I wanted time to think about Father and Vera and Uncle Josif, as if guilt might suffice to fill up the crumbling hollow in my breast. But my mind wandered. I kept recalling the way Azazel had held me on his lap in my dream, and how comforting it had felt to surrender my fear and shame to him. I wanted to feel his arms around me again.

The land around here looked very green, with swathes of scrubby oak and hornbeam, but it was a false lushness. This was proper limestone karst, the soil little more than pockets between the cracks of chaotic limestone boulders. Different to the bleak uplands I knew, but just as inhospitable to agriculture, and—I suspected—almost impassable on foot. A long way below our hillock, on the other side of the house from the steep little valley and stretching silver into the distance, was a huge plate of water ringed by hills. The shoreline looked rocky, and green islands studded the smooth sheen of the water. Lake Skadar, according to Petar—and the setting sun at my back put us on the western shore, pretty near both the sea and the southern border. Did Egan mean to get us out through Albania, I wondered?

He came crunching up the pebbly path to find me where I sat, on a very uncomfortable unmortared wall among the plum trees.

"This is," he said, "the most incredible country. This landscape..." He swept out a hand to indicate the hills and the lake and the mountains ringing us. "Just stunning. One of the most beautiful places I've ever been."

"Beautiful for a tourist means hard work for the people who have to live there," I said, but I smiled. It was nice to hear his appreciation. I stood up from the wall, dusting off the rear of my jeans.

"And their farmhouse—castle—whatever—how old is that? There's just so much history."

"Most of it bloodthirsty. Jelena told me the building was sacked by the Ottomans. I'm not sure how far back."

"Hm. Well, hopefully we won't be bringing any more trouble on their heads." Egan stuck his hands in his pockets.

"No." I couldn't help looking over my shoulder.

"Milja, don't worry. We've slipped out under the radar."

I nodded, determined to be positive. "What's *the* most beautiful place you have been to, then?" I asked him.

"Me? I'm a big fan of snow, actually. I think...Norway, under the aurora borealis. Mountains and fjords and those curtains of green light."

"Hah. You should try my home village in winter if you like snow. We can be cut off for four or five months. You can't believe that looking around you here, can you?"

"I certainly can't. How do you manage?"

"Thick socks. Lots of bean soup."

"Yeah...there is such a thing as too much bean soup."

"You don't have to tell me. Do you get much snow in Ireland, then?"

He shook his head. "Rain. That's why it's so green."

I nodded. "And d'you have a family, Egan?"

"I've got two sisters. Siobhan and Brigit." There was fondness in his voice.

I'd been wondering more about a wife or girlfriend, but I accepted what he gave me. "They're both younger than you, aren't they?" I said with a teasing grin.

"How did you know that?"

"Well. You're very protective. If they'd been older than you and given you hell, you'd be a lot less soft on girls."

Egan laughed out loud. "Oh, so we men are that simple, are we?"

I slapped at his arm gently in protest. "I didn't say that!"

"What are you saying then?" He was grinning.

"I just think that what happens to us when we're little shapes who we are. Deeply."

"Huh. How does that work with you then?"

I felt my brief effervescence vanish, and I looked away, letting out a long breath. "I grew up with a prisoner in our cellar. I first saw him when I was seven. And I knew he was there, right there under my feet, until the day I went away to college. Tied up, like this." I raised my arms briefly in a Y. "He didn't get older. Nothing ever changed. Always the same, every time I went down to see. He couldn't stand or turn over or sit up—he couldn't even scratch himself. Every moment must have been agony. And we were the ones who were told to keep him there." I blinked up at Egan,

113

my voice twisting. "How can a God who is Love do that?"

"Even to a demon?"

"To *anything*. I mean, why not just annihilate him, if he's that bad? Why the eternal torture?"

For a moment he didn't reply—not that I was expecting considered theology in response to my outburst. Then he said, "I can't even imagine what you've been through, Milja."

I sagged. "I can hardly believe it myself. Any of it. And now, being hunted like this..."

"You're been extraordinarily brave." He put a hand gently on my shoulder, his movement a little awkward. I recalled Azazel pulling me with such confidence into his embrace.

"What do you mean?"

"All this, and I've not even seen you cry."

I blinked at him, my throat swelling, but I knew there would be no release through tears. "I want to cry," I said. "I want to." I put my hand on his breastbone just to feel his warmth and solidity, and let my head droop. My skull ached. It seemed natural to rest my head against his chest.

With only the slightest hesitation, Egan's arms enfolded me. I let out a sigh: this was what I needed so desperately: comfort and absolution. Or, at any rate, the illusion of absolution. Someone to say, *It's all going to be okay* and *It's not your fault.*

He didn't say either of those things.

But he held me, his arms furled around my shoulders as if he would protect me from the whole world, and he stroked my hair. I felt the caul of tension slip from my scalp under his caress. His heart was beating fast and strong. He smelled of soap powder and warm skin. I wanted to stay there forever.

A crow in a tree nearby cawed bitterly.

What if Azazel is watching? I thought, and with that thought came cold fear. I pushed myself away suddenly; for a moment his arms resisted and then he backed off, looking confused.

"It's not safe," I apologized.

"What isn't?" His voice was rough.

"What if he gets jealous?"

"Who?" The light came on suddenly. "You mean your...?"

114

"Azazel."

Egan was holding himself with a curious tension. "Why should he be jealous?"

I blushed. I hadn't said anything to Egan about my vivid dreams. "He seemed...possessive. That's all."

"You think he's still...interested in you, then?"

"Maybe." There were unspoken volumes in that word: layers of confession and denial and defense.

Egan's mouth narrowed. "Well then, we'd better get back and not give him anything to worry about."

Jelena took us upstairs after sunset.

"Don't go that way down the hall—the floor is not safe," she said on the first landing, and I translated for Egan. She took us left instead, to a heavy door. "This is your room."

It was bare and smelled of dust and had one large bed. "Um, didn't you warn her we aren't married?" I said in English, trying not to smile and failing terribly.

"Ahhh." He looked a lot more concerned than me. "It didn't cross my mind."

"Don't worry. It's a big bed. We'll manage, I suppose."

"I suppose..."

I thanked Jelena, smiling through my blushes. She showed us two small flashlight lanterns on a table by the bed and told me, "Soon we will lock the front door and turn the generator off. If you need to piss in the night, there's a pot under the bed."

Oh, how startled Egan looked when I passed that one on...

Jelena turned to leave us. There was a small wooden crucifix by the door and I saw her pause and cross herself with an odd shrug of her shoulder before she disappeared down the hall toward the stairs.

"Well, this is a bit awkward," said Egan.

A part of me was disappointed that he looked more embarrassed than as if he were looking forward to taking advantage of the situation. Those dreams I'd been having had a lot to answer for, I admonished myself. "Well, obviously, we just keep our clothes on."

"Obviously." He folded his arms and nodded.

115

"Do you snore?"

"I...don't think so."

"That's okay then. We're good." I smiled brightly and kicked off my boots.

"Are we, um, *safe*? From your man there?" Was I imagining the tease in his voice? It made me want to rise to the challenge.

"I don't know," I said, affecting an air of innocent inquiry. "What do you think?"

Egan cleared his throat. "I think we should get as much sleep as possible. We've got a long way to go tomorrow, with luck."

I woke in the middle of the night, from a dreamless sleep for once—but with the urge to pee. I lay there for a while, hoping it'd go away and looking at the moonlight on the sheet spread over us both.

Egan didn't snore. Top marks to him.

I'd snuggled up against him in my sleep, just a bit. He lay on his back and my cheek and breasts were pressed against his shoulder and upper arm. My raised thigh was actually resting on his hand.

Oops, I thought.

Then *Aargh—I've got to get up.* There wasn't any way I was going to fall back into sleep. Nor, I was adamant, was I going to use the pot in the room with him. Nobody deserved to wake up to that.

Wriggling out from under the sheet, I groped for a flashlight and then the chamber pot, and stole in my socks out of the room. The hall was in absolute darkness, and seemed to yawn like a black mouth to either side of me.

Too public, I thought grumpily. Jelena and Petar slept downstairs, but what if they heard my footfalls and came up to investigate? I wanted to be behind a door.

There were other rooms opening off this corridor. I tried a handle, and the door creaked open. The room inside was empty—bare floorboards and no furniture at all—and moonlight shone in through the open shutters and the glassless frame. I shone the beam into every corner and then up overhead to check if there were bats or anything roosting up there, and I caught a glimpse of stars through gaps in the tiles.

Quickly, I did what I'd come here for. I was zipping up my pants when

I caught a pale movement from the corner of my eye and looked round to see a woman in the room with me.

It was a *really* good thing my bladder was empty at that moment.

I hadn't heard the door open or close again: she couldn't have followed me in from the hall. But she was pressed up against the door as if she'd just rushed in and slammed it against someone. She wore a long dress and there was some sort of scarf on her head; I could see her shoulders heaving. Then she backed off from the door and crossed herself. Her mouth moved, but I heard nothing. She looked wildly round the room—ignoring me as if I were not there at all—and then suddenly back at the door with an expression of absolute terror.

I looked too: I couldn't help it. She had me expecting it to burst in and a troop of soldiers appear. But the door didn't move. I looked back at the girl. She crossed herself again, backed up two more steps, turned—and then fled to the window. With a scramble she was balanced on the stone frame.

Then she jumped.

chapter nine

A SEA DREAM

N o!" I shouted as the night swallowed the girl.

"Milja!"

The door was open behind me. Egan stood there, shining his flashlight in my eyes as I turned to him.

"Milja—for God's sake don't move! *Don't move!*"

I looked around me, confused, and I went cold inside and out—colder than I'd ever felt. The bare floorboards under my feet were black and scorched and sagging with rot. Near to the window they'd collapsed completely, long ago, and a huge hole gaped just where the girl had run across. I was standing right next to a section where the joist had clearly given up and the floor had slumped like a suspended sheet.

But *I had looked* when I walked into the room.

I had looked but I hadn't seen.

"Milja." Egan stretched out his hand from the doorway. "Come here. Come on. Quickly now."

I walked toward him, my eyes so round they were nearly popping out of my head, and I felt the floor bend and sway under my feet with every excruciating step.

He grabbed me the moment I was within arm's reach, pulling me into the hall and crushing me against his chest. I clung to his waist, knotting my hands in the fabric of his shirt and burying my face against his breastbone as I started to shake.

"What on earth were you doing, Milja?" he asked.

I made a sort of tortured moan, which was the only thing that came to my lips.

"It's okay. It's okay now." He ran his hand over my hair. "Were you sleepwalking? The cat jumped on my face and woke me up—and then I heard you scream."

I didn't recall screaming. Maybe I had. "I wasn't asleep," I said. "I was wide awake. I really saw her."

"How did you get out on that floor? You could have gone straight through!"

"Did you?"

"Did I what?"

"The girl—did you see her? She ran and she threw herself out of the window."

"What are you talking about?"

"She didn't make any sound but I saw her. I think she was a ghost. I don't even believe in ghosts," I said desperately. "There's no such thing! When we die we go to God for judgment, don't we?"

"Milja...calm down. You were dreaming."

I looked up at him. "I wasn't. I was awake. What's happening to me, Egan?"

Angels and now ghosts—what was wrong with me?

He cupped my face in his hands. They felt warm. "All right. I believe you. Now come back to bed. Everything's fine."

He took me to bed, and I lay with his arm around my shoulders and my head against his chest for the rest of the night.

The next afternoon we went to the coast.

The morning was uneventful. Well, if you don't count the dream where I was kneeling between Azazel's spread knees, sucking away obediently as members of the U.S. Congress, looking uneasy and scandalized for the most part, tried to pretend we weren't there and get on with debating some finance act. Azazel even made a reasonable show of listening to the politics, I believe, though he also made sure to pull up my short dress

119

and expose my bare ass to the entire House. I was wearing a red velvet collar about my throat, and a red leather leash went from it to loop about Azazel's careless hand. It made me melt. Oh, I like giving head. I loved doing it to Ben, when we were engaged; I loved being able to give him the thing he craved. I loved the strength and the length and the excitement of the member in my mouth... And Azazel was in another league altogether. I ate him with true enthusiasm. I remember some man coming over to sit beside him and watch, saying with a sigh, "Can I have her when you've finished with her?" And Azazel laughing before answering, "I'll never have finished with her."

Uneventful if you don't count me having to pretend it was some nightmare that caused me to wake up in Egan's arms twitching and blazing with heat.

It's just a dream.

That was becoming my mantra.

I flung myself out of bed before instinct could catch up and make me run my hand over his oh-so-warm-and-solid body. I didn't even dare look at him as I pulled my boots on, though he woke with a grunt of surprise and stretched his back and stared around. Razor-edges of light were knifing through the slats of the shutters.

"Milja?"

"It's gone eight," I told him, determined to preserve some dignity. Not mine, perhaps—it was probably too late for that after last night's visions—but his. He didn't deserve me watching him as he struggled out of sleep. "See you downstairs."

But when I went into the kitchen Jelena was waiting with a big kettle of hot water on the propane stove, and when she saw me she poured it into two ewers decorated with roses under their cracked glaze. "There you go—you can take these up so you can both have a wash," she told me.

It wasn't really possible to refuse. She draped two tea towels over my shoulder and stuck a sliver of rock-hard soap in my pants pocket. When I asked, embarrassed, if she had some toothpaste to spare, she laughed and fetched me not just toothpaste but a toothbrush, still in its plastic packet. Words couldn't express how grateful I was, but I swore to myself that I was never again leaving a house without a toothbrush in my purse, not for as long as I lived.

The jugs of water were surprisingly heavy by the time I'd climbed back up the creaky wooden stairs. I was glad to see I'd left the bedroom door ajar.

Inside the room, Egan was talking.

"No, she doesn't," he said.

For a moment I froze, chilly doubt inveigling its way into my mind. It's not nice suspecting yourself the subject of discussion. There was no audible response to his voice, so he had to be on the phone. I was faced with the choice of standing discreetly outside and listening in, or barging in on the conversation.

The water was just too damn heavy. I turned my back and bumped the door open with my ass, backing into the room with the disingenuously cheerful warning: "Hope you've got your clothes on!"

Egan was standing by the window—fully clothed of course—with his phone to his ear. "Okay, that's fine," he said quickly. "I understand." Then he pressed the button to sign off.

"Hot water," I announced, pretending not to see the concerned look he had locked on me. I banged the ewers down on the side table with the set-in washbasin. "And soap and toothpaste. We'll have to share the brush, I'm afraid."

"Are you all right Milja? You shot out of bed first thing."

"I just...had a nightmare."

"Well, I'm not surprised, after last night."

"Yeah." I thought about the ghost and shivered. I was still absolutely sure I'd not been sleepwalking.

"D'you remember what happened?"

"Yep."

"D'you want to talk about it then?"

"No." Two could play at being stubborn, I thought.

"Okay then. Well, I've had a call," he said, rather unnecessarily.

"Uh-huh?"

"A good thing too, because this thing's nearly out of charge."

"So what's going on?"

"Good news. We've got our way out. We're taking a boat out from Budva tonight."

Budva is the biggest tourist town on the coast. I'd never been there. In

121

fact, apart from river ferries, I'd never been on a boat. I eyed him dubiously. "Where to?"

"Um." He moved closer, as if to reassure me. "Italy."

"Huh?"

"It should only take a few hours."

I shook my head, slowly at first, then with increasing vehemence. "That's no good, Egan! You've got a European Union passport, okay—that's fine for you—but that'll make me an illegal immigrant. And what the hell am I going to do in Italy?"

"Whoa." He held up his palms, placatingly. "Don't worry. Once we're on Italian soil you'll be absolutely safe from the guys following you. And don't fret about passports: I can get you any paperwork necessary. But you have to trust me."

That should have set alarm bells ringing—it would have, only a few weeks ago, when I was law-abiding and blameless. But I didn't live in that world anymore. I stared at him. It was slowly beginning to sink in that I was a fugitive, of a sort, and in an increasingly desperate state of vulnerability. The old rules were no longer enough to keep me safe.

"Will you trust me, Milja?"

Did I trust him enough to take the risks he proposed?

Did I have any choice?

"You'd better be sure you're doing the right thing," I said softly.

Egan closed his eyes, almost in pain, and nodded with lips compressed. "Yes."

"Because if this is some convoluted attempt at sex-trafficking," I said, my voice low and shaking, "I'm going to be *really* pissed with you."

I'd never seen a man look so shocked. "You...oh shite, Milja, is that what you think I'm after?"

"You hear about these things."

"For feck's sake." If he wasn't genuinely horrified and hurt, he was an actor of absolute genius. Even his pupils contracted. It was the first time he'd really sworn in my presence too. "No. Just *no*. I'm trying to help, here—you came to me..."

"I know." I touched his hand. "You're just..." *Too likable. Too honorable. Too nice. You haven't even made a move on me, and it would have been so easy. Would I have even have tried to say No?* "Like an answer to my prayers," I finished sadly.

Oh Egan, please don't let me down; I like you so much.

He swallowed. "Don't you believe prayers can be answered?"

"No. Not anymore."

"But you've seen an angel...you said."

I thought of Azazel lying in torment. "Maybe that's why."

We spent the morning helping stack a pile of cordwood, and then Petar took us west over the mountain range that stretches like a wall up the Adriatic shore, and down the long drop to the narrow coastal strip beyond, the three of us side by side in the front seat of his van. There wasn't much opportunity for Egan and me to talk, so we just watched the scenery. Which was spectacular.

How strange, that I'd never been to the part of my own country that's best known to the outside world. Never seen how the fragile green veil of foliage is swept aside there and the rock revealed in all its parched Mediterranean ruggedness, the yellowed grass contrasting with bright-flowering oleanders and dark pencil cypresses and red-tiled roofs. Never seen the clear turquoise waters of the Adriatic that lured so many tourists.

Petar dropped us off at the marina squeezed between Budva's fortified Old Town and its long, umbrella-packed beach. The great tilted wedge of St. Nikola's island loomed in the bay like a shark's fin.

"What are we looking for?" I asked as we walked past the ranks of yachts and rental boats—everything from scuba tours to pirate-themed booze-cruises.

"The *Grlica*. Have I got the pronunciation right?"

"Yep. It means the Turtle Dove."

We found it in amidst a cluster of boats advertising fishing trips. I eyed it dubiously—okay, so the Adriatic might not be the roughest sea in the world, but I'd have liked to see something a bit bigger. Worse, much of its length was open deck, presumably for fishing from, with only a glassed-in cabin at the back. A muscular, leathery-looking man stood on the stern, sorting out a selection of fishing rods.

"*Dobar dan*," said Egan.

"Hello, *Guten Tag*," he answered, knowing instantly that he was looking at a foreigner. "Do you want to go fishing?"

123

"Petar sent me. He said you could take us night-fishing."

The man on the boat straightened up, looking us over with narrowed eyes. Then he nodded. "Yes. No problem. Did Petar tell you how much it would cost?"

I didn't understand what it had to do with Petar at all, but I kept quiet and Egan answered for us. "He did."

"That's good." He nodded at the sky and grinned. "We leave at sunset then. We've got calm seas tonight. Be back here on time. With cash."

"Well, that gives us time to go shopping," Egan said as we turned our backs to the sea and headed into Budva. "I've got to buy a charger and feed my phone. And get some money out."

"Is this costing a lot?"

"Quite a bit."

"Well, have my euros," I said, passing him my cigarette packet.

He fended it off. "No you don't."

"It's not fair that you're paying for all this."

"I'm not taking money off you. Not now, not ever."

I thought of my stash of antiquities in Podgorica train station with an inner sigh. I'd been sitting on a small fortune, if only I'd been able to do anything about it. Some railway official was in for a nice surprise when the locker lease ran out.

So we shopped, and ate sea bream and black squid-ink risotto at a fish restaurant. A Russian tourist at a nearby table had one of those fashionable little dogs in her oversized handbag, and when it saw me it started howling.

"Shut up," I muttered—and it did, diving back into the safety of its designer satchel.

"You could make a fortune doing that," said Egan with a smile. "Milja the dog-whisperer."

I tried to look amused. How could I tell him that dogs now hated and feared me? It was as if I wore an aura of contamination that humans were blind to.

After dinner we returned to the sea front and boarded the *Grlica*. There were three crew members besides the one we'd already met, and no other passengers. Everyone made a show of presenting us with our fishing rods and showing us the buckets of bait. I pulled on my life jacket and hoped desperately that I wasn't the kind of person who got seasick.

Budva had seemed a tinselly, rather brash place from the little I'd seen of it, but as we nosed out of the marina I felt a pang of loss at our separation. I'd left the soil of my home country, perhaps for the last time, and now the town was nothing but a thinning line like a crust upon the waves. The island in the bay, and mountains beyond Budva, stayed in sight for a while longer, gilded by the sunset.

I thought of the little church under the cliff face, and snow, and eagles.

Our captain was right: the sea was calm as we headed west, though I quickly found that it was breezy enough to throw up cold spray if I stood at the bow, and that the stink of diesel fumes made me feel queasy if I went to the back where the engine was. So Egan and I retired to the cabin and I tried to get some rest on the padded bench.

Egan offered me the use of his leg as a pillow.

And that was the point at which *everything* started to go wrong.

I was in a dark place, underground. There was only one spot of light, off in the distance, so I headed toward it, feeling cool flagstones beneath my bare feet.

The light shone on Egan. He hung against a stone wall, cruciform, his arms spread wide by manacles and taut chains, wearing only a pair of jeans so old and faded and worn that the fabric was down to the weft in places; those jeans hung perilously low on his smooth hips, hinting at places I badly wanted to touch. His chest was bare, and scrawled with red letters I couldn't read. His head hung to the side as if in exhaustion, and his eyes were shut.

I bit my lips, unable to stop myself staring at a body just as solid and muscular as I'd imagined. Different from Azazel's long, lean frame, for sure, and with only a little sandy-blond hair on his breastbone, but just as enticing—if it hadn't been for the writing. It had been cut into his skin, I thought at first, but then I realized that it was written in scarlet lipstick. There was something uniquely cruel about that, I thought, as if it was intended to humiliate.

Egan, chained up and helpless. It was a combination that sent my heart thumping and my body into rolling waves of heat. It scared me and oh, I confess, it filled me with a sick, vertiginous longing that scared me even more.

I took a step forward. He opened his eyes.

"Milja?"

"Egan, it's okay."

His eyes opened wider. That was when I realized that I was dressed in that silly striped pajama jacket again, and nothing else.

"Oh," I said, and giggled in delicious embarrassment.

"Milja, what the...?"

"It's okay!" I held out a hand as I closed on him. "It's just a dream, Egan." Should my conscience have pricked me harder? But I'd dreamed like this, hot and vivid, several times now, and the sky hadn't fallen in.

No harm, no consequences. Lucky lucky Milja.

"A dream?" He looked wrecked, and nervous. Now that I was close enough, I could see that his nose had been broken out of true and there was a red mark across the bridge.

"Relax. Don't worry." I put my hand on his bare chest.

He jerked at my touch and shook his head slightly.

"What happened, Egan? Where'd the writing come from?"

"Writing?" He tried to follow my gaze and look down at his torso. "What does it say?"

I stared at the jagged letters, trying to make sense of them. Reading is always fantastically difficult in dreams, I find. "*We have seen,*" I announced at length. The words sounded familiar.

Egan took a deep breath, his eyes widening.

"What does that mean?" I asked.

He shook his head. "Milja, please get me out of here!"

"Don't worry," I repeated. "It's just a dream—it doesn't matter." Standing on tiptoe, I kissed him gently upon the lips.

Egan made a hungry noise in his throat. I felt his lips move against mine, sweet and soft, wanting me. Then, abruptly, he jerked away. "Milja, no!" he groaned. "We can't!"

"What's wrong?"

"Don't—just don't," he protested, not looking at me, looking anywhere but me.

"Shush." I pressed up against his body, my soft breasts to his torso,

126

and my bare thighs to his denim-clad legs. He groaned again, and gritted his teeth, but I felt the heat of him through the thin cloth, and I knew he was hard already and getting harder. "It's all right," I whispered.

"No. No it's not."

"I'm sorry," said Azazel in my ear, and I jumped half out of my skin. Without moving, I found myself six feet back from Egan's bound form again, and Azazel standing behind me with his hands on my shoulders. "Is she not pretty enough for you?" he asked.

Egan's jaw went slack and I watched the fear flood his face. I looked up over my shoulder and saw Azazel, smiling and complacent like always. This time, however, he wore wings—not bald and bat-like but feathered, as raven-dark as his hair, and huge, even folded.

My blood seemed to fill with heat.

"I think she's beautiful," Azazel said, stooping to kiss my cheek and jaw, running his hands over my waist and hips and ass. "Show him, Milja."

I raised my eyebrows, not understanding.

"Open that shirt," he murmured in my ear.

"Don't do that," Egan moaned. "Milja, you don't have to do what he says."

"Oh, but she wants to," my demon lover countered. "She wants to do what I tell her. And she wants you to see. Don't you, my Milja?"

My hand moved to the top button. "It's all right," I told Egan once more. "It's only a dream."

He made a helpless noise of protest as I slipped the first button, and tried to look away. By the second button he was looking in quick unwilling glances. By the third he had his eyes screwed tight shut. By the fourth he was watching, transfixed.

"There," said Azazel, taking the edges of the garment delicately and opening it up to show him my body from throat to thighs. He trailed his fingertips over the soft slopes of my bare breasts, down to the shallow curve of my belly, back to circle my nipples, down again to frame my sex. "Isn't she exquisite?"

I saw Egan's sharp intake of breath and the swell of his chest. The fabric of his pants was so thin that there was no disguising the other response of his body either: a heavy length strained visibly against the soft cotton.

I felt like I was melting under the heat of their attention. I was slippery and weak and soft as wax.

Azazel kissed my ear. "Kneel down."

Obediently, I slid to my knees on the stones. I kept my eyes on Egan's though, as if I could impart the last fading vestiges of strength through my gaze. Even when Azazel stepped to the side to take an approving look at the spectacle I presented, I kept my eyes on Egan's face.

"See: she does as she is told. She's mine to command. Open your legs, Milja."

I spread my thighs, slowly. There was sweat glistening in the hollow of Egan's throat.

"Play with yourself."

For the merest moment I hesitated, if only to appreciate the exquisite flush of shame that washed through me. My hand moved to the juncture of my thighs. I was fire, I was meltwater, I was the detritus swept along in the flood.

Oh God, Egan mouthed. *Please, God, no.*

"What's your problem, blondie?" Azazel sauntered toward him, great black wings flexing and pinions bristling like a canopy of living darkness. "Is she not to your taste?" He looked the bound man up and down, with exaggerated concern. "No, that's not it—not according to what you've got packed in those jeans right now. You like her well enough, don't you?" He glanced back at me, mischievously. "I think she likes you. Look how keen she is to show you."

My hand moved, snakelike. Egan licked his lips as if trying to speak, but no words came out. The hard points of my nipples stung. I watched his face and he watched me, and the air between us crackled and burnt.

But it still took me by surprise when Azazel leaned up against his shoulder and slipped one hand down the front of Egan's pants.

"No you fucker!" Egan howled, throwing himself back and forth in his bonds, but absolutely unable to escape. "No!"

"Language," Azazel reproved. "Aren't you the Nice Guy? The Hero? Though what a *gentleman* like you is doing with that sort of wood in his pants, I don't know. What would the lady say if she knew?" His thumb dexterously snapped Egan's button fly, one stud at a time, from top to bottom. "Are you shocked, Milja?"

I was stunned. Not by the sight of Egan's erection as such, but by the way it was brought into view, held firmly in Azazel's fist.

Egan banged his head back against the wall, teeth bared and the cords standing out on his neck. "Oh God oh God oh God," he groaned, his chest heaving. "Holy Mary, Mother of God..."

"Blasphemy, now?"

"Oh *fuck*."

"What do you think?" Azazel asked me. "Nice?"

I nodded, dizzy. He was handling the member in question with ruthless artistry, working it harder and harder.

"Come closer, Milja. On your knees."

I left off touching myself and crawled forward. I could see every humiliating detail: the ruddy swollen flesh, the sweat-soaked ringlets of Egan's pubic hair, even a scar just on the crease of thigh and pubis.

"Look at her," Azazel whispered in his ear. "Look at her."

Egan looked. His face was a mask of torment. There were beads of sweat running down his breastbone. But his pupils were dilated with arousal.

"Big, isn't it, Milja? Bigger than you thought, I bet."

"Yes," I whispered.

"Do you like it?"

"Yes." *Very much. It's beautiful.*

"Kiss it then, Milja."

I put my hands on Egan's thighs; they felt like rock. I looked up at the crucified man and I wanted to comfort his anguish. I wanted to take him in my embrace.

"No!" Egan protested weakly. "Milja—don't!" His legs were trembling with strain.

"Oh come on; it's a little late for modesty." Azazel was all darkness and glittering eyes and bared teeth. His wings stretched out, shadowing us. "Take it in your mouth, Milja. There...that's right. There's a good girl." He moved his hand off Egan and onto the back of my head. "Right to the back of your mouth. Oh, that's very good. Take: eat: this is my body..."

Egan made an indescribable noise.

My mouth was suddenly full of salt.

I woke up as Egan scrambled to his feet and threw himself across the boat's cabin onto the opposite bench. My head, which had been pillowed on his thigh, smacked into the damp plastic padding of the seat.

Disoriented, at first I didn't understand what I was seeing: his flushed face, his tousled hair, the spasmodic clenching of the hands he had no idea what to do with. He solved that last one by pointing accusingly at me. Words tumbled from his lips, thick with confusion. "What? *What?*"

"What's happened? I was dreaming..."

"*You said he didn't have wings!*"

The accusation hit me like a blow, and I cringed as I understood. "Egan?" I squeaked.

"Shite! Shite!" He lurched to his feet again and blundered to the cabin door. It let in a cold breath of sea night before it slammed, leaving me alone.

I didn't follow. I put my hands over my nose and mouth, like I was taking cover from the world. My face was burning and my stomach felt like it was trying to climb up the inside of my throat. And all the time my sex beat with a thick syrupy pulse, the glow of my erotic transport.

What had he seen? Should I be mortified? Should I be angry at the grotesque invasion of my privacy? I ran the events of the dream through my head, but just felt sick with confusion. *What had he seen?*

In the end, I had to go out and find him. Out on deck it was full night, the stars out overhead, the noise of the boat engine not quite masking the beat and hiss of the sea around us. The crew were lounging around the small wheelhouse, smoking and chatting.

"Where's Egan?" I asked.

Someone pointed forward. "I think he went to be sick." There were muffled snorts of amusement.

I didn't find it so funny. I made my way unsteadily up the deck—the sea didn't look rough at all, but still the boat moved in irregular rhythm that kept catching my feet out. Away from the shelter of the cabin, the night was cool, and only a few scattered lights on the horizon told us that we were not alone on the face of an illimitable dark ocean.

Egan was huddled right up in the bow, holding on to the inadequate rail. I wasn't surprised they'd thought he was seasick; he had his head resting on his folded arms.

"Egan?"

He lifted his head, just to show that he'd heard me, but didn't look round.

"Egan, what did you see?"

"What do you think I saw?"

I was glad of the dark; my face was blazing. "I was asleep."

"Me too." His rage had gone cold, and curdled to bitterness.

I swallowed, and bit the bullet. "You have a little scar, just at the top of your leg." *It's sort of sweet, sort of sexy.*

Egan stood up, turning. "You have a mole, just there," he said, putting one finger right on my breastbone. "In the middle."

"Yes," I said, weakly. It felt like he was boring a hole into my heart. "Oh crap."

"Yeah."

"It was a dream," I said. "Just a sex dream, I thought. I didn't know...I didn't think you'd..."

"A bit of harmless fun, was it?"

"It was a *dream*—you can't blame people for what they dream about! It's not under their control!"

"And yet you seemed to know exactly what was going on. You told me not to worry."

"I didn't know it would upset you—not the real you! For God's sake, that sort of thing doesn't happen!"

"Says the woman who consorts with demons."

"I..." I wanted to say *I'm sorry*, but I was worn out being sorry for my sins. "It wasn't me. It was him: Azazel. He puts me in these dirty dreams; he likes to mess with my head."

"Oh—this happens a lot, does it?"

I ran my hands through my hair; it felt salty and stiff with sea spray already. "Since I let him go free," I admitted. "Pretty much every time I go to sleep. It's like a game he plays."

Egan set his jaw, shaking his head. "Demonic obsession."

"What?"

"Tell me, do you enjoy it?"

"I...thought it was harmless."

"Sure, you certainly seemed to be getting into the spirit of things." His voice was ragged and cold. "Is that your...*relationship* with him, then? He pulls the strings, and you play the whore? And I'm just something to be used as part of your fantasy?"

Cold fire lit in my breast. "You weren't exactly an icon of chastity yourself, as I recall," said I with chilly precision.

He took a step back, and didn't answer. I reminded myself that he had only ever seen me as a helpless waif-girl, a victim of powers beyond my control. He didn't know my fantasies or my longings or my needs: only my fears. It must have come as a horrible shock to him.

After all, the deepest darkness of our imaginations is a private place, a secret between ourselves and God. That's what we're used to. If other people could see what we really thought...would any one of us be blameless?

What would your fantasies look like, Egan?

"Look," I said, painfully, "please understand. I never asked for this. I fell in... I'm out of my depth, Egan. This is something I don't understand. I don't know what's going on. In my head or out here or anywhere."

His voice was hoarse—still cold, but soft now. "Tell me how you feel about him. About this Azazel."

"What does it matter?"

"I need to know."

"I don't know how I feel." I stopped abruptly and shook my head. I *hated* it when people said that. I knew exactly what my feelings were for Azazel—however conflicted and contradictory they might be, there was nothing vague about them. It just took courage to face up to them.

"I..." I licked my lips. "What's the word in English when you hatch out a duck egg and the first thing the baby duck sees is a pair of green rubber boots? So it thinks the green boots are its mother and it follows them round all the time, and then when the duck grows up it tries to mate with green rubber boots and not other ducks?"

"Imprinting."

"Right. Well, that's what it is, I think. I grew up with him, Egan. He was always there, this big handsome naked man tied up in a cave. He was the center of our world. We couldn't leave, we couldn't let anyone else take the responsibility; he was the most important, incredible thing in my life. I fell in love with him."

It was the first time I'd voiced those words, even to myself. Confessing to Egan hurt like fire. I couldn't look him in the face.

"And now, when I see him, he is…" I spread my hands in despair. "I want him. He turns me on. Oh, that sounds so weak. He is just the most… My body reacts, it just goes straight past my head, and it has nothing to do with what he is. I just want him. Every time. I can't help it."

"I see." Did he sound angry? Or disgusted? Or contemptuous? I couldn't tell. "Do you love him, aside from the perverted sex?"

Why does he have to ask? I could feel the thump of my pulse in my wrists and belly. The weight of his gaze made me tremble. Egan was my champion and my refuge and this—this, far more than the dream—felt like I was betraying him. But I couldn't lie. He'd asked for honesty, and I had nothing else to give him.

"I'm *in* love. Is that the same thing?" My voice was a croak. "He makes me excited and stupid and crazy with fear. But I don't know him. How can you love someone, real love, unless you know them? Unless they are human?"

He bowed his head. "Do you ever see him outside the dreams? In the flesh, I mean."

"Not for a while."

"But you have?"

"Oh yes. He's real, if that's what you're getting at. He's solid."

"But the dreams are how he reaches you now."

"Yes. I think…I think I've had them for years. Since I was sent to America, for sure. But I never could remember them when I woke. Only since I came back here, since cutting him free…I remember the new dreams."

Egan snorted. "So you're saying he groomed you."

I felt like he'd punched me in the face. He must have seen that in my expression.

"What—did you expect me to say '*How romantic,*' eh?" His lip curled. "After our little ménage? That…*thing*, that piece of shite, is not some romantic hero. You do get that, don't you?"

"I…" Words choked me. Light danced on Egan's face, bleaching one half and turning the other to darkness. Men were shouting.

"He's just using you, Milja."

Men were shouting. Crewmen were running up the deck toward us. The light dazzled my eyes when I looked out to sea. "Egan? What's—?"

There was another boat, and it had a light trained on us. It was coming in fast, much faster than our fishing vessel.

"Get down below!" the sailor shouted, and we scrambled for the cabin.

"Is it the Italian border patrol?"

Egan shook his head. "I don't know—I thought we were still in international waters."

The new boat was sweeping in alongside, and there was a lot of shouting going on. The light trained on us was blinding, but I could hear voices, and the words were all in Montenegrin.

"They don't sound Italian."

Egan made a noise that was nearly a growl, pushing me behind him. "Not good."

Our captain cut the engine to a purr. The *thud-thud-thud* of waves beneath the hull dropped away. We stood in the center of the little cabin, facing the door. Shadows swooped across the frosted glass. I peeked past Egan's shoulder and listened to the orders being shouted.

"They're telling them to get down on the deck."

"Just stay calm, Milja. No one's going to hurt you."

The door opened.

"Out! Outside!" Men in dark clothes crowded the hatchway.

Egan grabbed my hand.

They gestured us out, and forward again up the side of the cabin to the open fishing deck. Egan surprised me by speaking clearly and calmly in Italian, which I couldn't follow. Unfortunately our new shipmates seemed to take no notice of his words either. I looked around wildly, trying to get my bearings now that the searchlight was averted. The crew of the *Grlica* were sitting on the wet deck in a huddle, their hands tucked beneath them, their faces wide-eyed and watchful. Other men—new men, mostly clad in heavy dark clothes with woolen caps pulled down over their ears—milled about keeping an eye on them.

Egan's grip on my hand was so tight it hurt, and I have never been

134

more grateful for pain. He kept on talking, addressing them in Italian and then in English. "Who is in charge here? Who do I speak to? Do you want papers? Is that what you are after?"

Then another man stepped to the front. I'd never seen him before, but he had a big beard and long hair tied back at the nape of his neck, and he wore an Orthodox clerical cassock.

"Ach," said Egan in dismay.

"Separate them," said the priest, nodding a heavy jaw toward us. The words might have been unfamiliar but Egan worked out what their import was instantly.

"Don't you touch her," he said.

Men closed in.

He let go of my hand in order to throw a fist. The first guy staggered and slipped over on the wet deck. Egan turned to face the next—but there were more opponents than he could possibly cope with and they didn't take it in polite turns. Someone grabbed him from behind and locked an arm around his neck, hauling him off balance and giving others a gap. They mobbed him, and in a few moments they had him down on his knees under a rain of punches and kicks. I was pushed off to one side and grabbed from behind by some burly man, and I screamed with rage and terror.

"That'll do!" A man—not the priest; a shaven-headed man with a face like a flat slab—brought the scrum to a finish. The others backed off a bit, revealing Egan on one knee, trying to rise but swaying wildly. As he lifted his head I saw there was blood all over his face.

"Egan!"

"Don't move," said Slab-face, pulling a handgun from his jacket and pointing it at Egan's head.

All the breath went out of my lungs.

"Search him," the priest ordered. Someone seized Egan's jacket and began to go through the pockets, finding his phone straightaway. Egan made a grab and got smacked in the head for his efforts, so hard that only the clutching hands of his captors kept him from collapsing.

I found breath. "Don't hurt him! Don't hurt him!"

"Now, now." The priest drew himself up tall, accepting the phone and Egan's wallet as they were passed over. "Let's have some calm here. We won't hurt him as long as you cooperate, girl."

"Let him go! He was just trying to help me!"

"Shut the fuck up," said the gunman to me. "He's not the one we have to bring back in one piece." He grinned and took a step closer to Egan, the weapon muzzle pointed directly at his face, and switched to English. "Unless you've got a hotline to the Egrigoroi too, friend?"

I had no choice, did I? I did the only thing I could think of. "Azazel!" I screamed: "Help me!"

Azazel heard.

He came.

chapter ten

AN EVIL CRADLING

O ur boat, wallowing in the water, shook from stem to stern under the impact of Azazel's arrival. One moment he wasn't there, and the next he was, crouched on top of the cabin roof, looking down on us.

All the electric lights went out.

He was not in a kindly mood. Behind him the starry sky wrinkled into rip-lines like the pinions of mighty wings, but the light that bled in upon us from that other place beyond was a deep red, and it lit the whole scene with a bloody crimson hue. His eyes caught that light and glowed like rubies, and a heat-haze shudder in the air made his form shimmer.

"Let her go," he said, with a voice of rocks rending a keel.

The slab-faced guy turned and fired at him. At that slight distance, he could hardly miss, especially with an automatic pistol. The roar of the gun was horrific.

I never saw Azazel move. He just suddenly had his hand out in front of him and he was opening it to look disparagingly at the contents. "I gave you the secrets of metal," he said. "You think you can use them against me?" He turned his palm and a dozen bullets dropped to the deck.

Around us, the surface of the sea began to hiss and fume, and bubbles broke the surface as the salt water began to boil.

Then he jumped down from the cabin roof—lightly, it seemed, but the boat groaned and shuddered under his feet. Tall and lean-hipped, and poised like a cage fighter on the balls of his feet, he turned toward me. Every step vibrated with pent-up violence. The air shook around him. The priest had found his voice and started to pray loudly, but Azazel took no notice.

Then the slab-faced guy stepped between me and him. Maybe he thought fists would work where bullets didn't. He never got the chance to try. Azazel's hand was on his throat in less than the blink of an eye.

There was a *crunch*. I will remember that noise in my nightmares until my dying day. It was the sound of a life being snuffed out.

The guy slid to the deck, feet drumming spasmodically, and there was red pumping out, there was red on...on...

On Azazel's hand.

Men were shouting in terror. I don't know how I had time to look in Egan's direction, but I saw his expression—mouth open, eyes full of horror—before I focused abruptly on the hand Azazel held out to me.

His hand was gloved in blood. It looked almost black in that crimson light.

"She is mine," he told them all.

The men holding me fell away. I stepped forward into his reach. Then I turned and stretched my own arms to Egan. "Egan, quickly! Come here!"

"Milja!"

Azazel's arm wrapped around my shoulders.

"Egan!" I screamed. "Save him too!"

The boat and the sea and the night *went away.*

My cry left me airless, but when I tried to inhale there was nothing to breathe—nothing at all in a between-space that seemed to go on and on— no air, no light, nothing beneath my feet. Panic swept me and I arched in Azazel's arms.

Then his mouth was against mine, and he was breathing into me. He tasted of smoke and pepper and ire, but he filled my lungs and held me safe. And when, all of a sudden, the world came back, and sounds burst on my ear and warm air smote my cheek and light made me shut my eyes, he still held me. His lips carried on moving against mine, but now with burning kisses. And my feet still swung clear of anything solid, because he was holding me up, taking my weight easily.

It was the first time he'd ever made me feel safe.

I broke the kiss, reluctantly, just to gasp.

"You left that late," he growled, kissing me again. "What if I hadn't been fast enough?"

I nodded frantically, pressing my lips to his and then rasping my cheek with his dark stubble. Relief had followed panic like the suck of a withdrawing wave, and it was nearly as hard to deal with as the fear.

"How did you get into that sort of trouble? What did those men want?"

That snapped me back to reality. I opened my eyes. "Don't you know?"

Azazel set me on my feet, holding me carefully until I was sure of my balance, and shook his head, frowning. We were on a rooftop, in a city. A street of tall, familiar-looking houses scrolled away behind me in the blue dusk.

"They want *you*, I think," I said numbly, looking around and not paying much attention to my own words. "Where is this?"

"You are home."

"Boston?" My voice shot up an octave. "Where's Egan?"

He shrugged. Without the trappings of his anger he looked human again.

"Is he still on the boat? Azazel! You have to go back and get him too!"

"Why?"

"Oh please—they have him held prisoner! They might kill him or anything!"

He lifted one dark eyebrow, still waiting for an explanation.

"For God's sake!" The exclamation was singularly inappropriate, but I pushed on. "He was trying to help me—he saved me over and over from those men. He was trying to get me out of the country!"

Azazel looked amused, and the tilt of his head was disconcertingly bestial as he started to circle me. "I'm not surprised. The reek of his lust is all over you."

That took me aback. My voice collapsed to a whisper. "That's not true. He's a good friend."

"So I recall." Sarcasm was certainly not beyond an angel's repertoire. "Such good men are hard to find, I understand. And he was certainly hard when you found him."

Oh, not that. "It was just a dream," I said through gritted teeth, "and that was your show anyway."

He laughed. "No. Not mine. How you furnish your dreams is entirely down to you. What was that thing with the ugly striped shirt?"

"But..." *What does he mean?*

"I enjoyed playing along," he admitted. "And you seemed to find it exciting."

I did, oh I did. Why was he distracting me when Egan was in terrible danger?

"That's all I wanted," Azazel said with a mockingly humble gesture. "Your pleasure is my pleasure."

I grabbed at the chance. "Then save Egan now. That's my pleasure. Please."

"You care for him?"

Goddamn. I was growing frantic. He seemed absolutely determined to lead the conversation astray. "Yes!"

All the amusement left Azazel's eyes, like a light going out, and he quit pacing. "Why? He is not me."

Under the glint of that whetted-steel regard I felt a chill. "I care for lots of people," I said. "Animals too. And places."

He loomed in over me. "But you love only me."

Love? You're talking about love, now? There was something oddly naive in his simplistic demand. Something desperately insecure. And that was not reassuring.

"Azazel, you can't tell people who to love. It has to be given freely."

"Hm." He nodded, his mouth twisted, as if my words carried an import that meant more to him than I knew, something dark and horrible. He reached out to touch my face, soft as the brush of black feathers. "But I love *you*."

Never had the declaration sounded more ominous.

"You mean that?"

"Milja, I never lie to you."

My voice shook. "If you really loved me, you'd save my friend."

I could not have picked a worse thing to say. It was like pressing the red button marked *detonate*. It was like pulling a trigger I had not known was there. The air crackled and darkness rose behind him like wings, as he grabbed my jaw and crushed in so close that for one horrible moment I thought he was going to bite my face.

"*Do not do that!*" he roared. "Do not *ever* do that! You are not God!"

Then he thrust me away, so hard that I staggered and went down, catching myself on one knee. When I dared look, Azazel was pacing back and forth, eyes wide, sweat beading his forehead. He wiped at his face as if trying to pull off something that clung to him, and stared at me. He looked horribly angry—and sick with fear.

"Don't," he began again, much quieter; "just don't..." He lost his thread. "I apologize. I am too rough."

"Yeah," I rasped. "That's an understatement."

"I don't want to hurt you, Milja. I don't want to see you hurt, ever. You are the one I love."

"Right."

"In the darkness, you were light. I reached out through the hurt... everything was cold and pain, and you were warmth and relief. Like a candle flame in the night. You *heard* me. You heard my voice and you held me and you soothed me and you loved me, and that was everything. The whole world. You were my strength and my hope and my God. My life. My love."

I shook my head, heavy with rejection. "I don't think you love me," I said. My voice was a croak, cold with rage. "I think you get off on me. I think you use me." I was remembering what Egan and Uriel had said. "You took advantage of a lonely girl because that was all you had to work with. You turn me on because that's what you feed off. You're just fine with me getting dirty with Egan, but only so long as I don't get so fond of him that I forget you. You're like some kind of vampire, only for desire and love, not blood. You're *feeding* off me, because it's what keeps you alive."

He took a step closer. "Isn't that what all lovers are?" he asked, and some part of me was startled to hear his voice tremble. "We love those who love us. It makes us happy when they are happy. We flourish under their affection."

"You think I feel any affection for you right now?" I didn't care how dangerous it was to say those words; they gave me too much satisfaction. "You're this horrible monster, Azazel. You kill people without a second thought." I flicked a glance at his hand, but there was no telltale blood on it anymore.

"I saved you," he said, looking confused. I ignored him.

"But you know what's worse? Underneath the monster, what you *really* are is just a selfish prick."

I braced myself for the explosion.

It didn't come. Azazel stood there and looked at me and just went still—far stiller than any human could. He didn't even breathe. Somehow, without shifting a millimeter, he made me feel like I was seeing him withdraw, pulling away and away and away, like a man falling from a great height.

Then there was a *crump* of displaced air and he was gone. Just like that. No threats, no spite, no cold passive-aggressive snipe at me.

Just gone.

A rumble of thunder rolled from west to east overhead, and big dark drops of rain began to fall. I saw the blackish blotches appear on the asphalt. A coppery tang rose from the wet dust. Only when the first droplet struck my hand did I realize the rain was warm—and red.

I was on the roof of my own apartment building in Boston.

It was raining blood.

And I had no way, no way at all, of finding or helping or reaching out to the man who had risked his life to save me, the man who I'd abandoned to die, an ocean and more away.

For a week, I barely left my apartment. For much of that week I lay curled up in bed with Senka the cat, staring blankly at the wall. I slept in fits and starts, woke up over and over in the middle of the night and paced about the silent rooms, then dozed again as daylight first grayed the sky. My head, even when it wasn't throbbing, felt like it was filled with wadded cloth, like an overfull laundry basket. My stomach churned and ached as I alternated between stuffing it with any food I could find and not eating at all. I lay on the sofa watching the shopping channels on TV, their mindless steady pap the only input I could bear.

142

On the few occasions I flicked by mistake to a news channel, the airwaves seemed full of disaster and omens. Vicious rebels surfaced in South America and the Middle East and were met with ruthless reprisals. Another hurricane swept through the Caribbean and grounded on Florida, swamping the low land and driving people from their ruined homes. An earthquake in one of the ex-USSR 'stan countries—Tajikistan, Uzbekistan, I don't recall which—flattened an ancient city and destroyed a World Heritage Site. Bird flu raised its head again in China. Evangelicals thumped their Bibles and predicted the Day of Judgment any time now and blamed gay marriages in California.

Was this Azazel's work—or was the world always prone to this chaos, and suddenly I was noticing?

Suzana hovered and fussed, prickling with frustration. I had no explanations for her—not for how I'd got back, or what had happened, or what was wrong, or what I thought I was doing right now. Certainly no explanation for that crazy-ass rainstorm on Boston that was the talk of the Christian Internet. I told her my father had passed away, but refused to confide in her or to make contact with my employer, or more likely ex-employer. And she desperately wanted to leave: she had tickets to Burning Man in Nevada with her boyfriend, it was a once-in-a-lifetime trip, and I'd arrived back just in time to screw everything up.

"Go," I told her wearily. We were pretty good friends as roomies go, but not so close I had any right to mess up her life. "I'll be fine."

For days the most positive thing I managed was to slouch to the store at the corner to buy milk and breakfast cereal, and I only did that when I found myself eating cold fava beans out of a tin because I had nothing else in my cupboard.

I didn't dream. Not the pellucid, burning dreams about Azazel anyway—just ordinary muddled visions of guilt and terror, in which I saw again the red-lit deck of the boat and Egan's horrified face. And heard him cry my name in despair.

I'd abandoned him.

And now Azazel had abandoned me.

I was full of such anger at first—bitterly angry at Azazel's stubbornness, and at his utter lack of compassion. Blame and guilt roiled inside me, gnawing at my guts. It was quite possible that I wouldn't be alive if it weren't for Egan, yet Azazel showed no gratitude to the man who'd looked after his pet mortal. He claimed to love me, but wouldn't do the one thing I desperately needed him to do.

I'd begged him, and he'd refused.

Well, not exactly begged him. More...

As the hours and the days wore on, a razor-edge of doubt began to creep beneath my righteousness, cutting it loose as a scalpel severs meat from bone. *You are not God!* he'd told me, his rage erupting out of nowhere. Almost like panic.

If you really loved me, I'd said... What was wrong with that?

What was wrong with trying to make him do the right thing?

Was he, I wondered, readying some sort of revenge now? It hardly seemed to matter to me. I was in such black misery I couldn't imagine anything I feared more. It was entirely my fault that Egan was in danger. I was as helpless now as I had been in the face of my father's passing, but this time the accusations came from within, not from any distraught relatives. This time I couldn't say *You've got it wrong, it wasn't me!*

It was me.

My self-righteousness fell away and I was left with the bare bones of my guilt. I was still angry with Azazel, but after I came across a book on Suzana's shelf at three in the morning, I couldn't even condemn him anymore. I started reading listlessly just because I couldn't sleep; it was the autobiography of a man who'd been abducted in Beirut and held prisoner in close confinement and near darkness for four years. Claustrophobia reeked from every page. The experience had left him with memories and mental scar tissue that it made me ache to imagine.

I closed the book hours later, my eyes dry and aching and my heart heavy. Dawn lay upon the city like a gray blanket. I weighed the prison imagery of the memoir like coins of a denomination I'd never used before and did not know how to spend.

Azazel had suffered his own captivity for millennia. *Could anyone come out of that undamaged?* I asked myself. Wasn't I simply asking the impossible when I demanded he act like any ordinary decent soul?

Later that day I had the dream—my one proper dream, and it wasn't even dirty, fortunately, because I found myself in no place to lose my clothes. I was standing in a snowdrift on a mountaintop—and I do mean mountain*top*, because below and all around me stretched a vast range of peaks, all bare black rock and sheer slopes of snow. I think it must have been just before dawn; there was enough light to see by but it was blue as an old bruise, and the wind was up and blowing snow, like smoke, from the top of the drifts.

I swear I could see the curve of the horizon.

Somehow, though it gave me no discomfort in my dream, I knew that we were so high up that there was almost no air to breathe. And it should have been unbearably cold, of course, but I felt this as nothing more than an abstract fact.

Azazel was sitting on an exposed crag of rock, his hands loose on his thighs, his head a little bowed. He must have been there some while, because the snow had drifted up against his back and rime had frozen in the hair that hung, fluttering against his bare cheek, in thick webs of frost. He was motionless but for the wind-blown edges of hair and clothes, yet his eyes were open—though it was hard to tell whether it was the incredible landscape they were fixed upon, or the pitiful patch of bright orange that lay in the drift before him. It took a long hard look before I was able to resolve that into a pair of legs clad in padded climbing gear, and a gloved and equally padded arm crooked about an oxygen cylinder. The top part of the body was buried in snow, rendering it faceless.

Azazel's bare feet, insensible to the cutting cold, seemed to mock the frozen corpse.

"What did he do to annoy you?" I asked grimly. The buffeting hiss of the wind snatched my words away and for a moment I thought he hadn't heard.

Then he turned his head to look at me, his mouth compressing to a hard line. For a moment I read hurt in his silvery gaze, before he stood without a word and walked away from me, over the top of the snow, leaving no prints.

"What did you mean, *You're not God*?" I shouted, but he gave no sign that he had heard.

I didn't follow. It wasn't my intention to stalk him, even in my dreams. I watched as he descended over a shoulder of the mountain slope and vanished. Then I looked at the body again and felt a pang of guilt. There

145

was an embroidered patch on the sleeve that showed a picture of a mountaintop, and in faded threads the letters *Everest* and *1986*.

It hadn't been entirely fair to blame Azazel for that, then.

Leave him alone, I told myself. *Just let him be.*

The next morning I rose early, drank a pint of coffee, showered (for the first time in what I shudderingly admitted was far too long), tied my hair up in a plait, packed a small rucksack with things I thought I might need, put out extra food for Senka and slipped from the apartment.

Stopping by the neighbor's opposite, I asked her to look after Senka if I was delayed coming back.

I'd made up my mind.

I went to the Serbian Orthodox church of St. Sava, which was where Vera used to take me, and I kissed the icon of the Archangel Uriel.

There was one way to reach Egan. If Azazel was too obdurate to help, there was one other who might.

"Uriel," I said softly, crossing my breast. The painted angel, depicted with the traditional flame in his hand, looked at me with sad eyes. "Will you talk to me?"

"And what exactly do you want to talk about?"

chapter eleven

THE BURNING MAN

I turned to see Uriel standing behind me. Though nothing like his icon, he was very much as I remembered: grizzled silver and painfully handsome, dressed in an expensive-looking gray suit but with a tie hanging loose down the front of his open-necked shirt, as if I'd caught him heading home from a hard day at the office.

He's not your friend, I'd been warned. Well yeah, I knew that. Uriel thought I was on Azazel's side in this age-old war. The side of the damned.

"I need help," I said in a ghost of a voice. He was an angel of the Lord God Almighty, and though somehow that didn't make him less scary, it gave me some faith that he would follow the rules. I just needed a fair hearing.

Maybe I'd have been better starting off by thanking him for turning up. His nose wrinkled with distaste. "Shouldn't you be asking your boyfriend, then?"

Ex-boyfriend, I thought, but didn't say it out loud. "He won't."

One perfectly arched eyebrow rose.

"He—we—did something bad. I need to fix it."

"You certainly do."

"I thought that since you are on the opposite side from...him...you might help set it right."

"Really? That's an interesting proposition. Did he send you to talk to me?"

"No. He doesn't know I'm here."

"Oh, I wouldn't bet on that. If you want to talk we'd better go somewhere else."

I couldn't help feeling a stab of suspicion. "Why?"

"We can be overheard here."

I looked around. There were some older women scattered about the nave praying, but it was far too early for crowds. I didn't want to go elsewhere; I felt safer here, for no reason I could justify on a logical level. "No one's close enough."

"This is holy ground. It's...public domain. Everything we do here can be heard. Do you want your boyfriend listening in?"

I chewed my lip.

"Come on, let's find somewhere private." He touched my arm, turning me toward the great church doors.

"Where?"

"Where would you like? Anywhere in the world. Your choice."

Nowhere outside the States, I thought. I wanted to be able to get back home under my own steam this time.

"Come on," said Uriel, slightly impatient, as we reached the door. "Pick somewhere you'd like to go."

My skull was stuffed with grubby laundry still, despite the coffee. I spoke the first idea that emerged from the jumble: "Burning Man. I've never been to Burning Man." *Suzana will be there, if he ditches me.*

"Fine."

I had sudden misgivings. "No, let's just go to the—" I began, but ended in a squeak as Uriel put one hand between my shoulder blades and *shoved* me out of the church, out of the sleepy weekend morning, out of Massachusetts—and into another place.

Desert air filled my throat, furry with dust and kerosene and incense. It was night—a late night—burning with neon, and I was somewhere high up and the floor was wobbling under my feet. No not a floor—a plank. I staggered against a scaffolding pole and caught at the metal, panicked. Far below me the ground winked with illumination, candles and lamps and glow-sticks moving like a slow sea, fireflies spinning in darkness.

Ahead of me a tower burned. Pearly water fell in an endless cascade of light. Moons bobbed and waltzed with ponderous grace. I was fifty feet above ground level in the narrow spire of a building of scaffolding poles and stretched white cloth.

I let out a long shriek and finished it with some choice swearwords, my hands springing sweat as they clutched at the struts. I could feel the poles vibrating, though I couldn't tell if it was the breeze that was to blame or the pounding of the drums that rose up from below. For a moment I felt like Fay Wray, tied up high over the heads of the crazed villagers and presented in sacrifice to Kong. I looked round wildly for Uriel.

He squatted on a level above me, on his haunches, the soles of his Italian shoes balanced on a horizontal pole, and only the tips of four fingers stretched to an overhead strut conceding any need for support. I'd meant to ask him what the heck it was his sort had about vertiginous heights, but the sight of him hunkered there like some Armani-suited bird of prey on its branch rendered the question pointless. He looked at the night landscape around with idle curiosity, and then his attention snapped back to rest on me.

"Well?" he asked.

"Well what?" I repeated in a near-hysterical wail, my brain still preoccupied with the question of whether I was going to fall to my death any second now.

"What did you want to propose?"

I shut my eyes. It didn't help: the structure beneath me just felt more flimsy and ephemeral, and I opened them hurriedly. "Can we go down?"

"Down there?"

"Yes!"

"Among *them*?"

"What's wrong with them? They look just fine!"

"Apart from the drunkenness and the fornication and the pride and the drug-taking and the Godless inanity?"

"You have a problem with people having fun?" I said faintly. It wasn't so bad, I told myself, as long as I didn't look down past my feet.

"I have a problem with disobedience to the Divine Will."

I decided to focus on Uriel's face. "And yet no problem," I snipped, "with drowning every living thing on the planet, or killing all the first-born children of Egypt?"

He raised an eyebrow. "My, you've been spending too much time with Azazel. He's been messing with your head."

"You think?"

"You believe that this is what the human race was made for, do you?—to live in a chaos of self-indulgence and an endless hunt for the next thrill, the next bit of fun, the next high, the next fillip to an empty, insatiable ego?"

"So what were we made for, then, in your opinion?" I couldn't keep the bite out of my voice.

"To love and obey God. And that's not my opinion, that's fact. I was there when it happened."

Angelic arrogance: it's like the squeal of nails down a chalkboard. "Funny how it keeps going wrong, then," I growled. "First the Watchers. The War in Heaven. Then us lot. You'd almost think there was a design flaw somewhere."

Uriel narrowed his eyes. "You came to ask my help."

The blustery wind went out of my sails. "Yes."

"I have to say you're not doing such a great job of it so far."

I lowered my gaze. My knuckles were white around the scaffolding pole. "Point taken," I admitted.

"So can we get back to the matter at hand? What did you want to talk about?"

"Egan—the man who was with me in Podgorica. At the church."

"What about him?"

"You know who I mean?—did you see him?"

"I didn't pay much attention, but for the sake of argument let's assume so."

Not what I wanted to hear. I clenched my jaw.

"When...when I was spirited away," I said through gritted teeth, still cautious about speaking Azazel's name now that I knew he could hear me; "when I was taken back to Boston, Egan was left behind. He shouldn't have been."

"So?"

"We left him, on his own. They were trying to grab me, but they took him—priests from the Orthodox church, I think—and I've no idea what they were going to do to him. Please…could you find out if he's still alive?"

"I might. Why are you asking me and not your surly sweetheart?"

"He's being…difficult."

Uriel grinned. "Really? You do surprise me."

"And you're an angel."

"That doesn't make it my function to play Facebook for you."

"But Egan's a good man—he helped me, and tried to save me, and he's decent and honorable and he doesn't deserve what we did. Please! He's one of the good ones!"

"And good men suffer all the time. In case you hadn't noticed."

"So you won't help him?"

"It's not my job."

I ground my teeth. "Aren't you one of the four archangels who stood up and opposed the fallen Watchers? I've read the *Book of Enoch*. You complained about them to God, and He sent you guys to take them down and put them all in prison."

Uriel's pale blue eyes seemed to catch the neon. They glowed as he looked down at me. "Raphael was the one who bound your master."

I let his description slide. "But your job is to oppose him."

"Yes. As the Almighty decrees."

"Well he did this to Egan. He rescued me, and he left Egan behind. That's wrong. You should put it right."

Uriel didn't blink any more often than Azazel did, I noted. "This earthly realm is mankind's to act in," he said softly. I lost my cool.

"Then *I* will put it right! But I need to know if he's alive! I can't do *anything* without help—I don't even know where to look for him!"

Uriel seemed to consider this. He nodded, shortly. "I'll take a look then," he said. Standing up straight on his perch, he dropped down onto my plank. The piece of wood was balanced across the horizontals, not fastened: it bounced wildly and tilted and I screamed.

Uriel's hand shot out and grabbed me by the tail of my braid, yanking my head back, pinning me. If I'd been able to cry, tears would have leaped to my eyes. All I could do was to let out a string of hacking sobs.

"Picture this Egan of yours, clearly," he ordered, leaning in over me.

151

I tried to comply. I tried to think of Egan, and not think about the way Uriel was pulling my hair, or about his pale luminous eyes staring into mine. I shut my own, picturing Egan's square face and the heft of his solid shoulders and the warm quirk of his smile, and everything about him that was different from the callous domineering of angels.

"That'll do." He released me.

I opened my eyes in time to see the contemptuous curl of Uriel's lip. "Don't go too far," he told me, as he stepped out sideways between two of the facing panels of cloth and fell. I saw his shadow flash downward—but there was no sound of impact, and when I craned my neck and stared down there was no sign that anything had struck the earth far below. The crowds milled and drummed and danced just as before.

"Oh hell," I whispered to myself. I was damp with perspiration, and it would have been nice to report that that was only due to fear. Nice, but inaccurate. I could feel my scalp tingling. *Those poor Neolithic women*, I thought. *They never stood a chance, did they?*

But now I was alone, up a construction that was never meant to be climbed except by its makers. My next and overriding thought: *I'm getting down off this.*

The climb wasn't actually that difficult. There were offset planks laid at each level of the scaffolding, so all I had to do was swing down from one to the next. As long as I didn't think about the drop below me, I was all right. Neon flickered, turning the night rainbow. A fragrant waft of marijuana rose to meet me as I neared the surface of the playa.

"What the hell?" a shadowy guy asked, frowning over his tin of beer as I hung at the end of my arms and dropped the last couple of feet to the ground.

"It's okay, all done," I mumbled vaguely, rubbing the dirt off my hands as I backed away. As soon as I was sure he wasn't pursuing, I turned and strode off as steadily as my wobbling legs would allow. I looked back up to see the building from the outside though: it was a white pagoda, an easy landmark.

Uriel, I figured, could find me if he wanted.

Then I wandered out into the crowd, shaking with gratitude for the solid earth beneath my feet, grateful even for the fine dust and the heat I could feel radiating off the desert floor. Ahead of me stood the two illuminated towers I'd first spotted from on high, one of fire and one of water; to my right was a boat surrounded by scrap-metal sharks—*a boat in the desert!*—and to the left was a huge naked dancer, lit blue from within her translucent skin, but there seemed no reason to hurry toward any of the installations. All around me wandered people in fantastical costume, not heading in any particular direction, just lighting up the night with their glow and their glitter. Huge luminous puppets of mantises and moths wended their way over the heads of the crowd. A robot head the size of a small house rolled its eyes and licked its lips and danced on spider legs. A charabanc styled as a top-heavy gothic mansion eased its way down a track lined by steel roses. Fire-poi twirled and hoops spun. Drumbeats mixed with the sound of several competing electronic dance tracks.

I remembered at some point to close my mouth.

A clockwork Lincoln in a stovepipe hat pushed a handcart up to me and offered me a slushie. "Tea, young lady?"

My mouth was parched from fear, and I delved into my pocket willingly. "How much?"

He shook his head, laughing. "No charge."

I took a sip, nervously enchanted by the gesture: iced tea in the desert. A second later I realized it might not have been the wisest of moves, accepting a drink from a stranger, but he smiled and moved off as if it were the most natural thing in the world.

Azazel would love this, I thought with an unexpected pang. The staggering left-field technology, the crazy-ass art—those women wearing nothing but fluorescent body-paint, *Yow!*—the sense of stretching for something unpredictable and unnerving and new, grotesque or beautiful or both.

He'd be so proud of what we'd done with ourselves.

I wanted him here, I realized. He would fit right in. Egan...not so much. Egan was too cautious and reserved for an anarchy like this. He'd distrust it. Not, I told myself, that I knew anything about what he did in his downtime, when he wasn't rescuing helpless maidens. But I imagined he'd like to be in control of the situation, whatever it was. He wouldn't enjoy being swept up and carried away.

He certainly wasn't in control now. I shivered, the hollow in my breast growing cold and heavy again. He was in hostile hands.

Be safe, Egan, I told him. *Be strong. Be alive, please.*

Hurry up, Uriel.

Holding my paper cup of mushy ice, I followed an eddy of the crowd into a space behind a row of silver camper vans. The rhythmic thunder was loud here; there was a circle of drummers, and in the center a black-clad man leaped and whirled in the firelight. My heart jumped: for a moment I thought—quite irrationally—that it was Azazel I was looking at. But his flapping black wings resolved into a cloak of feathers, his crowned head became a beaked mask, and his supernaturally huge strides became the bounces of a man on those metal spring stilts.

"Raven," he called, over the sound of the drums. "Raven summons you to the circle. Raven is wisdom and legend, the bearer of stories."

New Age nonsense, I thought indulgently, wandering closer to watch.

"Listen to the Raven. Look into the flames." He was whirling a ball of flame on a chain as he danced. "See down the ages, to the first times."

A blue-haired woman seated with a drum in her lap looked up at me, and patted the blanket beside her. I nodded and sat down, a little self-consciously. The slushie was making my fingers cold. I took another sip.

"Let go of the present," the Raven-dancer admonished. "The flat everyday, the two-dimensional, the gray ordinary, the world of things. Come into the world of words. Come hear the stories." The ball of flame whooshed past my face. "The sorrow and the love and the fear in the blood. Let the flames show you what is real. Let the Raven tell you truth."

Round and round went the flame, hypnotic.

"Let Raven take you back."

And once more: *whoosh*—and suddenly I *saw*. Not the fire-lit campsite or the go-go fairyland of the playa, but a riverbank with tall reeds under a hot sun and a broad sky, and two boys playing there. One was perhaps ten, the other a couple of years younger, and both were plastered up to their knees and elbows in mud. Both were laughing, and both extraordinarily beautiful—long black curls, golden-dark skin, dressed in short white tunics. I didn't doubt for a second that they were brothers. The eldest held up a handful of mud he had been shaping, and I saw that it bore the rough outline of a bird—a quail perhaps, or something about that size. A moment later that bird stretched out its wings and sprang into the air, wings whirring as it took off and flew away over the hissing reeds.

154

The boy threw back his head and laughed with delight.

"My turn, my turn!" the younger boy shouted, delving at his feet for more mud. His voice sounded as if it came from miles away. "I will make an eagle!"

Then there was a noise—a silvery shimmering noise as if of some unknown musical instrument—and both boys looked up, staring past me as if I weren't there, but as if something behind my left shoulder was. I saw the light on their faces turn gold. I saw a look of wonder in their widening eyes, and then a tentative smile dawn on the face of the smaller boy. Whatever it was they were looking at, it was wonderful.

"Who are you?" asked the eldest boy.

The scene changed, without warning. It was suddenly sunset, and I was standing with others on a raised platform among great carven stones. We were facing a woman, and she was dancing. The dress she wore was pinned at her throat but left her breasts bare to either side, and her long red hair was unbound and fell in luxuriant curls, whipping about as she tossed her head and wove her spine.

Suddenly the wind rose, whirling about us. Dust obscured the setting sun and pattered at our clothes. Everyone but me fell to their knees and pressed their faces to the floor. The dancer paused, confused, her chest heaving as if she had been at it for hours. Then she too knelt down and hid her face.

Azazel stepped from a fold of light into the bare space of the dance floor. He didn't look at me; he only looked at the dancer. Like all the other men in the crowd, he wore a long linen kilt and nothing else, but broken shards of sunset glinted around him like polished copper. I guess he was more showy, back in those days.

The sight of him made my insides cramp with need.

"Leave." With a wave of his hand he dismissed the audience, and they fled down the hill. Only the woman remained. She stood slowly, still panting from her dance. I was surprised to see how old she looked: her face was beautifully planed but weathered into wrinkles, and the sag of her big, dark-nippled breasts would have put her in her late forties if she'd been a twenty-first-century woman. I couldn't tell from this distance if her eyes were mismatched colors, but the lids were heavy and dramatic with kohl. For a moment she looked up into Azazel's face, and then she ran forward into his embrace. He kissed her with sweet, savage kisses.

A green pang shot through me, like I'd been stabbed.

Why show me this?

But Azazel, if this was his doing, didn't choose to spare me a glance. He cupped the woman's face in his hands and asked her something—the drums were too loud for me to hear what, but I could sense the urgency in the movements of his shoulders and jaw. She pointed away down the hill, her eyes widening with fear. Quickly he spoke again, and kissed her forehead, then pushed her from him.

I heard his voice this time: "Hurry!"

The scene changed again. We were back at the river, but it was a gloaming dusk now, and the moon was rising over shredded clouds. Azazel pushed down the reed-hemmed path, looking left and right.

And then he found what he was looking for.

I couldn't see it. My vantage point was low down, as if I were a rat hiding in the grasses. I only saw him stop and stoop and reach out to touch something on the ground. But I saw the change that came over his expression, and I have never seen anything so awful. And however long I live, I hope never again to hear a sound like the one he made then.

Then another noise washed over me—a metallic shimmer, like sunshine made music—along with a golden light. This time I could turn and look. It was a man in a white robe. No, not a man—an angel: I knew enough by now to recognize one when I saw it. He looked like some medieval warrior-hero from a Chinese movie, with black hair a silken fall as far as his waist, and high cheekbones you could cut yourself upon. There was a rope belted about his narrow hips: a dark and glistening rope that had made unpleasant stains on his pristine robe. Something about the sight of that…it made my heart curl up in my breast like it wanted to die.

Azazel took one look and threw himself forward, roaring. He burned as he ran, and black smoke flowed from him. In three strides he wasn't a man anymore; he was a huge black bull with eyes of fire and skin like a cracked lava flow, and the air shook with his heat and the thunder of his hooves. The other angel met him head-on: a bull of matching size, blinding white like sun on snow. The crash of their impact, directly over my head, shook the world.

I saw that fight, and yet I did not see it. I was too close, and my vision filled up with a thrashing confusion of limbs that changed and morphed. Hooves of bulls, paws of lions, claws and wings of eagles—and glistening scaled talons that might have been dragons or might have been something else. They fought in human form too, so fast I could not follow the flickering movements. The reeds around parched and burst into flame: the river steamed and boiled away, the earth cracked and heaved, groaning its protest. Blood flew as a red rain. Stars came out overhead and then fell hissing from the sky, striking the ground like mortar shells. By the time dawn broke, the country for miles around was a smoldering wasteland of soot and ash and upthrust rock.

Then Azazel struck the earth, facedown, crimson with blood from head to toe, flames still dancing on his flesh. A moment later I saw a bare foot, equally bloody, descend upon his neck and pin him.

"No!" I shrieked, lurching to my feet—and all around me the drums faltered and people stared. The Raven dancer, swaying on his stilts, stopped mid-declamation and looked at me reproachfully.

"Hey. Not cool. Don't interrupt."

As reality rushed back in to fill the void vacated by vision, I stuttered and blushed and stared.

"Milja, you're upsetting the nice people." Uriel's silken sarcasm was a cool hand reaching to me through the flames. I whipped round and stared into his sardonic face. It was actually a relief to see him.

"Bad trip," someone muttered nearby.

"Come on then," Uriel ordered, crooking a finger, and I wobbled toward him.

"The tea was spiked," I stammered, thrusting the cup at him. "I saw..."

"Watch the shoes!" he sniffed, dodging the drips.

"Uh...sorry."

Uriel looked down, curling his lip, and stuck a fastidious finger in the melted slush before licking the tip. "Bottled water, green tea, sugar, lemon juice," he pronounced. "It's clean."

"But I saw—"

"*Your young men shall see visions and your old men shall dream dreams.*"

"What does that mean!"

"You can't blame the tea. It's all you." He narrowed his eyes. "Why are all those people staring at me, Milja?"

The sudden change in conversational tack threw me into even deeper confusion for a moment. I turned a circle, slack-jawed, only to find Uriel wasn't wrong. The drums had fallen silent and everyone in the area was watching us, their faces distinctly unfriendly.

"Um... It's your suit," I muttered, as my brain finally caught up with my surroundings.

"My *suit*?"

"You see anyone else wearing one? You look like you're here on a drug bust."

Uriel decided to help matters by snorting derisively at this and rolling his eyes. Then he shrugged, and with the motion *changed*—just like that—his old appearance falling away from him like ash swept by a careless hand. Suddenly he was biker-booted and black-leathered from the waist down, gauntleted to the elbow—and that was all. The rest of him was bare, his hard chest sporting neither clothes nor hair, but he made up for that with a pair of huge folded wings whose feathers were such a pure white that even in firelight they made my eyes water. He flexed and shook them, fluffing the pinions for a moment before settling them into place.

"Do I blend in now?" he asked dryly.

I looked away.

The reaction from the people around us was a collective intake of breath so loud that I heard it—and then, uncertainly at first, a scattering of shocked laughter and applause that rose to a storm of appreciation. They didn't know how he'd done it, but in this place they expected wonders of art and technology. They believed in miracles.

What's more, they liked the results. Who wouldn't? His body wasn't middle-aged *at all*.

"Let's talk then," Uriel said, touching my arm to steer me away.

I didn't dare look at him. A dozen conflicting emotions were fighting it out inside me. I wanted to shriek.

"Now," he said. "This Egan."

Egan. Yes, Egan. Think about him—and not about how you're going batshit crazy seeing things that aren't there or how there's this bloody great gorgeous angel at your side who is *there and how much easier it would be if he put some goddamn clothes back on…*

"Did you find him?"

"Surprisingly easily."

"Is he alive?"

"He is. Not looking terribly happy, admittedly, but in reasonable shape."

My heart leaped. *Oh thank God. Or thank heaven. Or whatever.* "You really saw him?"

"He happens to be on holy ground."

"Is he being held prisoner?"

"I'd say that's what it looks like. A priest was asking him questions, and I'd guess, from his condition, that your friend has been reluctant to answer them."

My stomach lurched. "But where?" Turning to look at Uriel was a mistake, I realized. I tried to focus past his shoulder, on the wings.

He shrugged in irritation. "I don't know the name you lot give the place. Some monastery. What's your problem, girl?"

I blushed furiously. "Nothing, just…!"

"Oh for heaven's sake…" He rolled his eyes. "Can't you even manage to keep one of us in focus at a time? Brains between your legs, the lot of you."

I gritted my teeth. "Has it occurred to *any* of you to turn up looking, you know, *ordinary*? A bit ugly maybe? Perhaps we could have avoided the whole Flood and all, if you lot had just had moobs or bad teeth or beer bellies or whatever."

Uriel looked down his nose at me. "I am not ordinary," he said with hauteur.

"No," I said, defeated. "You're not. Hooray for you. Now help me get to Egan."

"Your logic confounds me. Explain. And do get on with it, please: I dislike being in material form. It…itches."

"Two minutes," I said with a ghastly grin that I couldn't stop. "Two minutes and you're complaining. You try a lifetime in a human body."

He glowered. "What do you want me to do?"

"I can't phone him: they took his phone away. I can't leave this country:

159

I've got no documentation. You guys could save him, but you won't. So what else can I do? Take me back to Montenegro."

"What are you planning?"

I told him.

Two minutes later I was standing in the Trg Republike square in Podgorica city, in the hot afternoon sun.

I fished my European SIM out of my knapsack and dialed Egan's cell phone. If this didn't work, I told myself, I would go through Vera and Josef.

But the phone picked up.

"Hello?" said a man's voice. It wasn't Egan.

My heart was pounding. "This is Milja Petak," I said. "I want to talk to Father Velimir."

chapter twelve

MENTAL RESERVATION

They came for me a couple of hours later, in a black minibus. I stood
up as the passenger door opened to disgorge one of Father Velimir's
sidekicks—the one with the red beard that I recognized from our meeting
in the park with Branko—along with a couple of other priests. They
looked agitated but pleased with themselves, and there was no mistaking
the way they looked down at me. I squinted into the interior of the bus but
the tinted glass wouldn't let me see if there were other occupants.

"Milja Petak," said the one with the rufous beard.

"Where's Egan?" I demanded. "You said you would bring him!"

"How were we to know this wasn't a trap? You might have been
waiting to kill us all."

The injustice made me gape. Me kill *them*—wasn't it the other way
round? I'd never threatened anyone!

Okay, so Azazel...in the boat...

Maybe they had a point.

"Father Velimir gave his word," I said harshly.

"And he'll keep it. Your friend is safe and we're taking you to him." He
indicated the vehicle. "Get in."

The moment I was inside someone grabbed my wrists and bound them
together with a cable-tie.

"That's not necessary," I said, my heart in my mouth.

"Shut up, witch."

They drove me through the city. There was one odd incident: we pulled up outside a drugstore and Red Beard—the others addressed him as Ilija—had a muttered argument with the driver, who was an older guy dressed in street clothes. I couldn't hear what it was about, from my place in the back wedged between two sweating overweight men in cassocks, but I did hear Father Ilija snap, "Well I can't do it!" After that the driver got out, went into the pharmacy, and returned a short while later with something in a white paper bag—and a face the purple of stewed beetroot.

We drove on, into the mountains. I couldn't see much past my minders and through the tinted glass, but I think we were heading north and then east, toward the Kosovo border—I glimpsed the minarets of more than one mosque before sunset caught us. At different points we drove through lush valleys and past a small lake, but the terrain eventually grew too steep and rocky for anything but shallow, swift-running rivers. The road turned to a track, and by the time we drove over a small bridge at the confluence of two stony streams and stopped, it was all but dark. As I emerged from the minibus I saw tall walls painted white and topped by towers. Mountains loomed around us, blocking out swathes of stars. Picked out by the bus headlamps, over the arched gate, was a painted relief of St. Michael casting down a hairy blue Satan.

A monastery, by the looks of it.

I was feeling quite sick with nervousness now, but I did my best not to show it.

Father Ilija unlocked the studded oak door and pushed it wide, before beckoning me forward. A man at either shoulder kept me on the straight and narrow, and they prodded me to the threshold.

"Go in," he said—and as I took that final step forward, everyone else took a step back. I paused and looked round at them, catching their dubious stares.

"What? Were you expecting me to burst into flames on holy ground, or something?" The pleasure I took in the situation was entirely out of proportion to the strength of my position. It was clear from their expressions that that was, more or less, what they had been wondering.

Father Ilija scowled. "Stay out of our heads," he growled, and shoved me hard.

Two tortoiseshell cats ran ahead of us, mewing, as the priests steered me across a dimly lit courtyard and up a flight of stairs. The impression I got of the building, as I was hurried through it, was of bare white walls, plain wood and austerity. And size—the narrow staircases up seemed to go on and on. It was almost a relief to be brought up short in front of a door, and to see Father Ilija knock upon it.

"Enter!"

Finally, I was pushed into the room within. Shelved from floor to ceiling, this was a room of books—but too cluttered and disordered to be a library. A private study, then. Sitting behind a desk that dwarfed him was Father Velimir, with his mild scholarly face and his long white hair. He stood up, pressing his back as if it ached.

I swallowed hard, fighting down the knot in my throat. This small, elderly man had killed my father. Inadvertently, perhaps.

Or perhaps not.

"Milja Petak," he said gravely. I wondered if they felt that saying my name gave them some sort of power over me. Not that they needed any— the cards were all in their hands.

All but one card, anyway. And I wasn't in any position to rely on Azazel.

But I wasn't going to tell them that.

"Where's Egan?" I repeated. I'm no action hero: I was sweating with fear. It was all I could do to keep my voice steady.

"Your friend is safe, and you will see him soon."

"You promised me!"

"And I will keep my word. He will be released, all in good time." He looked me up and down as he emerged from behind his desk, and I returned the favor with perhaps a bit more circumspection. After meeting Azazel and Uriel, there was nothing imposing about Father Velimir. He looked frail and somewhat spindly, except where the round of his belly pushed against his cassock. I used that thought to grab at my courage.

"Then," I said, "I want proof. I want to see that Egan's still alive and okay. And here. Show me. I want to see him."

He sighed, his watery eyes fixing on mine. "Very well then. This way." He led the way back into the corridor, and a cluster of lesser priests followed on behind me, prodding me between the shoulder blades to make me keep up. We set off again—going down this time, into the bowels of the building.

"Why are you treating me like this?" I asked, lifting my bound wrists as Father Velimir glanced back. "I offered myself in fair exchange. I won't fight."

"And we should believe the promise of a witch?" he answered. His voice was mild, almost sympathetic, despite the words.

"You people keep calling me that. I don't know what you mean."

"*And all the others together with them,*" he said, the lift of his chin warning me that he was quoting, "*took unto themselves wives, and each chose for himself one, and they began to go unto them and defile themselves with them, and they taught them charms and enchantments.* I have been doing my research, Milja."

I was pretty sure I recognized the tone of the *Book of Enoch*. "Defiled themselves?" I muttered. "Nice. Really nice. I'm not a witch, Father. I'm just a girl who..." But I ran out of words at that point.

"You are the mistress of the demon Azazel."

"He's not like you think he is," I said, but my voice shook and it sounded weak.

"Really? *And the whole Earth had been corrupted through the works that were taught by Azazel: to him ascribe all sin.* The words of God the Father Himself."

I was beginning to understand the 'scapegoat' epithet. "The *Book of Enoch*'s not even canonical scripture," I tried. "You can't take it literally, Father."

"And yet it describes our situation perfectly. Who knew? Who *could* possibly know, Milja, that your family was hiding this terrible thing for centuries? That you were keeping it secret even from the Holy Church itself? Such deception—such hubris. The kind of pride ascribed to Satan himself."

"That's not fair! My father was doing his duty!"

"His duty by whom? By what authority did he lie and steal and dissemble and stoop to simony? Your family do not even know who set the task upon them! It was not just sin piled upon sin, but a terrible risk.

And now look: *look what you've done*, Milja. Your lust and your weakness have released a scourge upon the world. A supernatural evil such as has not been seen since the days of the Flood." He shook his head, heavy with sorrow. "One we must fight to contain once more, by any means necessary."

"I didn't mean to…" I mumbled.

"And yet you must take responsibility. Or else the entire world will pay for your crime. Already your friend Egan has suffered terribly on your behalf."

He stopped abruptly. We were in a long narrow corridor, illuminated by fluorescent strip lights, that I suspected was underground. There were rows of heavy, ancient doors on either side, suggesting small rooms, and in fact most of them had open panels near the top. Monks' cells, I guessed. Outside one of them a man in civilian clothes sat on a folding chair, reading a newspaper. He shot to his feet as we approached, looking like he was glad to be relieved of his boredom.

"Here he is," said Father Velimir, signaling to the guard to slide back the viewing panel in the door. By standing on my tiptoes, I could look into the room beyond. I glimpsed a piece of large, static machinery—a boiler or a generator or something—and a single mattress on the floor next to it. Egan sat on the mattress, his head nested against one raised shoulder and eyes closed. It was hard to see the detail, but from the crook and the angle of his arm it looked like he was cuffed to one of the machine's pipes.

Egan, I moaned silently, my heart pounding. I turned to my captors. "Is he all right? Have you hurt him? Let me in there! I want to see him."

"And you can. But bear this in mind: we have rigged the metalwork to which he is bound," Father Velimir said, taking something out of a pocket in his cassock: a small black remote, like a TV controller. He didn't sound like he was issuing a threat; he sounded sad and gentle. "Be very clear about this, Milja. If you should try anything, and in particular if you should call your master, we will run several thousand volts through that pipe and it will kill your friend stone dead."

"More like crispy fried," muttered the guard, with a grin. Father Velimir ignored both my appalled look and the man's crassness.

"Do you still want to go in?"

I nodded, wordless with fear and outrage.

"Open it."

The cell door had a shiny new padlock on the ancient latch. The hinges yielded with a creak. The prisoner's eyes were open by the time I stepped in, and he was rising slowly to his feet. A steel handcuff scraped up a length of pipe. His right wrist was tethered.

"Egan?" I lurched across the room.

"Milja? Why are you here?" His voice was hoarse, his eyes wide. I closed enough to step onto the mattress and lift my bound hands to his face—bruised, haggard, unshaven—and he swept his free arm about me, crushing me to him, pressing his face to my hair. I could hear him panting and I could feel the bang of his heart against his ribs. "Milja, Milja," he groaned.

"Are you hurt?" I choked. "Are you okay?" He smelled sweaty and sour but I didn't care: just to be in his embrace was a staggering relief. I pushed away enough to look up into his face. "Oh God," I moaned.

His nose had been broken, and I remembered the blood all over his face, on the boat. The red split mark across the bridge hardly stood out against the rest of the darkening bruises, but I felt cold run into the pit of my stomach.

"What have they done to you?"

"What are you doing here?" he countered, looking beyond me to the doorway. "They caught you too? How?"

"Oh Egan." My hands slid over his chest, pushing at the edges of his misbuttoned shirt. I could see raw red patches on the upper part of his chest. A glance at the hand cuffed to the pipe showed me that his fingers were roughly bandaged and that he was missing at least two nails: the raw nail beds were bright and glistening. Impulsively, I caught his face as well as I could between my hands and kissed his cracked lips. The arm around me tightened. I could feel his body, hard and urgent and aching for release, against mine.

He groaned, shaking.

And then I realized: *this was what I had dreamed.*

The shock of recognition was enough to push me backward out of his arms. We stared at each other wildly. I could feel the race of my blood, the ache of inextricable pity and lust in me that responded to his duress and his captivity. And I could see him trying to master himself.

166

"Milja," he repeated, clearing his throat.

It wasn't precisely the same as my dream, of course. Egan was handcuffed, not chained, and his arms were not spread. He was wearing more clothes. But it was close enough for me—for both of us—to *know*. I saw the shame and the fear stark in his eyes. It nearly wrecked me.

"What have you done to him?" I shouted, turning my back because I could not bear to see the way Egan looked at me, and could not cope with wanting him right now, and did not dare face up to my horrible prescience.

Father Velimir stood in the arch, hands folded.

"What have you done to him, you bastards?" I rasped.

"You seem fond of your accomplice." He spoke in English for the first time, and I followed his lead.

"He's not my accomplice! He doesn't know anything!"

"So he tells us."

"None of what I did had anything to do with him—he came along later—he was just trying to be nice to me!"

"How often do men fall into that trap?" Father Velimir said, sighing, but it was definitely not a question. "Your demon master has taught you the arts of seduction. That was his specialty from the beginning, after all."

I wanted to laugh in his face—me, seductive?—but it just wasn't funny. I held to the important point: "It's not Egan's fault. You have me, like you wanted, so let him go."

"Or else?"

"Or *else*?" I was starting to panic. "For God's sake! Are you going back on our agreement now? That's not right!"

"A minor sin, some would say, in order to prevent a greater evil. And offhand, I cannot think of a greater evil than Azazel."

"Then you'd better not screw us about!" I spat.

"Enlightening." Father Velimir smiled thinly. "I'm not going back on our agreement. I just wanted to see how long it would take you to resort to threats, that's all."

I opened my mouth—and then shut it again. He had me.

"Look at it from our point of view, Milja," he said gently, opening his hands. "You're not a stupid young woman. I'm sure you see the logic. If

167

I let your friend go now, there is nothing to stop you calling your master to take you away again, just like you did on that boat. Or killing us all, at your whim."

I shook my head, dizzy. "I don't kill people!"

"The boat sank, Milja. Five men drowned. Besides the one with his throat torn open."

"Oh," I said, sickened.

"So you see: as long as we need you, we need your 'friend' Egan. When we have done what we need to do, then he will go free, and no further harm will come to him. Or to you."

The fear-sweat was gathering in my pores like acid. "How long?"

"A few months, I imagine. Preparations need to be made."

Months? *Months?*

Egan spoke up for the first time. His voice was rough and hard. "What are you going to do to her?"

Father Velimir grimaced. "We will need her, in due course, to summon her master so he may be bound again." He lifted a hand and beckoned to me. "Come here."

I cast Egan another glance, hoping that he had something to say, some argument that would change everything. But he only nodded, gnawing his lip, so I followed the priest out into the corridor, wondering if my legs would hold me up much longer. I'd looked no further than freeing Egan— I figured that Azazel was capable of taking care of himself. To have that goal pulled away from me into an unforeseeable future was unbearable.

"Let us be clear, Milja. If your master comes here before we are ready for him, your friend will die first. And if you flee or turn against us, he will die. So you must cooperate in everything we ask of you, however much you might wish otherwise. If you do that, your friend will live and go free."

I swallowed, though my throat had gone dry. "This is just so wrong, so sick," I said huskily. "Can't you see that?"

"You think we should lie down and let evil go unchecked?" Father Velimir drew himself up. "That would be easier, wouldn't it, than fighting back? But I've lived under tyranny, Milja. I've survived wars. I've seen the evil of men run wild, and I've witnessed genocide and mass rape, the destruction of holy places and the death of countless innocents. If that's what mere men do, how much worse your master?"

I stared at him, helplessly. The weight of history in this part of Europe was too great to argue with. The last of the post-Yugoslavia wars had finished only in the late 1990s. I remembered well the horrific reports I'd heard as a child. It was over now—but none of it was forgotten.

"If it's true that Azazel is such a threat, Father," I said, licking my dry lips, "then answer this—Why hasn't God Himself taken action? In the *Book of Enoch* he sent the archangels to bind the Fallen. Why hasn't He done that this time? Where are St. Michael and all the heavenly host? Why doesn't He act?"

Father Velimir snorted. "*Why doesn't God act?* Oh child—you think you're the first person in history to ask that question? You think they didn't ask it in Jasenovac and Auschwitz? It is the eternal question—but tell me who you are, to sit back and demand he clean up the mess you made? In mankind, in us, is the meeting-point of the spiritual and the material realms, Milja. When God acts, He acts through us. Your role, like mine, is to obey. Do you understand?"

I looked back at Egan. He had braced his shoulders against the wall in order to stay on his feet, and his look of despair was undisguised. That sight of him nearly broke my heart.

"Okay," I said. "I understand."

"Excellent." With something like a flourish, Father Velimir handed the black remote box over to the guard, while a priest closed and locked Egan's door. "You can stay down here for the moment," he told me, pointing at a room on the opposite side of the passage. "You'll be comfortable enough, I think."

The cell opened up for me was at least properly furnished as a room, not just a boiler house. There was a single bed, an icon of St. Basil on the wall, and a scarred writing desk and chair. But it was windowless and spartan and the sight of it made me shake.

"No," I said, trying to back out and getting a shove for my efforts. "Wait. Not yet. I need the bathroom." I wasn't lying either—it had been a long drive up into the mountains.

"See that she gets a bucket," Father Velimir told Father Ilija, with a grimace of distaste.

Then the men filed out and the door closed, and I heard the clunk and rattle of a padlock being applied to my door. I went over to the bed and sat on the hard mattress, staring at the whitewashed brick.

The first thing I did when I'd managed to gather my scattered wits was to take the chair over to the door and climb up to look out through the hatch. I could see the corridor, our guard reading his paper—and through Egan's matching slot, into his cell. I couldn't see him though.

"Egan?"

"Milja," he called. "What's going on? How did they find you? I thought you got away!"

"I came back."

"What the hell for? How could you be so stupid!"

"Well you're the stupid one, if you think I was going to leave you," I said, my throat swelling.

There was a moment's silence, and then, "Milja," but the syllables were broken and painful.

"It's me they want, Egan. You're just their guarantee of my good behavior." I couldn't remember how much of our conversation had been in English, or work out how well Egan understood the situation. "When they're done with me, they'll let you go. He said."

He promised me. I held on to that hope with slippery fingers, though by now I knew perfectly well how principled men could always find an overriding reason to act like bastards.

"You shouldn't have done this, Milja. I was trying to protect you! You should have just stayed away..."

"No," I said, shaking my head though he couldn't see it.

The guard, irritated by a shouted exchange in a language he almost certainly couldn't understand, stood up and approached me. "Get down and shut up," he ordered. "Or I come in there and I break your teeth."

I got down.

I shut up.

I spent a while gnawing through the cable-tie until it held only by a tag; I hoped that it would snap easily if I really needed my hands free. Then I lay on my bed for hours, thinking. Imagining what might happen if I broke and begged Azazel for help. Imagining what might happen if I didn't. Remembering what Uriel and Father Velimir had both said to me about suffering and the importance of obedience. Recalling my strange vision I'd had on the playa—only a few hours ago, but half a world away.

Everything churned around in my head, mixed up.

They kept the lights on all night but I still had my wristwatch and it was after three in the morning when I suddenly realized what it was the priests wanted from me.

I understood.

I wish I hadn't.

Loki.

I sat up, sweat running across my skin, and shoved my fingers into my mouth to stifle the noise bursting from my throat.

I spent the rest of the night pacing up and down my tiny room, unable to sleep, wishing I could cry just so as to relieve the pounding in my head.

They brought us breakfast the next morning, and it was surprisingly good—fruit and bread and cheese and ham. They even brought me a bowl and lukewarm water to wash in.

An hour later Father Velimir paid a visit, with an entourage of priests that included, to my discomfort, the priest with the gray-striped beard that Egan had knocked cold in Vera's hotel bedroom. He still carried a greenish bruise on the side of his head and round his eye, and he looked at me from that swollen socket with cold dislike. Father Velimir, on the other hand, looked furious.

"You're not pregnant!"

I wasn't the least surprised at his accusation. I recalled the red-faced trip to the drugstore in Podgorica, and the removal of the covered bucket of pee from my cell this morning. I glared at him from my seat on the edge of the bed, red-eyed with sleeplessness and loathing.

"No," I said clearly, speaking English so that Egan could understand, if he was listening. "I'm not pregnant. Has that screwed up your plans? No half-human baby that you can murder and make into rope."

Father Velimir's mouth dropped open. I kept talking.

"And that's the only thing that'll hold a fallen angel, isn't it? Chains won't work, ropes won't work, stone cells won't work—they can probably teleport out of set concrete for all I know. They were tied up using bits of *their own children.* And that's what you want from me, you piece of—"

He jabbed a finger in my face. "Why? Why aren't you pregnant? You fornicated with him, didn't you? You lay with him!"

171

"Hell yes."

"Then his seed is in you!"

My words hissed out between my bared teeth. "What century are you stuck in, Father Velimir? Progestogen coil. Itty bit of plastic. I've been wearing one for years."

He flung up his hands. "Ah—what should I have expected? The God-given instincts must be dead in such a breast!"

"My instincts?" I snarled. "*You* were planning to kill a baby! How does that square with your Godly conscience, eh?"

"It is written of the Fallen: *The murder of their beloved ones shall they see, and over the destruction of their children shall they lament.* It's the will of God, girl."

"Not my God," said I vehemently. "My God is Love—He doesn't tell us to kill children."

"Yet He told Joshua to do exactly that to the Canaanites. He told Abraham to do it to his own son. He slew all the firstborn of Egypt. Sometimes," said Father Velimir, with a look of dignified sorrow, "we must do hard things for the sake of obedience. Sometimes He commands those who love Him to wield the knife. It is the ultimate test of our devotion."

Something stirred in my memory, but I did not have time or the wit to chase it down. I was too flabbergasted.

"Go fuck yourself, Father Velimir," I said.

It wasn't exactly theologically astute—but then how can you argue with True Belief? Anyway, at those words the gray-bearded priest stepped in and struck me across the face so hard that he nearly knocked me off the bed. I scrabbled at the blanket, drooling with shock, my ear ringing—and my eyes burning with tears, at last.

No, not tears.

"Look at her," said someone in hushed horror as I struggled to sit up again and turn a defiant face to them. "Look!"

Confused, I wiped at my wet cheeks. All of a sudden the back of my hand was red.

"Tears of blood! What's wrong with her?"

"Is she a *tenatz*?" someone else asked anxiously—referring to the vampires of local folklore.

"Hush!" Father Velimir signaled for calm. "Her flesh has been corrupted by his demon seed. Enoch has warned of this: *And the women of the angels who went astray shall become sirens.*"

Sirens? I thought dizzily. *What the hell?*

"In which case," he added grimly, "perhaps her own flesh will do just as well as her Nephilim child's. Since we have no other option now. Bring her."

"What? What?" I started to shout. "You said you'd release him!"

He caught my face as his priests hoisted me to my feet. "Don't be afraid, girl. We don't want to kill you. Your legs will probably do. We need ligaments, sinew, skin… Look upon it as blood money for the men you have killed. Justice."

"Justice!"

"Animals retaliate. God dispenses forgiveness. In the human realm, Milja, all we have is justice."

I was scooped through the door, my toes dragging on flagstones. "That's not justice, you twisted fuck!" I screamed.

"If not," he said, bringing up the rear and eying me with equanimity, "then I trust and believe that Almighty God will forgive me."

I lost it. I broke my cable-tie and twisted in my captors' arms and stuck a finger as hard as I could in someone's eye and kicked and screamed and punched.

Like I said, I'm not an action-movie heroine. I might as well have fought a host of archangels, for all the good it did. All that happened was I got slammed against a wall hard enough to knock the breath out of me, and punched several times, and ended up on the floor throwing up my monastic breakfast.

The world spun around me, blooming dark and light as I tried to focus.

I could hear Egan shouting.

"Get up," said Father Ilija in a gruff voice, grabbing my clothes between my shoulders and pulling me so hard that the fabric seams creaked and snapped.

"Stop it! Stop it! I'll tell you!" It was Egan's voice, almost cracking with the strain of his bellow. "I'll tell you how to catch the angel! I know how to do it!"

Slowly his words sank in. By the time I was on my feet, dangling from

Father Ilija's fists, Father Velimir was staring through the hatch in Egan's door.

"What?" he demanded.

"I know how to catch him! I'll tell you! And it will work, but you must keep her unharmed—you need her!"

What on earth is Egan up to? I wondered groggily.

"How do you know anything about this?"

"*Vidimus.*"

The word meant nothing to me, but Father Velimir frowned. "Open the door," he grunted.

The cell was as I remembered. Egan stood, straining against his hand-cuff chain, eyes wide and fixed on me. "Don't hurt her," he gasped, "or I swear you can go burn in Hell before I tell you."

"Talk," said Father Velimir. "You've got thirty seconds to convince me you know anything at all."

Egan talked, quickly. For about thirty seconds. In a language I didn't know at all—but the word *Vidimus* was repeated.

Latin? I guessed, flailing inside. I could feel the world slowly crumbling away beneath my feet.

"Get him out of that," growled Father Velimir. Whatever it was he'd heard, it had made him angry—coldly, grimly angry. Two priests went forward: they seemed practiced at what they did. One got Egan bent over in a headlock, his free wrist twisted up behind his back, while the other unlocked the cuffs.

"Did you know?" Father Velimir turned to me, his voice soft, one eyebrow raised. For a moment he reminded me strongly of Uriel. "Did he tell you where he was taking you? Do you *know* who he works for?"

"A bank. He works for a bank." My lips felt numb.

"You idiot girl." The words were loaded with bitterness.

I looked into Egan's face as they forced him upright. "You told me you worked for a bank," I whispered.

"I'm so sorry, Milja," he said, shaking his head, his gaze slippery with shame. "*Mentalis restrictio.* Technically, yes…I'm on their payroll."

"Tell her."

Egan looked sick. "The Vatican Bank."

chapter thirteen

THE CAGES

Extraordinary. You almost got her out from under our noses. And once in Rome…your people would have taken possession of the Watcher, wouldn't you?" A muscle twitched in Father Velimir's cheek. Suddenly his head snapped sideways, like a hawk fixing on a mouse. "Put her in his place."

Clamping a hand over my mouth, Badger-Beard bundled me onto the mattress and secured my wrist in the steel handcuff, all before I could think straight.

"We have a change of plan, for the moment," Father Velimir told me. "Now he's ready to talk, let us see what he does know."

"Milja," said Egan urgently. "Don't lose heart: you'll be okay." Then they pushed him out into the corridor and the door clanged shut on the sound of the priestly party retreating down the passage.

Okay? *Okay?* How was I going to be okay? As I knelt there on the mattress, panting, with bloody tears smeared down my cheeks, I had never felt less okay. My body was sending up distress flares of pain from all the places they had roughed me up. I could feel my split lower lip swelling with every thump of my racing heart. And I could feel the raw hole in my belly that was left where the warm core of trust had been torn out.

Egan was Catholic. Of course he was. Of *course*. I should have seen it, shouldn't I—an Irish mother and, judging from his surname, a Polish-American father? And he'd crossed himself the wrong way round, left to right, as did, come to think of it—I could see it right now in my mind's eye—motherly Jelena...in the second of the "safe houses" he'd taken me to. Houses with crucifixes, but no icons.

His network. His "friends." His inexhaustible bank account.

Quoting *Job*. And Dante's goddamn *Inferno*.

Appearing out of nowhere in Podgorica, just when I needed his help. He must have been following me.

"Peter sent me."

The Vatican? Dear God...

How long had they been watching me?

If I had any excuse for not recognizing the obvious, it was because I'd never really met any Catholics, so far as I knew. There are hardly any here in my homeland—most fled over the border into Croatia in the 1990s—and certainly none in our village. I suppose I'd probably bumped into some in America, but I'd never been near a Catholic church or discussed religion with fellow students or work colleagues. My personal experience of Catholicism was on a par with that of Moonies and Hare Krishna devotees.

I just hadn't thought.

But now it seemed only too clear.

He'd sought me out deliberately, from the beginning. He must have. Planting the seeds, inveigling his way into my trust. A handsome guy it was easy to like. So that when everything went wrong and I needed someone to turn to, he was there—a shoulder to cry on, a strong arm to lean upon. It must have been like a gift to him.

He'd known all along, I realized, sliding farther down the slope into my pit of despair. He'd known about Azazel. It had taken no leap of faith at all for him, when I'd tentatively confessed that I'd freed a fallen angel—I'd just assumed, quite wrongly, that he was struggling to believe me.

It explained why he took the whole story so calmly.

It explained everything—including the way he acted around me, as if he were wearing some sort of invisible chastity belt. I was, as far as he was concerned, contaminated goods: the girl who'd consorted with devils.

He'd played me from start to finish.

Dear God—had he *picked my pocket*, back at Logan? Had he taken my passport just so we could meet?

He hadn't been my friend. He'd been my courier.

Smuggling me back...to Rome. Where they'd be waiting for me with a nice cozy cell in Vatican City, no doubt. Much like this place, in all probability.

I put my free hand to the pit of my stomach, pressing hard, as if I could fill up the empty space inside, as if pressure would stop the hurt.

He'd seduced me. Not into bed, sure—but into trusting him and liking him. And risking everything for him.

I'd come back here and given myself up to the men who hated me, for him. For a man who had intended to betray me all along.

I squeezed my eyes shut and let out a whine of pure pain that somehow went on and on. Then I bent right over and pressed my face into the mattress and mouthed his name, over and over, like I was trying to vomit something from the back of my throat. I didn't care about being overheard. The pain overwhelmed everything else.

I cried tears of blood. It hurt, but it was better than not being able to cry at all.

And when, in the depths of my blame and my self-loathing I mouthed Azazel's name too, I didn't think, at first, what the result might be.

They'd promised to throw the switch if I summoned him.

I opened my eyes. My heart ran like a fast engine. I raised myself from my sticky fetal clench and looked around the room.

He wasn't there.

I wondered if the guard was listening from behind the door, a sweaty finger on the button and his heart in his mouth. The hatch was closed.

I could call him. I could call Azazel. I could beg his help. And maybe he was still listening, despite our last fight. Maybe he'd come and snatch me away, in the twinkling of an eye, if only to prove to us both that he was right and I was wrong.

But more likely the guard would press the switch, and the monastery electrical supply would surge through the cuff and my body, and then I'd twitch and smoke and fry. I'd seen that kind of death in American movies. It looked agonizing.

I looked up the length of my arm at the pipe and the inert furnace. I wanted to be brave. I wanted to defy them all.

But I was too afraid.

And I didn't trust Azazel. I didn't trust him to be fast enough. I didn't trust him to care.

I knew then that I was wholly on my own.

I was tethered to that metal pipe for five days.

I could stand, or kneel, or lie down, and I could swing round to use the plastic waste bucket, but I couldn't so much as walk around the room. I made myself stand for hours, just to keep my legs working. I made myself do push-ups and squats. I made myself eat and drink everything they brought me.

I had a lot of time to rage—at myself, at God, at Egan and Azazel and the priests. I had a lot of time to regret. I had a lot of time to think about the things I'd been told.

I had time to recall my recent dreams, with their portents and significance.

Perhaps I understood, in my captivity, a little of how it must have been for Azazel—though I had none of the physical pain to bear that he'd had, and though my butchered children were no more than notional possibilities. I lay there in the fluorescent glare, eyes open, and imagined his agony.

And in the end I understood, I thought, his fury with me. Why he'd lost it, up there on the roof of my apartment.

You are not God!

Sometimes, the priest had said, *He commands those who love Him to wield the knife. It is the ultimate test.*

Abraham, ordered to butcher his only child.

The God that Father Velimir worshiped was very much the same as the one Azazel rebelled against, it seemed to me. The Pantocrator: the almighty, all-powerful king. An absolute ruler, never to be questioned, and one who demanded not just obedience but extraordinary proof of it.

Lying there, staring at the wall, I thought I understood at last what Azazel had reacted against. *"If you really loved me you'd... Save Egan. Do what I tell you. Obey my commands. Fall down in worship. Stay away from all women. Slay your own son."* I'd spoken carelessly, assuming a right to command him. But the kind of "love" that demanded obedience, that set tests, that attempted to exert control in its own name—it must burn him like acid.

I hadn't thought.

"You are not God!"

Azazel's experience of divine dominion would be enough to drive anybody insane.

That wasn't my God though. That wasn't the God my father had taught me, in our simple little house or our lonely church. Father's God was one who manifested through the world in intimate passionate love for all His creation. "Closer than your own heartbeat," Father had said to me. "More affectionate than any friend, more just than any ruler, more loving than any father, more a part of us than our own limbs."

Father's God was infinite Love.

Except...except that my gentle, musical father had been a jailer and a torturer too. He had obeyed his calling, out of Faith. He'd not had the answers, so he'd trusted to a higher authority. He'd let God—or custom, or history—make the decisions.

The dismaying possibility occurred to me that the difference between my father and Father Velimir was not one of kind, but only degree.

That night, I dreamed of Azazel.

I was somewhere dark, and it was raining. It wasn't falling directly on me, but on a tin roof over my head, and the noise was insistent and ominous, like the roll of drums at an execution.

Lightning cracked the sky. A pale glare reflected off the sheet of mud that covered the earth and was already filling my shoes. I saw Azazel, soaked to the skin and with his filthied white jumper hanging off his shoulders like a flag of surrender, leaning against an outer post of my shelter, barely under the protection of the corrugated metal roof. He had his back to me. I saw buildings farther away across the flooded stretch of earth—drab buildings patched together out of tin and wood and thatch and mud, and I wondered how they ever held up under the onslaught of this sort of weather. I saw other things too, on the ground, but I didn't want to look at them.

After the lightning, darkness once more. But I could pick out Azazel's form silhouetted against the reflective sheen of the earth.

"Azazel?"

He hunched a shoulder. "And now you're following me. Come to gloat?"

"No."

"Come to beg my forgiveness?"

That was a lot closer to the mark. I said nothing, and he turned so that he could look at me. That red glow of his eyes from the shadows made me shiver. "Where have you been?" he asked.

The reek of alcoholic spirits rolled in like a wave. He had a bottle in his hand; I could make out its outline as my eyes adjusted to the night, and I could hear the slurring of his words.

"Are you drunk?" I asked, quietly appalled.

"You going to tell me off?"

"No. I just…didn't know angels could get drunk, that's all."

"And you're *such* an expert on angels," he said sourly.

I bowed my head, stung.

"Where've you been? Where are you, Milja, when you're awake?"

"Don't you know?"

He bristled. "I'm not omniscient!"

"But I'm on holy ground. It's a monastery."

"And I told you before: I have no connection with the Christ-cult."

I frowned. "But I thought…holy ground is public domain. I mean— that's what Uriel said. He said you could overhear everything said on holy ground."

"Uriel?" He snorted, and took a swallow from the bottle. "That's what that kiss-ass told you?"

I nodded.

"Uriel has made few friends, in his position. If he was worried about being overheard, I suspect it wasn't by me."

Unease pricked my insides. "His position?"

"Uh-huh."

"What's that, exactly?"

Azazel waved the bottle. "He's the Accuser. The Adversary." He peered at me as if trying to read my reaction, and shook his head. "Well, last time

180

I knew him, anyway. His job is to uncover dissension within the Court of Heaven. Secrets and sins among the Sons of God. He sets traps. Keeps us on the straight and narrow." He hunted for words. "Like an internal police force, you know?"

"No, I didn't know." I'd found Uriel arrogant, snobbish, vain—but quite humorous, in his way. He made me nervous, but I hadn't really disliked him.

"Well stay out of his way. If he can think of a way to get at me through you, he'll do it."

Too late, I thought. *Way too late.* I'd played right into Uriel's hands, I was starting to suspect.

"Unless that's what you want," Azazel added grimly.

"What do you mean?"

"You want me locked up again?"

"No! Azazel, no!"

For a moment his prickly, defensive stance held, and then he relaxed a little. "Then what do you want, Milja?" he asked.

I want you to save me. The words sat on my tongue, and I could neither spit them out nor swallow them down. "If Uriel came up against you, what would happen?" I asked, deflecting the question.

He shrugged with drunken over-expressiveness. "He's an archangel, but no warrior. It's all yap yap yap with him. I could take him apart."

"Good," I whispered. But what if Egan was right in his boast? What if there was a way to trap one of the Fallen?

I moved toward him. "Azazel, do you know what *vidimus* means?"

"In what language?"

"Latin?"

"*We have seen.*"

Of course, I thought. I had, after all, heard those words before. "But what does that mean? What is it?"

"It's an old word for a sketch-plan for a stained-glass window. Why do you ask?"

I wasn't sure. But the phrase had occurred and recurred in my dreams long before Egan spoke the words out loud. Something about it creeped me out.

"Just something someone said," I answered weakly. If Azazel didn't know about Egan or how he'd betrayed me, I didn't want to tell. My shame was too bitter, and Azazel would only laugh at me. It was better he didn't know.

Lightning went off like a flashgun. It lit Azazel's tall form—all angles now, all lines of starvation, his eyes pits, his collarbone stark above the bloodied line of his top. It lit the miserable little village. It lit the things sprawled in the puddles. I cringed.

"What is this place? What happened here, Azazel?"

"It's a bear village."

"A what?"

"A bear village. They go out into the forest around here and they catch bears. Black ones with a white blaze on their chests. They bring the bears back and they put them in cages, really tiny cages where they can't turn round or stand up or anything, and they stick an open tap through a puncture-wound in the walls of their bellies, into the gall bladder, and they harvest the bile, drip by drip. For fake medicine." His sullen growl shifted to an almost childish delight. "I set the bears free. They were hungry. I told them they could kill anybody they liked." He looked around us, tipsily bemused. "What a mess."

"Oh Christ."

"One more time: nothing to do with him."

"Azazel...these were poor people. Families. Just trying to make a living."

That produced a derisive snort. "I really don't care."

I chewed my lip. "Other people will catch the bears before they get far enough away. They'll all be shot or put back in the cages."

"I don't care about that either."

"That's not true," I said, very gently. "You couldn't stand to see them caged and in pain."

He considered this. "Then I'll do it again," he announced. "And again. Until all the bears are free or dead." He smiled, with a wild mirthless satisfaction.

"Is dead better?"

"Better than the cages."

I reached out and touched the back of his wrist, just the merest brush of fingertips. "Do you understand why I couldn't leave Egan, then?"

He looked down at my hand. His voice cracked when he spoke next. "What do you want, Milja?"

"I want to say sorry. I didn't mean to hurt you."

He touched me gently on the cheek, his fingertips cold. Lightning flickered again, a long-drawn-out stutter. I could see the new gray in his hair, the shadows of exhaustion around his eyes. "Milja..."

I could not do it to him. I could not throw myself on his forgiveness and beg his help and draw him into whatever trap awaited. I didn't know what Father Velimir and Egan were plotting—for all I knew Egan might be lying to the priest just as he'd lied to me—but I could not risk that. I couldn't see Azazel trapped again, not for my sake.

"That's all," I whispered. "I understand now. I'm so sorry. I shouldn't have said those things. Now I have to go."

"Go?" He drew himself up taller. "You came back. I...can forgive."

"I'm not staying. No. Find yourself a nice girl, Azazel," I said quickly, before my resolve could weaken. "Be gentle with her. Let her grow to love you."

He grimaced, bewildered.

"Just don't get her pregnant though—they'll use that against you."

His fingertips traced the lines of my face, like he was blind and trying to see me. "Why aren't you like the other women, Milja?"

"What do you mean?"

"They were all proud to be with me. Proud to be loved by a Son of Heaven. How is it that I'm not good enough for you?"

I shook my head gently, though inside I could feel my heart tearing itself to shreds. "You'll find someone like that," I promised. "Plenty of women would..." I'd been about to say *sell their souls for a guy like you,* but it seemed a really unfortunate choice of words. "Just not me," I finished; "so you must stay away."

He lowered over me, washing me in alcohol fumes and broken dreams.

Don't kiss me, I prayed. *Please don't kiss me. If you do I will break, I will not be able to hold back, I will give up to you. And you will take charge and come to my rescue, because that is what you are like—and then they will have you, because that is what they have planned all along. Everything for them depends on us being lovers. I am your weak link. I am your Achilles' heel.*

"I could be better, if I tried," he offered uncertainly. "All I need is for you to love me, Milja."

That nearly killed me.

"No, no," I said, my voice hoarse. "You're an angel. Don't stoop like that. We're just apes, remember?"

"You are creatures of infinite wonder. You are climbing to the stars. We…only fell."

"You didn't fall; you jumped. Don't you forget that." I hardened my voice. "Fight your way back, Azazel—don't just stand in the rain having a pity party. You look pathetic."

His hand recoiled. Red light flared in his eyes.

"That's…cold, Milja."

I hated myself. "It's the truth."

"You will kill me."

And that was true too, if Uriel's words could be trusted at all. It was, quite literally, Azazel's fatal weakness: he needed to be loved.

"They will bury you again," I said through gritted teeth, "unless you stop feeling sorry for yourself. And if you need someone to love you, then *go earn it*. You're no more entitled than anyone else."

Lightning flashed, filling my vision with his bleached-out face, beautiful and ravaged. Then darkness returned, and when I blinked away the blooms of color in my eyes he was gone, and only the fallen bottle lay at my feet, spilling its contents to mingle with the rain.

I woke up in my cell, my socks wet with mud.

On the fifth day, at six in the evening, my guard of the day brought me in a bucket of water to wash myself, and a clean dress.

"Make yourself look respectable." His name was Ratko, which suited him better in English than in Montenegrin, where it meant "happy."

I stared at these offerings and rattled my handcuff meaningfully against the pipe. With my right hand tethered, getting changed was impossible.

"Fair enough," he said, and came to unlock me. But the moment I was free he took out his gun and pointed it at my face. "No tricks," he said, as he retreated a few steps.

"You can't shoot me," I countered. "Father Velimir needs me."

The muzzle of the handgun dipped to a different angle. "He doesn't need your pussy."

I clenched my jaw, outmaneuvered.

"Get on with it, girly."

It made me feel like my stomach was full of barbed wire, but I obeyed, glaring. Getting undressed in front of this wiry, hard-faced man was nothing like being stripped in public by Azazel, in my dreams. It wasn't titillating. It wasn't even shameful, to be honest. It wasn't sexual at all, not from my end of things, though his smirk certainly suggested that he was finding some entertainment in the exposure of my grubby flesh. I just felt cold and vulnerable and angry.

I washed as quickly as I could and pulled the dress on over my still-damp skin, leaving my unbearable underwear on the floor. At least the dress, though faded, was clean—though it was the sort of sack-like floral smock a middle-aged woman might have picked, and I'd not normally have been seen dead in such a thing.

Once I was dressed my guard locked me up again and took away the key. He made sure to lean against me in the process, breathing hard, though he didn't quite get as far as groping.

I pictured Azazel's hand around his throat, squeezing.

Half an hour later, Egan entered the cell.

That took me by surprise. I stood up from my mattress, inhaling deeply as if it could fill me with words, my heart flip-flopping over. He looked better than the last time I'd seen him. At least they'd given him a black clerical shirt and let him clean himself up, and the bruises were fading. But his mouth was compressed to a thin line and his shoulders were tense.

His eyes were all sorts of blue with pain.

Standing there in my thin flower-sprigged smock, I found myself starting to shake. All those vitriolic monologues I'd rehearsed in my head whilst alone—they were still there somewhere inside me, but filed away. I wasn't ready for him, weirdly. Some stupid part of me still wanted to throw my arms round his neck.

"You knew," was all I managed to blurt. "You knew *all the time*."

Egan opened his mouth, hesitated, and then nodded. "Yes. Some of it."

His admission was like lemon juice poured on a wound—the harm was already done and known, but the fresh pain was out of all proportion. It seemed to run right through me. I wiped at my face, looking away, momentarily speechless.

"Milja, we're going outside now, and it's really importan—"

"How long? I mean—from the beginning? You were following me when I flew here?" It wasn't coming out the way I'd imagined.

"We, um…you'd been watched. Your family. A long time. I mean, centuries. We knew there was something there. We just didn't know what…who. You came to the States, and we watched. When you suddenly headed home…"

The familiar soothing confidence had gone out of him. He was all hesitation now, picking his words like they were steps through a minefield.

"You were sent to take me?" My voice was raspy.

"To keep watch. To find out," Egan said, not meeting my eyes. "To act…if necessary." He was ashamed, I realized. That, oddly enough, gave me fire.

"You played me, you lying bastard," I said. "You *used* me. Dear God, Egan. I hate you more than I hate Father Velimir."

His eyes were narrowed and glistening wet. "I deserve that."

"Where were you taking me?"

"I was going to keep you safe. You're not going to believe me—"

"Too right I'm not."

"—but I was trying to help you. I have tried all along."

"Safe? Where? Rome, like he said?"

He nodded.

"You were going to hand me over? Your lot instead of this lot? Were you hoping for a sweet little Nephilim baby too? Was that your plan?"

"Milja…"

"Different shovel, same shit," I spat.

His mouth twisted. "I would never have let anyone hurt you."

I laughed at him. "Yeah, right!"

"Milja, I promise I wouldn't, I mean, you and me, we have become…I wouldn't harm you. Ever."

"Bull!" I sneered. "You would have done what you were told, just like everyone else in this setup. *Just following orders.* That's what you people do."

Egan blinked, and swallowed, and did not answer.

"I thought you were my friend," I said. It was the cruelest reproach I could think of. "I really liked you."

I had the satisfaction of seeing him wince, no more than a tic around the eyes.

"Milja," he croaked, "we have to get him, the Fallen, recaptured. The priests here are right about that. You've no idea how dangerous he—"

"No!" I rasped. If he'd been within reach I would have hit him. "Don't you dare say that! I know him better than any of you—don't you tell me what he is!"

"He's a creature of darkness," Egan soldiered on grimly. "Great evil, and immeasurable power. Don't be fooled by the way he looks. He has to be taken down. We are not meant to share the Earth with that kind."

"Can you hear yourself, Egan?" I was in despair. "Can you hear what you sound like?"

"I know this is hard for you—"

"No. You know squat. You're just so afraid of what you don't control that you'll do anything to crush it, even if means working with Velimir and these bastards. Did you hear what they were planning to do to me?"

"I heard." He moved in closer, to the edge of the mattress, fists clenched.

"And you're still working with them?"

"Milja, what I am doing right now is keeping us both alive," he rasped. "You shouldn't have come back for me—"

"You think?"

"It didn't matter that they had me. Now they have you." He blinked hard. "What choice do I have? I had to give them what I knew. So they're going to do it now. They're going to call him, and bind him. That's what we all want." His voice became stern. "And you're going to do what they tell you, Milja, because that is the only way they are letting you out of here in one piece. You *have* to cooperate. Do you hear me?"

I shook my head, my face crumpling. "This is wrong!"

"Remember, he is not a human being—not a real one. That's just the way he's chosen to look."

Oh—that's what my father said, when I was seven, that very first time.

187

"I don't care!"

"You don't have any choice. Neither of us does. If we don't go along with this then you'll never be allowed to leave this place. Is that what you want?"

Openmouthed, I shook my head.

Egan opened one fist and showed me the familiar handcuff key. "I'm going to let you out now, and take you upstairs. Please, don't do anything rash. They're watching us every step of the way. They're ready for the fight. You have to let this play out, Milja, and give them a chance to fix things the way they were."

He reached for my bound wrist, and I didn't try to stop him. My own despair was as great as his, and for a moment I even found myself wondering if he was right. Egan's hand slid over mine, wrapping my fingers up in his warm grasp, squeezing tight. The touch of his skin made me want to cry out. He was so close I could feel the heat of his body and smell the laundry powder on his borrowed shirt.

Gently, he fitted the key into the little lock. I swayed, my footing uncertain on the sprung mattress. With a click the steel slid open and fell away. Suddenly he abandoned the handcuff key and reached to touch my hair instead, clasping the back of my head, bending his own so that our foreheads met.

I should have been relieved that I was no longer chained, that they couldn't fry me with the flick of a switch. But the only thing in my mind was Egan, the smell and the feel of him and the promise of his touch. In the middle of all my rage and pain, some part of me wanted him to fix it all—to say the magic words, or to do some unimaginable thing that would change and justify everything. I wanted it all to be revealed as a terrible misunderstanding.

I wanted him to be right.

"Milja, please, don't think about him," he whispered; "just concentrate on staying safe." He took my freed hand and pressed it to his breastbone. Under the shirt I could feel the swift hard pounding of his heart. "If you're hurt then it's all for nothing. You should not have come back."

I couldn't answer. I couldn't think. The scent and the heat and the solidity of him made my head swim. My heart ached, its rhythm matching his.

"I've messed this up so badly. I shouldn't have let..." He cut himself off.

"Let what?" I whispered. His blond scruff was almost a beard now, scratchy against my skin as he pressed his lips to my temple. The hand not occupied holding mine to his chest was tracing the fall of my hair, and his thumb sought the curve of my cheek.

"I'm so sorry, Milja. None of this is fair—and none of it is your fault, I know that. I just wish things could have been different."

You cannot do this to me, I thought faintly. *You cannot betray me and ask forgiveness. You can't use me to entrap my lover. You can't be my enemy and my only hope.*

But the priests had made a good choice sending Egan in to free me. When he murmured, "Come on," and he put an arm round my shoulders and drew me toward the cell door, I went docilely. It was a strange thing, maybe, that I would argue and argue with Azazel, but I couldn't bring myself to fight Egan. Or maybe I was just too worn out by that stage.

Outside in the corridor they were waiting for us—many men: priests and monks and laymen in rough clothes. It was hard to imagine why such an entourage was necessary—there were too many for me, I thought, and not enough for Azazel. Three of the burliest priests carried filigreed silver caskets before them with an air of solemnity. The boxes didn't match, though they were roughly of a size—a little over a foot long.

Ratko trained his gun on us the moment I opened the door.

"Ah, Milja," said Father Velimir, who had reverted to his usual mild, implacable gravity. He even gestured me politely to walk beside him, as if I were some visiting European royal come to look round his monastery. "This way."

But they put Egan to the front of us in the procession, an armed man at his shoulder. The threat was still there, just unspoken.

Should it still work? I wondered, as we walked in silence through the halls and passages of the complex. Should I care what happened to Egan now? I'd come back to save him, but he had turned out to be not worth saving. At least, that was how I ought to see it, if only I could be hard-headed and not confused by leftover feelings that refused to go away.

What options were left for me? I'd told Azazel to go away and forget me. That was the only way to be sure of his safety. If I let them use me

189

in whatever ceremony it was they had planned, would it work? I wasn't cocky enough to think they couldn't make me cooperate—they'd shown every willingness to hurt me. But would Azazel even bother to answer my summons?

And if he did, was there anything the priests could really do to bind him? Egan had promised, but Egan wasn't to be trusted. He'd demonstrated that clearly enough. He had his own masters, his own agenda. Was he lying to the priests now? Was he just playing for time?

Yet despite everything, I couldn't bring myself to want them to hurt Egan, any more than I wanted them to recapture Azazel.

My thoughts went round and round in circles as we climbed stairs and came out, eventually, into a long passageway with shutterless windows to either side. This was a very old bit of the monastery, I realized, glancing at the unplastered stonework and the rough and broken tiles beneath our feet. We were walking the length of a wall. The windows to the right seemed to overlook the main courtyard of the building complex, several stories below. The ones to the left looked out into sunshine and at a rough hillside across a great gap. The ravine was on that side. The ravine and the shallow stony river I could hear very faintly.

Unconsecrated ground.

I thought of the ghost-girl flinging herself from the tower window to escape the unseen soldiers. An act of utter desperation, and yet of courage.

A piebald cat slunk in the angle between floor and wall, beneath the windows, staring up at the procession of priests. It looked at me with green eyes and mewed.

Maybe, I thought, the priests were right. Maybe I was turning into a witch or a siren or whatever it was they called me. Maybe that accounted for the besotted cats and the terrified dogs, for my inability to cry real tears, for the ghosts and the campsite visions and the prophetic dreams—and even the traffic lights changing when we needed them to. Maybe I could do something after all.

Something will happen, I willed, clenching my jaw. *Something will happen to distract them all. Something, something, yes, it will.*

One of the priests at the front of the group stumbled. I didn't see what tripped him—a monastery cat perhaps, or just a broken floor tile catching his sandal-toe. But he fell, and the heavy silver casket he carried slipped out of his hands and crashed to the ground.

Everyone gasped in horror. For a moment, all eyes were on the fallen man and the box.

That was my moment. As if in a dream, I slipped away from Father Velimir and darted for the window to my left. Everyone else seemed to be moving in slow motion. The crumbling sill was an easy leap and scramble. The late afternoon sun was in my eyes, blinding me.

Whatever happens, Azazel will be free, I thought.

I jumped out into the empty air, screwing my eyes shut.

"Azazel!" I screamed, as I fell. It was pure terror.

The fall went on and on and on.

Then there was a tearing noise, a wind in my face, and suddenly hands caught me, bruisingly hard. All the air rushed out of my lungs. I fought for breath as the sun dazzled my eyes and I came to terms with the fact I wasn't dead, wasn't falling, wasn't smashed across a rocky hillside. I was held safe in two strong arms, clasped against a hard male body.

My borrowed dress was rucked up to my waist.

"Azazel!" I gasped in relief, lifting my head from his chest as he set my feet down upon solid ground. I didn't care about my bare ass.

But it wasn't Azazel.

It was Uriel.

chapter fourteen

WE HAVE SEEN

I pushed against his chest, getting to arm's length but no farther: one hand was hard on my shoulder.

My skirt slid down to hide my legs again. I think we were both grateful for that trivial mercy.

"Uh-uh-uh," the archangel admonished, wagging a finger in front of my nose. "You don't get out of this that easily."

My mouth hung open. For a moment I had no idea what to say. I looked desperately around me, and then up. The monastery wall towered overhead. We were standing on a tiny lip of ground where cut stone joined to the earth of the cliff face, and a narrow goat path ran along the boundary. To my left, so close that I was practically leaning against it, loomed the ancient ecclesiastical stonework. To my right the ravine fell away in a jumble of savage rocks down to the river. One step separated the two—one step, and Uriel's hand grasping tight my upper arm. My legs folded under me and I staggered—but he held me upright, sighing in exasperation.

"Get a grip on yourself, girl."

I hung my head and dry-retched. It was the shock—the leap, the survival, the dashing of hope—but Uriel grimaced and spun me to face away from him. "What does the Scapegoat see in you?" he complained.

"What are *you* doing here?" I asked weakly. He was dressed as a priest, and the somber garb suited his refined face very well.

"Making sure that everything goes according to plan."

"What plan?"

"The only Plan that matters."

Shouted words tumbled down the wall onto our heads. The priests of my entourage were leaning out of the passage window, staring down at us. I could see Father Velimir's white hair blowing around his head, far overhead.

"She's all right!" Uriel called up. "I caught her!" He shook me slightly to demonstrate that I was still in one piece.

How the hell anyone could believe I'd fallen forty or fifty feet through clear air and been snatched to safety by a random passerby was beyond me, but I guess they accepted the evidence of their own eyes.

More shouting. Arms were waved.

I shut my eyes.

"Walk," Uriel instructed, with a push that woke me from my stupor. He set me going before him along the goat path, the fingers of one hand resting on my shoulder as we walked, to remind me that there was no escape. The path, hardly wider than our feet, sloped upward. We were heading upriver and up the valley, I realized, toward the back of the monastery and away from the gate and the road. Where the wall kinked there was a tiny sally-port, and I guessed we were aiming for that.

"You want them to recapture Azazel?" I asked.

"Of course. The Divine Order must be restored."

"It's not going to work."

"Really?"

"Their plan...whatever it is."

"Hmph. Don't be too confident. A bunch of pathetic amateurs, relatively speaking, but they somehow seem to be getting their act together now."

Egan, I thought, bitterly. *He's instructed them.* For a while I bit the inside of my lip and kept silent. Then I tried again. "Azazel"—I spoke the name clearly and deliberately now, for this might be the last few moments it would do me any good—"won't come when I call. He'll see it's a trap— he's not stupid."

"Oh, that's where you're wrong, Milja. He was the Serpent's right arm—the muscle: never the brains of the bunch. That first time, when Raphael was sent to take him down, he could have run. He could have warned Samyaza and all the others. They could have regrouped and stood against us. They were outnumbered two to one, certainly, but oh, it would have been a real battle. Instead…your idiot boyfriend went looking for his bastard children all on his own, and Raphael was waiting for him."

"That's not idiocy. That's what a father would do."

"Sentiment, then. Call it what you like, it's a weakness. Without their general the Egrigoroi were doomed. We trussed them like sheep."

"*We?*" I sniped. "According to the *Book of Enoch*, the only thing you were entrusted with was warning Noah to build a big boat. Not exactly heroic."

Uriel grabbed the plait of hair at the nape of my neck and jerked me to a halt, slamming me back against his torso and pulling my head back. "Don't be rude, monkey-girl," he said softly in my ear. "I am the Light of God. I am the power that stands before the throne of fire and crystal, my feet upon the paths of lightning, the stars at my right hand and my left."

Despite the painful stretch of my throat a harsh wild laugh burst from me.

"What?" he demanded. "What's funny?"

Archangel or not, didn't he see how sexual this looked, the way he was holding me? "They're all watching you from up there, Light of God, and your hard-on's jabbing my ass."

Uriel thrust me away like I was poison—so recklessly in fact, that I stumbled and nearly slid sideways off the precarious little path. He caught the back of my dress to stop me falling, and the seam under my arm split. I had to push myself upright with my hands on the walls.

I risked a look at his face. His eyes were narrowed and he was pale with anger.

"You've got a real problem with the human form, haven't you?" I muttered through the dust coating my tongue.

"Not for much longer. Believe me, by nightfall this will all be over."

"And God will pat you on the head and tell you what a good boy you've been?"

He lifted his head. "Get walking."

"Azazel said you were a kiss-ass," I muttered.

"Azazel is nothing but a penis on legs. Azazel can say what he likes with his mouth full of sand and blood and a thousand tons of rock sat on his head for the rest of eternity."

His urbane gentility had slipped somewhat, I thought. *"Blessed are the merciful,"* I quoted sourly, *"for they will obtain mercy."*

Uriel smiled a thin smile, and pointed up the track. *"Blessed are they that mourn.* Remember that tomorrow, Milja, and count those blessings. Now walk."

When we reached the little postern gate it was already open for us, held by a breathless priest. I stepped through into the tiny courtyard beyond and Uriel gave me a hard shove between my shoulders, sending me to my knees on the flagstones. From the scrum of black-clad figures filling the space, someone pushed forward and grabbed me.

"Are you okay, Milja? Are you hurt?"

It was Egan. He looked sick and angry. Well, at least they hadn't shot him for my disobedience.

"I'm all right," I said dizzily, as he pulled me to my feet, his arms around me, and glared at Uriel.

"Get off her!" The guard with the gun was right at his shoulder, and reaching for him.

"Leave them, Ratko," said Father Velimir grimly. "Let his blood be on her, and hers upon him, if either should fail us again." He looked at Uriel, frowning. "Father...? What happened?"

Uriel bowed, addressed him as "Holy Father," and the two men began to talk. Part of me was really curious about how Uriel was going to explain his presence away, but Egan wasn't going to give me peace to listen.

"For feck's sake," he demanded of me, "what did you go and do that for!"

"I know, it was stupid," I said with a curl of my lip. "Suicide being a sin, and all." I straightened my dress and looked arch. "And I was doing so well otherwise."

He blinked like I'd slapped him, but he didn't let go. "That's not the way out of this!" he insisted.

"It was looking like a top option."

"You have to stay safe!"

"Yeah well, you would say that—all you care about is recapturing Azazel."

His mouth twisted. "That's just not true, Milja."

I wished I believed him. But it was far too late for that. I shook my head. "Well, it doesn't really matter what you want, does it? You're not in charge. You're not even their expert demon-catcher anymore." I jerked my head at Uriel. "He is."

"Who's he?"

Uriel heard us, looked round and lifted an eyebrow. "Just a mendicant," he said, in English. "One who has seen...more than you have."

Egan stared, his mouth compressing to a thin line.

"We will proceed," announced Father Velimir, looking annoyed that he was no longer the focus of attention. He waved his hand and the procession rearranged itself, Egan and I getting shoved toward the front. My would-be protector held onto my arm as we climbed a flight of steps.

"Your man there—who is he?" he asked in a low voice.

"He's an angel of the Lord." I didn't care if he believed me anymore.

"Say again?"

"An angel. He caught me in midair."

Egan gave me a wide-eyed look, but only moistened his dry lips.

"Swap you. What's in the silver boxes that's so important?"

"Relics." He twisted to look back at Uriel, like a man in a nightclub who'd been told there was someone famous by the bar. Doubtless all the priests would have reacted the same way, if it wasn't for the fact we were conversing in English. "Nails from the True Cross. Gathered by St. Helena in Constantinople. Scattered across the churches of the Eastern Patriarchy."

I felt a wash of relief as the information sank in. "They won't work," I said, actually blushing with heat, too thrilled to consider whether I should keep the information to myself. "I've seen him, Egan. I've seen Azazel walk happily on consecrated ground. He's not scared of the Church. He lived thousands of years before the Incarnation."

"They'll work."

"They won't! He told me, Christ is nothing to him one way or another!"

"They will work." The emotion in his voice was not stubbornness, nor even ironclad certainty. It sounded, if anything, like despair. I felt the hairs rise on my neck. As the head of our procession reached the shadowed cloister at the top of the stairs and we stopped to await Father Velimir, I turned to look Egan in the face, bristling.

The expression there…

My skin crawled.

I saw despair. I saw knowing. I saw receding depths of horror, as if his eyes were pits down into places of darkness and loneliness that I could not imagine.

If I were a painter, I thought, Egan's face would be how I depicted Judas.

"You've seen them in action, have you?" I meant to sound biting and sarcastic, but my voice shook.

"Yes," he said softly. "We have seen."

"Take your places, everyone," Father Velimir commanded, puffing a little at the top of the stairs. He was, after all, an elderly man. The group fanned out, and I obeyed as my guard Ratko directed me, jerking the muzzle of his gun for emphasis.

We were in an enclosed courtyard or cloister, not terribly large, and rather old by the looks of things. It was stonework not brick that towered on all four sides, cutting out all but a square of the evening sky overhead, and the pillars around the portico on every side were carved of single pieces of stone. They put me out in the middle of the open space, and I watched the priests arranging themselves around the perimeter. There were several cats scooting about underfoot here too, but everyone ignored them. Father Ilija of the red beard had one of the boxes, I noticed, and so did familiar Badger-Beard, as well as another bulky, strong-looking priest. They laid them down at their feet and opened the caskets. Then Father Velimir went round from box to box, praying and swinging an incense holder over what lay within. The sound of bells and chanting was like a summons from my childhood.

"This is the oldest part of the complex," Uriel said, appearing at my left shoulder and making me jump slightly. "Thirteenth Century, some of the lower chambers."

Egan, still holding my right arm, gave him a hard stare and then looked away abashed.

197

"They've emptied all the rooms now," Uriel continued serenely, "and walled up all the exterior windows. When this is done today they'll back-fill the whole thing with crushed gravel and sand, and slab over the roof. No one will come near your master ever again."

I imagined Azazel pressed under the tons and tons of stone, unable to twitch even a finger, blind and breathless, sand scouring his eyeballs, his bones and teeth splintered by the pressure. *He will die*, I thought, feeling nauseated. *Eventually. If he has no one to sustain him. But maybe that's better than the alternative.*

A dirty ginger tom trotted up and began to twine round my ankles, staring like I was going to feed it caviar.

"Explain to me again," I said through gritted teeth: "You're the *good guys?*"

"Of course," answered Uriel. "*Fear God and keep His commandments, for this is the whole duty of man.*"

"Ecclesiastes 11," said Egan, with a sideways glance. Clearly he didn't like being left out of the conversation. Maybe, I thought, he'd like me to introduce him. *Uriel, this is Egan Kansky, Vatican spy. Egan, this is the Archangel Uriel.*

"Why are you lot always quoting the Old Testament?" I asked bitterly. "Did you never read past that part? Why is it never *Love your enemies?*"

"Me, I'm strictly old-school," said Uriel. He put a hand on my shoulder. "But you want something from the New Testament? How about—*For He hath judged the great whore, which did corrupt the earth with her fornication, and hath avenged the blood of His servants at her hand.*"

My mouth sagged.

"The Book of Revelation," he added helpfully, before letting drop the afterthought; "Although, to be fair, that scrawny ape John was out of his head on fly agaric when he had his vision."

"And you're quoting somewhat out of context," Egan said in an icy voice.

Uriel switched his full attention to the Irishman for the first time, and smiled benignly at him over my head. "You like her, I can tell." His eyes shone with disingenuous warmth. "Take my advice: don't waste your time. You're never going to live up to a Son of God in the sack."

Egan's whole frame stiffened, and I heard the intake of his breath.

I was almost relieved that Father Velimir chose that moment to turn round, raise his arms and announce, "Let us begin."

Father Badger-Beard started to sing, and one by one the men around us joined in. If there's one thing Orthodox priests can do, it's sing, and the stone walls threw back the intertwined tones of their slow, magisterial chant. Those deep sweet notes took me back instantly to my father's church, to the hymns of the Divine Liturgy, and I felt the hair stir on my neck.

Spinning from heel to heel, Uriel backed off toward the perimeter cloister. "God bless," he mouthed to us in a stage whisper, and I swear he dropped a wink.

I'd really like to see Azazel punch him one, I realized.

My armed guard was right behind me. "You," said Ratko to Egan. "Hands behind your head."

Scowling, Egan complied. His raised elbows made points like the tips of folded wings. "Milja, just get this over with quick," he told me in a low voice.

You think it's going to be quick, burying him alive? I wanted to ask. But I turned my gaze away.

The cat fawning at my feet yowled. With an irritated grunt, Ratko booted it clear across the courtyard. I watched, sickened, as it hit the flagstones and lay spasming, its ribs staved in.

"You bastard," Egan said softly.

I'm not sure that Ratko understood the English phrase, but he certainly recognized the tone of voice. "I'll do it to you if you don't shut up," he said in Montenegrin.

"Egan, be quiet," I whispered, shaking.

"Milja," called Father Velimir. "This is your chance. Take a step away from the darkness, toward the light. In the name of the Father, the Son, the Holy Spirit—call the Fallen One here to face his just punishment."

I wiped my sweating hands against my thighs. "No," I said. Not with any hope of truly defying him, but simply because it had to be said, at least once.

Father Velimir nodded, very slightly. I thought it was at me. But it was at Ratko. Without any fuss he caught up my left hand in his, lifting it. The movement was so casual, so gentle, that at first I wondered what he was doing. I actually saw him bend my little finger back before the strain registered.

"No!" I squeaked. He twisted my wrist and the pain shot from my finger-joint up my forearm all the way to my elbow, like molten metal running through my bones. My mouth fell open.

"For God's sake!" Egan protested—but Ratko's gun-hand shot out. Without letting go of me, he clubbed Egan casually across the side of the head with the barrel, sending him staggering.

I cried out.

Egan fell to one knee. Ratko pulled me round, twisting my hand up behind my back, to face the man I'd given myself up for. He snuggled into me from behind, his breath noisy in my ear, his gun-arm hooked over my right shoulder so he could accidentally press his pistol against my breasts.

The pain in my arm was excruciating.

"Milja," said Father Velimir sadly. "Call him."

I screamed.

I felt my finger-bone snap. The pain filled my world.

"Azazel!" I shrieked, when I could shape my cry into words. "Azazel!"

For a while I was so blinded by agony that I didn't know what was happening. When the world stopped flashing red and white enough long enough for me to make out figures through the haze, I saw Father Velimir looking from side to side. Ratko had let go of my hand and transferred his grip to the scruff of my neck, holding me at arm's length so that his could point the gun left and right in turn. Everyone was looking round.

There was no sign of Azazel.

I knew then that he'd given up on me. My demon lover had abandoned me. Just like I'd told him to.

A part of me was relieved, despite everything.

In the middle of my dry sobs, I looked at Egan, who knelt with one hand to his temple where he'd been struck, looking like he was trying not to keel over.

"I can't," I rasped. "I told you, didn't I? He won't come."

"Milja?" Father Velimir sounded hurt, like I had disappointed him deeply.

"He's not coming!"

"That's not good enough, Milja."

"He's not coming. I can't make him. He doesn't want me anymore."

"Try again."

Ratko pulled me back into his embrace, his crotch pressed against me from behind, his arm over my shoulder again. My broken hand wasn't involved this time round, allowing me to clutch it to my abdomen. But the muzzle of his gun was pointed straight at Egan's head.

"Try harder," he suggested.

"I can't make him come!" I panted. I could feel his disgusting hard-on digging into me. I was looking right down the length of his arm into Egan's face. At point blank range my Judas had no chance of survival.

He'd betrayed me, and now he was on his knees at my feet. He was looking up at me with eyes swimming with pain, but there was no fear there. His face was oddly calm.

"Milja," he whispered. His mouth moved in a sad smile.

Ratko's finger curled around the trigger, slowly.

"Azazel, please help me," I moaned, and I meant it with all my heart.

The sun went behind the mountain then, and shadows deepened. There was a moment in which the whole courtyard held its breath. Ratko spun me, scanning the perimeter.

No. He's gone for good.

"You are wasting our time," Father Velimir announced. "Ratko, finish him."

The gun will not fire, I told myself as the black metal pointed back at Egan. *The gun will not fire. The gun will not fire.*

Ratko pulled the trigger.

The gun went *click.*

Sweat was running off me under my dress. *The gun will not fire.*

Click. Click.

"Shit," Ratko said, in consternation. He dropped me, turned away, worked the mechanism to eject the magazine and slapped it back into place.

The weapon went off with a roar. I saw the puff of sand as the bullet ricocheted off the stone floor and then it *spanged* off the stonework somewhere behind my head. Even Ratko flinched. Then he turned back, eyes blazing.

But by that time I had my arms wrapped around Egan's neck.

I don't even remember making that decision.

Snorting, Ratko started to circle us, trying to get a clear line on Egan—but I twisted too, keeping myself in the way. *You can't shoot me, you bastard: you need me.* And as Ratko hesitated, one of the priests cried out in terror.

We all turned.

It was the dying cat. Dying, or more likely dead—in fact I really hope it was dead, though it was still moving. It had split in half down its belly: a line like a razor slash from which red light was pouring out in a fan shape. And through that tiny, impossible slit, the whole of Azazel's towering frame heaved forth like a rumple-winged butterfly shouldering its way from a chrysalis.

"Azazel!" I howled. "It's a trap!"

Azazel lifted his head, looked at me and smiled. It was an expression that made my bowels cramp with fear.

He looked terrible. Worse than the day I'd freed him from beneath the mountain, by some margin; his hair was grizzled, his face gaunt, his eyes sunken in orbits blue as bruises. As he straightened up he held himself awkwardly as if everything ached, and even his clothes looked ragged. It hurt me just to look at him. Some strange part of me, through the fog of pain and terror, was wailing *Why didn't he listen to what I told him?*

But dishevelment and exhaustion didn't make him look any less threatening. The light in his sunken eyes was red. Darkness lurked in each crease and shadow of his form. And as we stared, from the empty air he unsheathed a sword of fire—a blade of living, flickering flame that made the air around it ripple with heat.

The men with guns—there was at least one other apart from Ratko, though in that confused space the most I was aware of was the bang of the shots—opened fire. It achieved precisely nothing, as far as I could tell. Azazel didn't bother catching the bullets this time; he just ignored them. His glance moved contemptuously over the men all around, and then he started toward me.

Shadows streamed from him with every step, smoking the air.

He looked like the Angel of Death.

Ratko, only a couple of paces from me, reacted remarkably calmly, considering—in his position I'd surely have been wetting myself. Firing carefully and methodically, he stooped and grabbed me up, his hand biting into my arm hard enough to quell any question of resistance. He jerked me in front of him as if I were a shield.

Azazel didn't even slow.

Not until Ratko put the gun to my head, anyway.

Azazel stopped, sword half-lifted. Overhead, thunder rumbled from a clear sky. Behind his looming angular form men were milling about for position, as irrelevant as mice so far as he was concerned. I glimpsed red-bearded Father Ilija scooting forward from the cloister shadows, his hand raised.

Something in it.

"Bet you're not faster than a bullet," Ratko warned, backing us both away.

"Behind you!" I cried.

Azazel ignored me. "Put her down," he told Ratko, "and I will not make your loved ones pick your balls out from between your broken teeth."

I'd somehow imagined a nail from the True Cross as a shiny six-inch thing like you'd buy from a hardware store. Instead it was a good foot long, thick as a man's thumb, dark, with a T-head.

"Azazel!" I screamed. "*Behind you!*"

"Fuck you," said Ratko. The muzzle of the gun was hot against my temple. "Fuck you, fuck her."

Egan hit him.

I only worked that out in retrospect. Egan, discounted and ignored, came in from the side and knocked Ratko's gun-hand up. I felt the muzzle rake my skin and then the shot went off over my head, loud enough to make my ears ring. I was flung aside and fell, looking up just in time to glimpse Egan twist Ratko's arm taut in a double-handed lock and then, with a savage economy that left me stunned, break the elbow.

Ratko screamed.

Azazel roared with rage, and the building shook.

I twisted to look that way. I saw Azazel standing with his head back, his throat stretched taut. He took one staggering step forward. Then he pitched onto his knees.

Behind him stood Father Ilija, his eyes as round as coins, a hammer raised in his fist.

Standing up between Azazel's shoulders, black against the dirty white of his sweater, was the brutal iron spike of the Holy Nail.

As I watched, Father Ilija smashed the hammer down on the nail-head one more time, driving the iron through Azazel's spine.

Chapter fifteen

THE ADVERSARY

A zazel!" I screamed.

My angel did not fall easily, or quietly. Howling, he twisted in his agony, striking backhanded behind him. The burning sword was a tear in the fabric of the world: it cut through Father Ilija as easily as it cut the air, and the priest burst into flame.

He didn't have time to run. He barely had time to shriek. He was a column of black ash and glowing cinders in less than a second. Then he was nothing—dust crumbling to the floor, and a plume of greasy black smoke.

Even the singers shut up at that point, the antiphony choked in their throats. I heard Father Ilija's hammer strike the flagstones. I heard Father Velimir scream, "Now! Now! Take him!"

Azazel, crumpled upon the ground, writhed in torment, trying to reach behind him for the iron staked through his back. Even so, it took some courage for the next priest—the bulky badger-bearded one—to run in and hammer the point of a Holy Nail through his splayed ankle. The metal went through flesh and bone and into a crack between two stones, the note of the hammer changing as it struck resistance.

The ground shook, and did not stop shaking. Overhead, the clear sky went red, dousing us with bloody light. A huge swathe of plaster fell from the portico roof, knocking two priests flat.

Azazel lashed out at Father Badger-Beard, who stumbled back barely in time to escape the tip of the sword. His priestly beard smouldered, crisping up.

"One more!" Father Velimir shrieked. "Keep singing!"

But the choir in the shadows were worried about more than keeping their places in the chorus. Plaster and chunks of stone were falling from the ancient building. Men scattered as the earth bucked beneath us. I rolled onto my knees, trying to regain my feet, just as Ratko hit the ground flat.

He and Egan had been fighting, I realized dimly. There was blood leaking out of Ratko's mouth and his wide eyes were unfocused.

Good, some part of me thought: *serves him right.*

Then Egan stepped up and pinned him with a foot on the chest. Egan had got hold of a gun—the one Ratko had held to my head, presumably—and he held it in his unbandaged hand and pointed it straight down at the fallen man.

He shot Ratko in the head, twice, with utter deliberation and perfect accuracy.

It's not like they depict it in the movies. There's a lot of blood in a human body.

If I'd been in my right mind I would have screamed, I guess. I would have probably thrown up. I would have felt *something*—something more than shock. But all I could think about was crawling away, crawling toward Azazel.

He'd stopped fighting. The sword of fire had vanished. And there was a third nail in him now—through the back of his right hand, through the stone beneath. He was pinned hand and foot, slumped on one hip, head drooping.

"Azazel!"

"Stand your ground!" Father Velimir was shouting. "We've done it! He is defeated! Stand your ground!" But pillars were splitting and great chunks of coping stone were crashing into the courtyard, and the priests were running this way and that. We knew about earthquakes in my country. We knew we should never get caught indoors during a quake. And it sure didn't *look* like victory for the forces of good: black flakes of ash were falling from a sky the color of coagulating blood, and the earth was groaning. Dirty smoke coiled up from the fallen angel's body like he was about to burst into flames.

Nobody stopped me crawling over to Azazel. Nobody wanted to be anywhere near him. He was motionless but for the heave of his chest.

"Azazel!"

He lifted his head. His eyes were red as burning coals, but it just made him look blind. The noise that came out of his throat was an animal groan.

It was all wrong, I thought. It was just so wrong. They should not be able to take something so beautiful, so powerful, and cripple it like that. I put my good hand to his cheek—and then snatched it back; his skin was hot enough to hurt. The world shook around us.

"Milja?" His voice was not human.

"Don't give up," I sobbed, as I pushed myself to my feet on the shaking ground and cast about me. My unbroken hand was stinging from Azazel's touch. I saw the claw hammer that Father Ilija had dropped when he died; the wooden handle was scorched but intact. Grabbing it up, I lurched into position at Azazel's back. His knitted jumper was melting onto his skin in crispy black holes. The head of the nail stood out between his shoulder blades.

"Milja!"

It was Egan's voice, wild and despairing. I looked across the courtyard, through the rain of ash and dust. Blood was pooling about his feet, unnoticed; his hands were at his sides—but he still had the gun in one of them. He looked as pale as a corpse.

He shot Ratko. Dear God, he just killed a man and now he will shoot me, to save the world.

"Milja, don't do it! Walk away from him! It's finished!"

My face was all twisted up with hurt. I shook my head. And I waited for him to lift the weapon and point it at me.

Egan stood motionless in the midst of chaos, his eyes imploring. Then, with a sag of his shoulders, he hefted the gun, and my heart caught in my throat.

He snapped the safety on and cast the weapon away. The expression on his face as he looked away from me was all but unbearable.

My eyes burned. But I could waste no more time. I hooked the claw of the hammer under the roughly beaten T-bar of the Roman nail, and I stomped a foot down on Azazel's back, and using my broken hand and my

207

burnt hand and all the strength of my body, I hauled as hard as I could.

It was agony. It seemed to go on forever, but maybe it was swift and smooth as far as anyone watching was concerned: time seemed to be stretching around me. Every heartbeat was a distinct thud in my breast. Heat flared up through the sole of my foot. I felt the square-shafted nail grate against bone as it slid free, inch by resentful inch: a length of forged iron as long as my forearm, crimson with the blood of angels.

Azazel screamed.

The nail swung loose and fell to the floor. I sat down hard as my legs gave way, and slumped forward, trying to see his face.

He twisted round, his hellfire eyes seeking mine.

"Azazel," I told him, "I love you. I've loved you all my life. Get up and fight." Scrabbling forward gracelessly, I pressed my lips to his.

They burned.

They burned my breath away.

I felt the air being sucked from my lungs. I felt the strength being sucked from my bones and the light from my eyes. I fell backward on the stone as the shouting and the growl of the earthquake grew faint and muffled in my ears. I saw ash hanging in midair and men standing open-mouthed, caught motionless in time just like the people in the hospital corridor, a lifetime ago. It made them look like they were singing. Maybe some of them were.

The back of my head bounced off the floor. I hardly felt it.

With his free hand, Azazel got a grip on the Holy Nail through the other palm. He pulled. I saw the sinews cord in his forearm. I saw the nail, which had somehow been driven right into the stonework itself, resist.

But Azazel was strong now. Azazel was burning. He let go of the iron and hooked one set of fingers around the other, and he pulled. If the metal would not yield, then flesh and bone would. Raging, he pulled his trapped hand upward, and pulled the broad T-head right through it.

I saw the bloodied head of the nail reappear beneath his torn palm. It must have made a hole as big as a dollar.

I smiled.

Darkness was closing in on me. *I'm passing out*, I thought, immensely relieved.

The next thing I knew there were arms around me, pulling me up into a close embrace.

"Milja?"

Azazel?

I opened my eyes—but it was Egan who cradled me to his chest. I was glad to see him unhurt. The ground was no longer shaking, but the world was red and dark and the stench of burning meat was horrible. I coughed, but there was no air to draw into my lungs, just smoke.

"Jesus Christ," said Egan in a hoarse voice, looking over my head. "He's killing them all."

I managed a turn of my head, a half glimpse. Egan wasn't lying. I didn't want to see more, so I shut my eyes. In my private darkness it took me a moment to work out what was going on, as Egan scooped me up with one arm beneath my knees and lurched to his feet.

"No," I said, but I didn't even know if it was loud enough for him to hear over my coughing. He carried me though the smoke and the screams. "No," I repeated as we reached a door in the cloister wall, and he put my feet down so he could wrestle the latch one handed. I started to struggle, pulling out of his arm. "I want to stay with him."

"Not right now you don't," he said, pushing me against the stone. "He's going crazy, Milja. Sure, let's get at least one door between us and the carnage?"

I didn't argue with that. The stinking smoke seemed to close my throat. I let Egan bundle me through the doorway into the staircase beyond. He hooked an arm round my ribs and supported me as we staggered down the flight. Now we were out of the melee, I could hear that my ears were still ringing from the gunshots. Broken stonework littered the steps. When we reached the first door—it looked vaguely familiar and I guessed we were retracing our route up to the courtyard—the collapsed lintel stone had wedged the oak shut.

"We should get outside," I said. "This building isn't safe." Talking hurt: my throat felt raw and when I put my fingertips to my mouth I could feel my lips were puffy with blisters. The hand with the broken pinkie finger felt like a balloon full of hot water.

He burnt me. He burnt me but he got free and now he's taking his revenge. He could have run. He could have taken me and run, but he'd rather kill.

My stomach roiled.

"Not that way, though."

We plunged on down the stairs, took the next door and found ourselves in the high corridor of many windows.

This was where I tried to kill myself.

Egan pressed onward, pulling me.

"Where are we going?" I asked, as my brain caught up with the situation.

"Anywhere safer than this. Your man's got a bit of a temper, you notice."

"Says *you?*"

"What does that mean?"

"*Ratko?*" I was still in shock. I mean, you'd expect stuff from a fallen angel, but...not from an ordinary guy. This couldn't be normal, could it? I mean, there've been plenty of unsavory stories about the Catholic Church over the last few years, but since when have they been employing stone cold hit men?

"He put a gun to you," Egan said grimly. "Not acceptable."

I stumbled and he pulled me closer, not slackening his pace.

"Stop." I dug my heels in, bringing us to a halt. "I'm not leaving with you. I'm not going anywhere you want to take me."

Egan turned to face me, running one hand across his head. His hair was stiff with sweat and plaster dust. "I'm not...taking you," he said, hoarse with exhaustion. "Forget that. Forget Rome. I just want to see you safe."

"Please," said another voice querulously. "Please don't leave."

We looked back down the corridor to the door we'd just come through. Father Velimir stood there. He was holding a gun—*the* gun maybe; I'd seen Egan cast it aside. The old priest didn't look comfortable with it: his hands shook as he raised the muzzle and pointed it straight at me.

And then Egan rammed into me, knocking me against the wall. The gun barked. Egan fell.

Father Velimir had the grace to look shocked at what he'd done. He even paused to cross himself. And when Azazel's hands appeared from the darkness behind him, descending upon his shoulders to lift him from his feet, Father Velimir's expression remained appropriate.

Even as he burned.

The gun broke from his ashy fingers and smacked to the ground. Black cinders kissed the stones, smoking.

Azazel stepped into the corridor, dusting off his hands, and smiled with dark satisfaction.

I couldn't look at him. I looked down instead. Egan sprawled across the floor at my feet, staring wide-eyed at the ceiling. There was a red hole in his chest, just right of his breastbone.

"Egan?" I dropped to my knees.

Blood was bubbling out of his mouth. He was trying to breathe, and not succeeding. The hole in his chest was making a wet sucking noise instead.

"Egan!" I didn't know what to do. I grabbed his face between my hands, babbling in my panic. His pupils had contracted to pinpoints. "Egan! Don't! Stop it! Stop it!" Like it was his fault. "You can't do that!"

Can't die.

Can't step in front of the bullet meant for me.

It makes no sense. We are on different sides here.

"Milja." Azazel stood over us, stinking of smoke, looming like a pillar of fire and shadow. "Is this the one you wanted me to save?"

He doesn't know. He doesn't know what Egan meant to do to me. He doesn't know Egan was working to entrap him. That the Holy Nails were his plan. Azazel doesn't know.

I nodded.

With a flick of his fingers, Azazel motioned me aside and hunkered down over Egan's supine form. I crawled backward, out of his way, shaking. Egan looked up into Azazel's face. There was no expression on either one of them that I could read. Azazel put his hand on Egan's chest.

"Be healed," he said.

There was a smell of frankincense.

I flinched as Egan convulsed and began to cough—great racking coughs that spat a spray of blood. His back arched, and then he rolled onto his side, and then with one final gory eructation a metallic blob shot out of his mouth.

211

A hand slipped around my throat, gentle as feathers.

Azazel nodded, seeming pleased with his work, as Egan, gasping, groped for the tiny object he'd just coughed up, and held it before his streaming eyes.

The bullet.

"You are whole again," Azazel said. "Everyone else here, all your enemies, they are dead now. You are safe."

Egan blinked hard, trying to focus on the angel squatting over him. I've no idea what he was feeling. Relief? Gratitude? Resentment? I'm pretty sure fear was in the mix. Wiping his mouth with the back of his hand, he nodded without speaking.

"So," said Azazel, standing. "I leave you to sort out the fine detail. We are going."

"No," said Uriel. "You're not."

Azazel looked up to see me staring at him mutely, clasped from behind in Uriel's arms, the archangel's hand round my throat. I saw the satisfaction melt from Azazel's face, leaving a cold darkness behind.

"Let her go," he whispered.

Egan grasped the new situation and began to shuffle backward across the floor, out of the firing line.

"An interesting standoff, isn't it?" said Uriel. He was holding me with my back to his chest and my carotid artery under his hand, without any roughness or cruelty, but with absolute control.

Azazel clenched and unclenched his hands, slowly. I expected him to blaze up—but he'd gone dark and still instead. "No," he said. "You have already lost this battle, Uriel. And you know it."

"I have your lover."

"What good does that do you?"

"You want her. You need her. You will do just as I command, to keep her safe."

Azazel shook his head. I could feel the hair stirring all over my scalp as an electric charge swept the room.

"Take her from me, and I will hunt you down. I swear this, Lightbringer. I will hunt you down, if I have to burn Heaven to ashes to do it."

"I'd like to see you try."

"I will find you and tear you into pieces—and I will *eat* each bloody shred. I will devour you, Uriel. No one will recall your beauty or your grace: you will be only a noisome thing lodged in my bowels, forever. But you will keep me fed, so that I won't even need her. Is that how you want to spend eternity?"

"Big words, from the last rebel left standing against the Heavenly Host," Uriel said, but I was close enough to him to feel the quiver of his breath as he spoke.

Azazel snorted. "You have no host. If you were able to call upon backup, you'd have done it long before now—and not had to rely on some mob of witless humans." He shook his head, a sneer twisting his lips. "You've finally dicked them all off, haven't you, Satan? Not one of them's prepared to help you out, are they? Not Raphael. Not even Gabriel."

"Satan?" I squeaked through my constricted throat. I was so shocked I forgot to keep quiet. "Uriel—Satan?"

Azazel frowned, distracted. "I already told you," he growled. "The Archangel Uriel—the *Adversary*. Satan."

Uriel's lips brushed my ear.

"*I. Never. Fell.*" He strung each whispered word like a bead on a wire. "Think about that, Milja."

Then he stepped away, his hands slipping from me so gently that it was almost a caress. I staggered sideways to a wall, grabbing at the stonework, setting my back against the strong, simple, unchanging rock as I looked from face to face. Azazel, dark and smoldering with menace. Uriel, silver and wry and just a little wary. Egan, blood-spattered and wide-eyed.

Uriel raised his hands. "You've got her. For now."

"Come here," Azazel ordered me.

"No, Milja." To my surprise, it was Egan who spoke. He was trying to push himself to his feet, and he looked pale with shock still, but I couldn't fault him for lack of courage. "Please. You don't have to do what he tells you."

Azazel raised an eyebrow.

Uriel folded his arms and looked impressed by this ape-man's bid at suicide.

"You have a choice," Egan persisted. "You're a human being."

I hesitated.

"Does she have a choice?" Uriel asked Azazel, whose mouth was thinning into a line of displeasure.

Do I?

"You want to go with me," Azazel told me, as if it were an axiomatic truth.

I do... But still I hesitated.

Egan spread a bandaged hand—bandaged, but no longer hurt. "He cannot love you. He's not human. He is cut off from the grace of God, and there's no true love left in him. Just darkness and lust and a need for dominion."

I swallowed. "He came to save me." *When he was weak, and dying, and I'd told him I did not want him. He risked everything. He risked eternity.* "He saved my life."

"Well, we've all done that," said Uriel dryly. "We're practically on a roster."

"Milja," growled Azazel. My hair was crackling with static.

"Please," Egan repeated. "Think what you're doing. He will destroy you. It's his nature."

He looked so lost and hurt that it made my heart ache.

I looked at Azazel, my eyes full of questions.

"You are mine," he said, slowly, as if he could not comprehend the alternative Egan was trying to present.

"She is *not*," insisted the Irishman. "We belong to our Creator, and to no one else."

I took a step from the wall, impelled mostly by the instinct to get between Azazel and the sweet idiot who was practically begging for cremation.

"Milja," said Uriel, urgently; "if you go with him, you are putting yourself on the losing side of history. They lost last time, and they will lose again. And the punishment that will fall upon you will be beyond anything you can imagine."

I glared at him. "You think threats are the way to a girl's heart?"

"It is simply fair warning. Can you doubt that, after everything you've seen? But it's not too late for you to change sides."

I looked from angel to man to demon. Azazel, who had said least of all, stood with hands clenched together before him.

He looked so unhappy.

214

"I don't know," I told the other two. "I'm in the dark about so much. I don't know if he's right about God and stuff. I don't know if he's on the right side, and I don't know if he's a good guy. But I know you two both deceived me. And given the choice between him and you two liars, I'm going with him."

I stepped into Azazel's reach.

chapter sixteen

WHAT WILL YOU DO?

U riel rolled his eyes and vanished, in a flash of light.

Egan bit his lip and bowed his head.

Azazel's embrace furled about me, soft as soot, strong as iron chains. We went.

We went to a place of blue shadows and darkness, a place that smelled of stone and damp and incense. But I didn't have time to look around me, because Azazel turned me to his face and kissed me. I felt his mouth press my blistered lips, and I winced.

"You're hurt?"

"Just—"

I broke off as he kissed me again. It was like balm: a sweet cool tingling flowed through me as my blisters shrank and vanished. He swept his hands over my face and shoulders, smoothing away scratches and bruises, and the smoke-scraped rawness of my throat. Then he ran his hand down my left arm. I couldn't help gasping in warning as his hand approached my wrist, but he took my crooked swollen finger and caressed it gently back into place, and all the pain ran out of me like water.

I curled my fingers, testing their strength, and laughed.

"What?" he murmured.

"Nothing. I just didn't know you had that kind of power. I thought..."

"What? That I'm only good for fire and brimstone?"

Something like that. I pictured Egan again, coughing out that bullet from his lungs, the flush of life returning to his ashen skin. I put my hand on Azazel's cheek. Stubble rasped my palm. "Thank you. For saving Egan."

"And for saving you?" he asked.

"Yeah. For that too." I smiled in a wobbly way. "You came back for me even when I told you to stay away." I stretched up and planted a kiss on his cheek. He steadied me by slipping his arms around me, his hands on my waist and back to pull me against him.

"I'm not good at taking orders," he reminded me.

Our lips were so close that our breath was tangled. It made me light-headed. "You walked into a trap."

"For you."

"That's not a good enough reason."

"Yes. Yes it is."

I ran my hands tenderly over his beautiful, drawn face. "Don't do it again."

"Don't tell me what to do." There was laughter in his growl.

Unable to hold back any longer, I brought the conversation to a halt by kissing him full-on—my lips to his lips, my body rubbing hungrily up against the hard wall of his. Oh how I wanted him: the touch and the taste and the strength of him, the rough stubble as well as the smooth skin, the fear and the might of him.

His mouth was like the first sip of strong spirits, taking my breath away with its sweetness, sparking a burn that flared through me from head to toe. His hand caught my ass in a heft that nearly lifted me from my feet.

"Tell me," he groaned, looming over me, pressing me off-balance. I had to cling to him. "Tell me, Milja."

"I love you," I admitted—and groaned as he caught my lip in his teeth, the pain tiny but exquisite. "Is that what you want to hear? I love you."

"That's what I want," he agreed. One hand moved to cup my breast through the thin cotton dress. Thumb and fingers closed about my erect nipple, pinching it. "And this. I want this." He tugged until I whimpered, arching. "And this." His grip on my asscheek became entirely improper as his fingers delved into the cleft, bunching the cloth of my skirt. "I want all of it."

He wasn't lying—the grind of his erection against the softness of my belly was uncomfortable verging on painful. I whimpered.

It was all the invitation he needed.

Covering my mouth with his, filling me with ravening kisses, he backed me up through that shadowy room until my ass collided with a hard edge. A table of some sort, draped with a cloth, I noted dizzily, unable to see, unable to look down, unable to escape his hungry mouth. He lifted me up to sit on the table edge and thrust his hands up my skirt, stroking up my thighs with heavy, kneading pressure.

"Open," he growled.

I obeyed, spreading my legs. He touched me between the thighs, and his hand actually felt cool against my own heat. I shivered and cried out softly as the thrill rippled through me. For a moment he went still—all but the slither and caress of his fingertips.

"Wet," he murmured, his voice thick with pleasure. "Very wet."

I think I was blushing, there in the darkness. I nodded.

"You want me."

"Yes."

"You want this." He took my hand and pressed it against him through the cloth of his pants, making it very clear what he meant.

"Yes," I answered, though my own voice sounded faint. It was one thing to be debauched by him in dream after dream. Here, now—in the flesh—was another proposition entirely.

He'd only had me once before. He'd been so rough.

His forehead was pressed against mine, his breath burning my lips with each word. His fingers were relentless in their slow, teasing caress. "Don't be frightened."

"I'm not frightened," I lied. "Please don't hurt me."

"Hurt you?" It was getting harder to tell through the red fog of my physical arousal, but I thought I felt a dew of perspiration on his upper lip. "Do I not give enough thought to your pleasure?"

218

"You're too much," I whispered. "Too big for me. Too strong. Too fierce."

I wasn't talking about his cock. Not entirely.

"Oh my love." His voice was coal and darkness and soot-black feathers. "I can't promise that. Not to hurt you."

I kissed him, eyes closed, nodding.

"But you will take it. Because you can. And I will make pleasure from your pain. I will give it back to you as diamonds."

I slid my hands up under his knitted top, wanting to feel the beat of his heart. My palm brushed the huge, ancient scar on his torso, and he groaned. Then he pulled away from me—long enough and far enough to wrench his sweater off over his head and cast it aside. He stretched his back, standing tall.

There wasn't much light in here—a blue gloaming of a fading evening through grimy panes, that's all. I could barely make out Azazel's outlined form, pale against the deep shadows. I had to explore his torso by touch, running my hands over his ribs and his scar, up to the burr of hair on his chest and down to the hard V of his hips, over the vertical slit of his navel—yet he'd never been born, I reminded myself; never earned that umbilical mark—and the muscled planes of his flat stomach. I felt him shudder when I touched the ridged scar tissue, and I could not tell in this poor light whether it was in fear or pain or joy.

"Milja." There was a gloss of sweat on his skin. He was rigid with tension.

Without a word I pulled at the buttons of his pants fly, releasing the thing I wanted, that I feared—the thing that had brought down angels and condemned mankind and drowned all the world in a Flood. Such a stupid, insignificant trigger for a war in Heaven, in the greater context. And yet...it seemed big enough in my hand.

"Stroke it," he told me.

Hot and hard, like new-cast bronze. A weapon raised defiantly against God Himself.

Beautiful. I am not ashamed to say that.

"Kiss it," he whispered, just as he had in my dream.

I bent forward from my perch and nuzzled it into my mouth. You see, that is the difference between me and Azazel.

219

I *like* to obey orders.

"Yes," he said softly, as made I my throat into a sheath and took his length as far down as I could. "Yes," as he wound his hands in my hair and pulled me tight to him. "Oh...Milja."

At the corners of my eyes, light bloomed. Warm lamplight, point by point, swelling and filling the darkness. *Candles*, I realized, too busy with my task to look around me. *He is lighting the dark.*

But when I had him at my mercy and the slabs of his thighs were quivering under my hands, he surprised me once more. With a firm grasp of his hand in my hair, he pulled me up—openmouthed—and in one ruthless motion pushed me over onto my back upon the table.

Oh yes, his grip hurt, but it was a good, good pain. It gushed through me like a rushing storm. It sparkled like diamonds.

Now I could see properly. Now Azazel loomed over me, both illuminated and shadowed by the flickering candle flames all around us. His skin glowed golden and tiny reflected flames danced in his mirror-eyes. He drew up my legs, wrapping them about him, and then he took hold of the front of my awful frock and in three jerks tore the cloth all the way down from neck to hem, to lay me bare.

I was still gasping from the abrupt change of position, and from the sweet and utterly possessive pain of his grip in my hair. I did not stop gasping as he took himself in hand and guided hard male to soft female flesh, but I cried out as he entered me. And I arched my back as he laid one hand upon my mound and the other upon my breasts.

His self-control came as a surprise. He was keeping his distance— only his hands upon me, his length in me, body leaning over mine—and holding back. Gliding with slow, deliberate strokes as his thumb slithered across the nub of my clit and his hands played with my breasts. It was as if he were teetering on the brink of a great abyss, stopping himself from falling. The brace of his hands against me was the only thing holding him on high.

White-hot delight shivered through me from the tugged points of my nipples, from the juncture of my thighs, from deep inside. I felt dizzy: tiny beneath him, huge as the world, all perspective gone. The candles hung around us like constellations. And as I looked up at his face above me, haloed with his unkempt hair, intent with concentration, golden and dark, light and shadow...I fell instead, blazing like a star wrenched from the firmament.

Rapt with my pleasure, Azazel watched as I twisted and gasped and shuddered beneath him. His lips moved in silent echo of my cries.

But when the last tremors rippled through me and died away, he forgot mercy. He didn't give me time to recover. He ran his hands over my slick and shuddering body and lodged one on my hip for a good grip. Then his weight came down over me like the slow press of a mountain on the spaces beneath the earth.

I lifted my knees and wrapped my legs tight about him as he began to thrust. Every stroke was an earthquake. He beat the breath from my lungs. His hair hung in my eyes, and the surge of his breath was a growl in my ear. I couldn't see his face anymore, but my blurred gaze took in the faces above me and over his shoulders: the sad eyes and the glimmering halos and the hands raised in blessing.

And I knew them. I knew this place, those frescoes painted upon the arched and plastered ceiling. I knew Michael and the hidden key he guarded. I knew the smoke-darkened Pantocrator in bearded majesty. They were as familiar to me as family photos.

He'd brought me home.

We were in the tiny church my father had tended all my life. And Azazel was fucking me upon the church altar.

"Oh!" I cried, my eyes widening. Even now, even with him, the blasphemy was a shock that struck me to the core.

Darkness and lust and a need for dominion.

To him ascribe all sin.

Public domain.

And I knew. This wasn't just pointed and deliberate sacrilege; it was giving the finger to Uriel and anyone who might be watching. All the Hosts of Heaven. The fallen angel pounding the sex of his witch on the altar of the Most High, for all the universe to see.

All of them, watching.

I came again then, screaming, and Azazel cried out with me and held back no longer, pouring out his lust to mingle with mine.

He lay over me for some time afterward, kissing me as I sobbed with shock. Then he scooped me up and turned so that it was his butt propped on the altar slab, my legs around his waist and my arms around his neck, and he cradled me there as if he would never let me go, his arms tight about me, his face buried in my hair, his fingers soothing my quivering skin.

Tender as a guardian angel. Gentle as the eye of a hurricane.

"I'm going to have to find some clothes. You...sort of finished this dress off."

Azazel nodded. His eye was half on the nightscape beyond the open church door.

"You won't leave me, this time?" I asked in a tiny voice.

"Not this time."

My breath caught. I couldn't read his face or his voice. Was it a promise, or an apology, or some sort of dark joke? But I didn't dare ask. I bit my lip and turned away, plucking one of the lit church candles from its sconce.

It would be the last time, I suspected, that candles were lit in this mountain chapel. The last time I came back here. I ducked through the inner door into my old house, moving through the darkened familiar passages as if through a dream.

Father's study. The hall. Down to the bedroom. My old bedroom, tiny and snug and simple as a child's picture.

I set the candle upon the dresser and rummaged through the mothball-scented drawers. I'd left some clothes behind when I went to America, I knew. Things just a little too small for my eighteen-year-old body, or too worn, or so old-fashioned that I did not dare show my sophisticated cousin Vera. Hand-me-downs from my mother.

I found a dress of hers in the wardrobe. It was prim and respectable, the dress of a priest's wife. I didn't think I'd ever worn it, to be honest. But I slipped it on now, settling its soft cotton fabric over my bare shoulders.

It smelled of lavender and mothballs. I could imagine it was the smell of my motherland.

Somewhere in another room, a male voice began to sing.

I thought it was Azazel at first. I'd never heard him sing, but I assumed he could; he was an angel, after all. I hunted out a sweater to go over the dress.

It was only when I stepped out of my bedroom that I realized the song was a hymn. And I recognized the voice as that of my father.

The light danced as the candle shook in my hand. My heart raced so swiftly that it left my thoughts standing.

Back, back, to the study. He had tried to confine his books there, though they'd spread out and taken territory in every other room in the house. The walls were lined with shelves.

I stood in the doorway. My father sat in his favorite armchair, and he was cleaning off some small piece of machinery—a distributor cap, in fact—with a rag. And singing. Just like he used to when I lived here.

When he was alive.

"Come, my Light, and illumine my darkness.
Come, my Life, and revive me from death.
Come, my Physician, and heal my wounds.
Come, Flame of divine love."

He had a wonderful voice. Most Orthodox priests do: singing the Divine Liturgy is a vital part of their duties.

"Papa?" My throat was swollen and the word had to squeeze out, thin and shaking.

He glanced up at me and smiled. "Little chick."

He looked just as real as anyone does by candlelight.

I walked into the room, step by wobbling step, and knelt beside his chair, just like I used to when I was small. He watched me, his smile a little troubled.

"Papa," I said, resting my head against the upholstered chair arm. "I've missed you."

"Milja," he chided gently, and put his hand on the top of my head.

I could *feel* him. His touch was light, but it was there. I shut my eyes, feeling dizzy. I'd have been in floods of tears, if that were still possible for me.

"Papa, I have done terrible things. Please don't hate me."

He stroked my hair, very softly. "Milja, you are my daughter. Whatever you do, I will not hate you."

I made a noise in my throat that defied description.

"Shush, little chick. Nothing in the universe could stop me loving you. You know that."

I bit my lip and nodded. My shoulders shook. I kept my eyes closed. He stroked my hair as I took breath after breath, and slowly the tension ebbed from me, and slowly the world stopped spinning. His touch was so light that after a while I couldn't be sure it was there at all.

I opened my eyes. The candle had burned down two inches in the draft from the church door. My father had gone.

They were right about me, I thought. *I am a witch.*

I went back out onto the rock ledge at the front of the house. It was night now, though not quite full dark. The sky overhead was clear, a magnificent royal blue except toward the silver west. The brightest of the stars were out already, along with a narrow sliver of moon. Venus, the Evening Star, shone like a distant lantern, even brighter than the moon.

Azazel stood there on the edge, looking up at the stars. He'd buttoned up his pants but had given up on the rags of his sweater and was shirtless, his shoulders broad, his longish hair black as midnight against the skin of his nape.

He'd waited. I let my fists unknot.

He had waited without, apparently, any sign of impatience. Any ordinary guy would have wondered what on earth was taking me so long— but maybe time looked different to him. For a moment I wanted to blurt out what had happened, but the words gathered in a choke in my throat. Seeing my father again meant everything to me, but less than nothing to him.

He'd hear my news with amused indifference, was my guess. And I didn't want that. My heart was brimming over.

He looked so handsome. And for once, so calm. As for me, I felt... light-headed, as if a great weight had been lifted from my whole body. My fingers tingled like blood was running back into cramped joints.

I walked up and put my hand on the small of his back, feeling the firm smooth muscle and the strong pillar of his spine. I brushed my hot forehead against his bare shoulder—and I said nothing.

"They were my brothers once," he said, still looking up, but slipping his arm around me. "We walked together across the lapis floor of Heaven."

I sucked my lower lip. "Do you miss it?"

He didn't answer.

"Where will we go?" I asked. "You're free now. What will you do?"

Azazel looked down into my face then, and brushed his lips to mine.

It was a long, considered kiss—not hungry, not joyous, but full of deliberation. It caused appetite to stir again within me, but also a sense of trepidation. I could feel his thoughts, moving like great oceanic predators beneath the dark pelagic surface.

I put my hand on his cheek. He turned to kiss the palm.

Then he took a deep, slow breath, and let it out. When he spoke his voice was quiet, but there was iron in it too.

"I'm going to release my brothers. The ones enslaved in darkness, beneath the earth. All of them."

My heart jumped. "Azazel?"

"I will set them free—and then we will rise up and defy Heaven."

ABOUT THE AUTHOR

"It's always the quiet ones..." **JANINE ASHBLESS** (janineashbless. blogspot.com) may be the living incarnation of this universal principle. On the outside she is shy and respectable, living quietly in Yorkshire, England, with her husband, where she enjoys walking her dogs and gardening.

Look closer and you might find her running around the woods at night, slaying orcs with her trusty LARP sword. You will certainly find her thinking about sex—because she is living her dream by being a writer of fantasy erotica and steamy romantic adventure—and that's "fantasy" in the sense of swords 'n' sandals, contemporary paranormal, fairy tale, and stories based on mythology and folklore. She likes to write about magic and mystery, dangerous power dynamics, borderline terror, and the not-quite-human.

Janine has been seeing her books in print ever since 2000. Her three short story collections are *Cruel Enchantment*, *Dark Enchantment* and *Fierce Enchantments*. Her more outrageous novels include *Wildwood*, *Red Grow the Roses* and *Named and Shamed*. If you prefer passion mixed with tormented romance, try *The King's Viper* or *Heart of Flame*. She's also coeditor of the nerd erotica anthology *Geek Love*.

Janine loves goatee beards, ancient ruins, Minotaurs, trees, mummies, having her cake *and* eating it, holidaying in countries with really bad public sewerage, and any movie or TV series featuring men in very few clothes beating the hell out of each other.

Her work has been described as "Hardcore and literate," (Madeline Moore) and "Vivid and tempestuous and dangerous, and bursting with sacrifice, death and love" (Portia Da Costa).

Happy Endings Forever and Ever

Ordering is easy! Call us toll free or fax us to place your MC/VISA order.
You can also mail the order form below with payment to:
Cleis Press, 2246 Sixth St., Berkeley, CA 94710.

ORDER FORM

QTY	TITLE	PRICE
_____	_____	_____
_____	_____	_____
_____	_____	_____
_____	_____	_____
_____	_____	_____
_____	_____	_____
_____	_____	_____
_____	_____	_____

SUBTOTAL _____

SHIPPING _____

SALES TAX _____

TOTAL _____

Add $3.95 postage/handling for the first book ordered and $1.00 for each additional book. Outside North America, please contact us for shipping rates. California residents add 9% sales tax. Payment in U.S. dollars only.

* Free book of equal or lesser value. Shipping and applicable sales tax extra.

Cleis Press • Phone: (800) 780-2279 • Fax: (510) 845-8001
orders@cleispress.com • www.cleispress.com
You'll find more great books on our website

Follow us on Twitter @cleispress • Friend/fan us on Facebook